His hand burned...
and that pain, fr...
absence, it grew uneve...
ing the pain, crashed...
liquid spilled onto the table, ran along the lines of energy. Onan staggered back. He saw Akeem fall back. The others, rather than pulling away, were drawn into the lights, now spinning and whirling crazily. They leaped from the designs and the sigils onto the bare center of the table and became a small cyclone of light, drawing in toward a circular point in the center.

"No!" Onan cried out. He leaped for Akbar, and then, before he touched the other man, he stopped himself. Something was wrong with Akbar's skin, his face. He had become translucent, fading, and then returning to clarity. Onan turned and saw that Ghazalan was the same. The center of that glowing whirlwind brightened again, and Onan turned, diving away and covering his head. "Down!" he screamed. "Get down!" He had no way to know if Akeem had heard him.

There was a great flash of light. His hearing and his sight left him. For a long moment it felt as if he floated off the floor, hovering, and then, with the strength of a charging bull, an explosion of energy rippled out from the table, lifted him, and slammed him into the wall. As his mind fell to darkness, he saw the light sucked into a smaller and smaller point, then disappear into the center of the table. Akbar and Ghazalan shimmered, whirled, and along with the light, flashed out of existence as the room joined Onan in darkness.

JURASSIC ARK

DAVID NIALL WILSON

*For Trish, Katie, Stephanie, Will, Zach, Zane,
Brittany and Joshua. They put up with a lot from me.
And for the cats. They have me surrounded.*

FOREWORD

Every time I sit down to write a new book, I find that I did not really have a grasp of the story itself until I was immersed in it. A lot of authors have explained, most more eloquently than I, that, not unlike readers who will discover what we have created as they turn the pages, we discover and experience them in a very similar manner while writing.

A few years back I wrote a book with my wife, Trish, a very talented author. It was pure satire. The president and his press secretary at the time had repeatedly referred to a massacre at "Bowling Green," an event that never happened. The president also said that he'd heard Frederick Douglas was "doing fine things." We didn't want those things to be forgotten, so we wrote Remember *Bowling Green: The Adventures of Frederick Douglass, Time Traveler.*

That book turned out exactly as expected. It was funny with some action and some heart, and it had a message we hoped would reach people. We have donated every cent of the author's royalties to the ACLU. None of this is germane to this introduction, though, except to say that when I first thought of the title Jurassic Ark, I thought it would be a follow-on alternate history satire about the ridiculousness of the world Creationists posit, with men and dinosaurs walking the earth together, and all the species of the world gathering to get on a great wooden boat less than 6000 years ago. I expected to knock it out in a few weeks. Then I started to write.

This is not that book. This is nothing like what I expected to create, but I believe it is something more. I fell down several research rabbit holes involving the flood myth. Yes, I believe it's a myth. No, I neither believe in magical gardens with talking snakes, or organized religion. What I discovered is, those are not what is important about this story. What is important is the characters, the incredible emotions involved in the belief in a great prophecy, the knowledge only a few would be saved, and the wonder of things beyond understanding intruding in our lives.

There are giants in this book. There are tidbits of myth and folklore. There are dinosaurs, sorcerers, righteous men, and strong women. There are men who have lived for centuries, and stories, handed down from father to son, since a beginning of time that feels ancient beyond reason, but that, in the context of this book, is only a few thousand years.

The heroes will not necessarily be who you believe. The reactions are not those of Biblical stereotypes, but of men, women, and children. At least one question the young at heart have asked again and again will get an answer, even if it's no more real than the story.

It's an adventure that I spent nearly a year living inside my mind. I'm inviting you in. I hope you'll enjoy the stay.

David Niall Wilson
Hertford, NC
2012

Prologue

Ezra wished he'd not ventured so far from the city walls alone, but he'd promised a particular herb to Master Balthazar and misjudged both the heat of the day and the difficulty of the journey. Dusk was approaching quickly, and though he was well prepared for the weather, the desert could be harsh and cold by night and there were other dangers.

He had about an hour before the guards would close the immense gates and lock him out for the night. There were shelters outside the wall, but there was no circumstance under which those gates would open once the sun disappeared. Even Master Balthazar, who was both rabbi and healer to the lords of the city, would not be able to entice the guards to break that curfew. Nor would he be likely to try.

Ezra broke into a trot. He was used to long, difficult journeys, and he had plenty of water. It was a shame he couldn't have risked a camel, but the scent of it would have been too strong, and too tempting.

That passing thought sent a shiver across his sweat-slicked skin. Suddenly, the immensity of the open desert at his back overwhelmed him. He felt the intense gaze of thousands of eyes pushing him across the sand. The walls of the city looked tiny and distant. He knew he had only a couple of miles to cover, but it could have been a thousand.

His sandals and robes scuffed across the desert floor and his mind created echoes from the sound, bouncing them off dunes and rocky outcroppings, whispering them through brush and scrubby trees. The day's heat rose in wavy, surreal shimmers that teased his senses with flickers of motion.

Ezra turned and glanced over his shoulder. He thought he caught a shadow of movement behind a large stone, but it did not repeat. His throat was dry, and he wanted to stop and take a drink, but he'd lost control of his limbs. His legs churned, and he gulped in ragged breaths. Instead of slowing, he broke into a full sprint. He was a mile from the gates, but the shadows had grown long and the sun had dipped. Sunset in the desert was not a gradual thing. It was sudden, final, and the weight of it pressed down on his heart.

The gates drew closer; the walls loomed tall and forbidding. He knew they should feel welcoming, but they would close. He knew, suddenly, they would close before he made it through, and he would be left outside. Alone.

He looked back again. This time, overextended limbs, and a mind awash in terror, visions, and thirst, failed to maintain his balance. He tumbled face first, into the sand, tasting the grit on his tongue. There was a sudden flash of light behind his eyelids as the pain jarred him back to his senses. He lay there, just for a second, then rose to his knees. He scanned the desert carefully and took off at a slightly slower pace. He was within sight of the guards on the walls, and he knew they would let him pass. There was time—barely—but enough. He allowed himself a small smile and focused on the open gates.

They began, very slowly, to close. He glanced up at the walls, raised his arms, waved, and calling out as loudly as his tortured throat would allow. He sprinted toward the gate, trying to gauge whether he would reach it in time. His mind reeled. He was certain that he heard sounds behind him, skittering footsteps, heavy clicks, or perhaps nothing more than the echoes of his own frantic footfalls. Remembering his earlier fall, he did not glance back to see.

Inside the main gates, there was another, smaller wall. It was covered by a metal cage anchored to heavy blocks of stone. That smaller gate was always closed, until the watch was certain who, or what, sought entry. Ezra considered looking back a final time, then pushed the thought aside as he realized it would matter not at all to his survival. He threw every ounce of his strength into a final dash and dove forward, oblivious to the approaching gates on either side and the imminent possibility of being crushed. Suddenly the night, and the shelters beyond the wall, were no choice at all. He screamed, and dove through the closing gates.

Behind him, something screamed. It was loud, high-pitched, and not remotely human. He felt the booming thud of the gates slamming shut and, as he rolled to his feet, turning frantically. The massive doors had closed on the neck of a creature with massive, razor-lined jaws and reptilian eyes. Just for a second, it seemed the thing would withstand that pressure and press forward. There was no fear in its eyes.

Then the gates ground inward. There was a snap. The huge, scaled head dropped to the sand, rolled slowly, and came to rest at Ezra's feet. He dropped to his knees, head in his hands, fighting for breath.

"Next time you are out," a voice called from above, "come back early, and don't travel alone."

Ezra glanced up. Two men in leather armor, armed with great swords and flanked on either side by long, viciously sharp metal lances grinned down at him. He tried to return their smiles, but he knew the expression was likely more of a grimace. His voice failed him. It was all that he could do to stagger to his feet. He turned toward the smaller gate and took a step forward.

"Not so fast," one of the guards called out. "You aren't leaving that thing here. Perhaps your master will have a use for it, but you'll have to wait for a cart and men to help you load it. The public byways must be kept clear for those who use them during the proper hours.

Ezra turned and glared at the lifeless, reptilian head lying behind him in the dirt. He leaned back against the inner gate in exhausted resignation. He hoped Master Balthazar *did* have a use for the creature, because otherwise it was likely to cost him another year of apprenticeship to pay for the disposal.

"Maybe," the guard called down with a laugh, "you should pray and offer thanks. I don't believe I've ever seen a man move quite that fast."

This time Ezra did grin. He dropped to the sand, back to

the gate, and settled in to wait for a wagon to be sent around. He checked his bag and was pleased to find that—at the very least—the herbs he'd been tasked to find were safe. It was shaping up to be a long night.

Chapter 1

Noah stood on a hillside beyond the compound that was his home, staring off toward the city in the distance. Between the forest's edge, and the walls of the city, barren desert stretched hot and empty, sending heat vapors into the morning air. Behind, and above them, the hills rose, filled with trees and valleys. Visions, half-formed and ethereal, spun through those mists—mirages that drew men to their deaths.

It was early. Inside, the morning meal was being prepared. Men were waking and readying themselves for a day's work. Soon it would be time to meet, and to pray. Noah's place would be at the head of the great table, leading those prayers, but for the moment he sought the silence of the hour just before sunrise, when everything glowed like molten metal and the great beasts were only sluggishly rising from their pits and dens.

He felt closer to his Lord at moments like this, where the voices and clatter and sinful arrogance of the world fell away. Those he could speak to of his faith, those who truly believed, had grown so few that he scarcely spoke in public and avoided the city as though touching his boots to its streets might corrupt him, or the air might steal his soul.

He felt the weight of his years. Five hundred of them, each spent in a world less Godly than the last. The temples were in disarray. The Holy Days had become times of debauch and sin. He was now mocked for his piety, scorned for his faith, until just the mention of his name brought laughter.

He shook these thoughts from his head and took a seat on a fallen log. He emptied his mind and closed his eyes. When he opened them again, he saw that the desert vapors had shifted. He would have shut them out again, but he could not. Something caught at his breath, widened his gaze, and drew him in. Something moving in the morning air, tantalizing him with a form that remained just beyond his sight. He was so entranced by the sight that when a voice spoke—not with words, but with images in his mind—he was barely startled. He sensed a presence, a warmth beyond the sunlight of the day.

Noah opened his mouth to speak, but words proved beyond him. He thought to push off the log and stand, but found that, though he still felt his limbs, they wouldn't obey his commands. He fought against the visions filling his mind, fearing some sort of possession, or evil, but as moments passed, that sensation melted away, replaced by a fear of an entirely different kind.

"Lord?" As with the voice invading his thoughts, the word formed without the necessity of lips, or sound.

The visions shifted, and he tried to concentrate. He saw a palace, domed in gold, tables littered with flagons and goblets, spoiled food, and around that table men and women in every form of sinful intercourse. He saw a temple, dust on its floors and dim, flickering candles burning low. There were no faithful in attendance. He saw men with men, men with women, and boys, women with women, and all together. He saw armies and fields awash in blood, pulsing, as if each new outrage were triggered by a single beat of his heart.

"It must end."

Those words emerged from the visions, clear, like a whispered pattern in a great rushing wind, or syncopated thunder in tones that made sense. There was no time to wonder at the manner of the speech. The images continued to assault his senses, and he reeled, tried to pull away, failed, and watched as the world of men and flesh poured across the heated sand and seared his eyes.

"Everything is poisoned. Everything is broken and bent, warped and rotten. I cast my creations from Eden to have them violate every gift, ignore every commandment, and worship the things I most despise. I will end it. I will cleanse it. As you would wash away the sweat and dirt of a hard day's work, I will bathe the world and wash away their corruption. I will make this world new."

Tears flowed down Noah's cheeks as he watched abomination after abomination. Sin after sin. He saw men, and women that he knew, others from places so distant he didn't recognize their features, or their manner of dress, but everywhere it was the same.

"They have turned from me," the voice whispered so loudly the words filled the world and blended with the images. "The lives of men are long, and the longer they live, the further they corrupt the flesh and the life given them. I will no longer suffer it. When I have finished, the days of men will be no more than one-hundred-fifty years. You have sons who would already be dead."

Noah tried to remember his life when only a hundred years had passed and found that it was difficult. The decades blurred, and the visions compounded his confusion.

"Please..." he managed. It was not directed at any one thing, but at the totality of it, the bombardment of evil, the necessity to concentrate on the words, the thudding of his heart at the proximity of his Lord.

The world silenced. Where he had seen cities and throngs, orgies, and wars, he saw a slowly rolling expanse of water. It stretched on and on. He could make out no land, no shore on the far side.

Another shift, and he stumbled, as he found himself standing—not in the forest, but on the deck of a great vessel. It rose and fell with the waves, and his stomach took a moment to adjust.

"You will build it," the voice said. "You will build it, and you will bring on board seven of every animal the law names clean, and two each of the rest, male and female. You will carry the future of the Earth until the waters have washed the evil away. You and your house will survive. You will carry beasts, cattle, birds. You will know what is proper. Each thing you need will be made available to you. Your faith must sustain you."

A voice cried out. It seemed incredibly far away, but Noah heard his name...recognized it as Shem, one of his sons. He fought to retain the visions, reached out, and found his arms were his own once more, and his voice.

"My Lord..."

The light of day had grown bright, and the sun shimmered off the sand. Noah nearly dropped to the ground as his mind juxtaposed the sensation of standing on the ship with the reality of sitting on a log. He righted himself, just as Shem came into sight.

"Father?"

"Find your brothers," Noah said. "Your mother as well. Gather the family."

"They are at the table," Shem began.

"Do as I say. All of them. I have had a vision. I have spoken with our Lord. Bring them to me."

Shem stared at his father. Just for a moment, his eyes flickered with something that might have been doubt or resignation. Then he met Noah's gaze.

"Yes, Father."

Shem turned, and disappeared. Noah also turned, staring out toward the city, but there was no sign of what he'd witnessed. The sand glistened in the brilliant sunlight. The heat waves danced and shimmered, but they contained no visions. He turned his gaze to the heavens, just for a moment, and then followed Shem back to the walls and halls of his home, wondering what he was going to say...and if anyone would believe him when he did.

Chapter 2

Master Balthazar's shop was a curious conglomeration of esoteric items. It held scrolls, books bound in leather and lizard skin, bottles and jars of various sizes and shapes filled with liquids, powders, and all manner of strange concoctions. Some of it was old. Some of it was so ancient that it stretched back to the very beginning of creation. There were a few very well-protected and preserved containers that, while the words had never been spoken, Ezra believed must have come from Eden herself. Those gates were long closed to men, but there were other sources. Master Balthazar might be a Rabbi, but he was also a very shrewd man—he knew how to find things, and he knew what to do with them once found.

It came, at least in part, from nearly five hundred years of life, but there were plenty of elders in the city, and Ezra found the majority of them no wiser than men of only a few hundred years, or even less. It seemed that age and wisdom only walked hand in hand to a point, and then, if one were to continue to learn and achieve, he was on his own.

The head of the creature that had nearly ended his life the night before was now mounted on a large spike in the back workroom of the shop. Rather than being displeased, Balthazar had been thrilled with its acquisition. He'd left Ezra to run the day-to-day business and closed himself off with an assortment of knives, saws, containers, and a small stack of books. Ezra hadn't questioned his master, or his luck. He had no idea what there might be of value in that great, scaled skull, but whatever it was, he was more than happy to have no part in its extraction. Instead, he prepared the herbs he'd been sent to retrieve, and handed out remedies for toothaches, allergies, fever, and insomnia to the slow but steady stream of customers who wandered in.

Others were looking for more intimate services. Help in their love lives, or vengeance against those who'd done them wrong. It was all well and good to heal, and to support the spiritual health of the city. The real money was traded behind closed doors. Ezra believed that was what would come of his near-death. Whatever that beast was good for could *not* be Godly. He also knew that he should be upset by this, but his life was a good one, and he found Master Balthazar's wit unendingly amusing—particularly when he was waxing poetic on the sins of the well-to-do and royal. Five hundred years might not ensure wisdom, but they brought a lot of insight.

In any case, a godly man would have left this city in terror. The joys of the flesh, dreams induced by mead and herbs washed away the day-to-day misery of men and women alike, drawing them into shadows and guaranteeing sparse attendance in the Temples.

He moved around the shop, stocking shelves where necessary and straightening displays. It was early, and he didn't expect a rush of customers until much later in the day. He stopped by the window and glanced outside. Several groups of men and women had gathered, chattering away about something, hands flailing descriptively. A pair of women broke off from one group and hurried toward the shop. Ezra backed away from the window and stepped behind the counter so as not to be caught snooping.

News traveled very quickly in the city. One of the main entertainments was gossip, and when crowds gathered to discuss *anything* this early in the day, it had to be good.

The women slowed as they approached the store, leaning in close to one another and continuing to whisper. Ezra made a show of stacking containers filled with various scented oils, examining them as if looking for just the perfect arrangement, watching casually out of the corner of his eye as the women glanced back over their shoulders, then slipped in the doorway where they turned to face one another, out of sight of the groups on the street.

"He's crazy," one said. "It's finally come to it…what of his family?"

"Hush," her companion said. "He is a God-fearing man. He has heard the word of…"

"Don't be ridiculous," the first woman cut her off. "If he has heard voices, they are in his head. Five hundred years of denying himself pleasure, of seclusion? He is mad."

Ezra desperately wanted to speak. He wanted to ask who they were talking about, and what had happened, but he knew better. They were more likely to give away the gossip in their private discussion and, barring that, more likely to ask what he thought if he feigned indifference. There were only a few they could be talking about. Those who'd lived five hundred years were common enough, but those who had denied themselves pleasure and closely followed the ways of the temple were much scarcer.

In fact, just before he heard one of the women mention the name Shem, he guessed the truth. It was Noah; something had happened with Noah, and that was bound to be good for business. Gossip was good for business. When something stirred the population, they wanted to talk about it, and that meant going into the streets, interacting with people, asking questions, and buying things.

Ezra turned to the two women and smiled. He cleared his throat.

"May I help you?" he asked. "Is there something in particular…?"

They turned, as if he'd caught them at something. Ezra was careful to keep all emotion from his smile. A merchant, just trying to be helpful.

"I…" the first woman said. Her eyes swept the shop and locked onto a counter piled high with scented candles. She hurried over to it, leaving her friend behind to face Ezra.

"A lot of people on the street this morning," he said. "More than usual."

She glanced at her friend, swallowed, and then nodded. She met his gaze, and, as if letting him in on one of the great secrets of the universe, she asked, "Have you not heard?"

He lifted an eyebrow and held his silence.

She checked the door, glanced at her friend again, then leaned close and spoke softly.

"It's Noah," she said. "He is claiming to have spoken to God."

"That is hardly news," Ezra said, widening his smile.

"This is different," the woman said. "He believes that an end is coming—to everything. He claims that he will build an ark — a great boat to carry his family and..." her voice dropped, "animals. He says the world will end in a flood, and he is chosen to be the only survivor, he and his family."

"That will be a boring world, indeed," Ezra said. "A boat? There is no water within two days' travel deep enough to keep one afloat."

"He will build it in the forest," she said. "He even claims to have been given specific dimensions. He's quite mad."

"How will he decide what animals?" Ezra asked, honestly interested.

"He has been directed 'by Jehovah' to carry seven each of all beasts that are clean, and two each of every other. At least that is what we heard."

Ezra turned and glanced over his shoulder toward the workroom where Master Balthazar was cutting, chopping, and disassembling the head of the beast. He shook his head.

"Mad indeed if he's being literal. I wish him luck getting those outside the walls onto his craft without sinking it and feasting on his cargo, not to mention his family. Putting aside his odd fanaticism regarding the Temple and the Law, I've always thought he was a reasonably sane man."

"He has lived alone too long," the woman said. "Some say he is seeking attention."

"That seems the opposite of what he has sought until now," Ezra said, "But who knows what goes through a man's mind?"

The younger of the two women cast a glance at him that suggested she might have an idea on the subject. Ezra blushed, but smiled.

"In any case," he said, "a project of that size will require a massive undertaking. Even with such a large family as his, it will take a hundred years."

"Noah is not a poor man," the first woman said. "He will pay for the services of those who can build."

"No doubt your master will be flooded with requests for various charms...pain killers..."

"More likely," Ezra said, "he will be called upon for love potions to help woo Noah's sons and his daughter, ensuring space on his prophetic craft."

They all laughed, and the women, after purchasing small bundles of incense and herbs, returned to the street, leaving Ezra staring after them, wondering what to make of their story. He knew he'd have to report it to Master Balthazar as soon as possible. If the stories were true, there would be money to be made, and Ezra knew that if anyone could figure out the best way to take advantage of that, it would be Balthazar.

He returned to his duties, running over possibilities in his mind, and ignoring the sounds of Balthazar's tools drifting out from the workroom.

Chapter 3

The noise in the streets re-doubled, and then fell away completely. Ezra stepped back to the window to glance out and saw that the crowds were parting. Striding down the center of the street was a tall, bearded man. His eyes were dark and piercing. He did not smile, nor did he glance to the right or the left. He ignored the gathered men, women, and children who parted to let him pass, falling back to point, whisper, and rush off to spread the word. His path led straight to the shop's door.

Ezra did not hesitate. Despite the order not to disturb, he ran to the workshop door and pounded on it. There was a muffled shout from within. He pounded again. A moment later, the door swung wide, just as Ezra had pulled back his arm to strike again. Master Balthazar glared out at him.

"What? In the name of all the gods, what do you want?"

Ezra knew he had only moments. He described what he'd learned from the women in as few words as possible, and even as the door to the shop burst open, he managed to add a last comment.

"It's Noah, Master, he is here. In the shop."

Then, without waiting to see if Balthazar would follow, Ezra turned and hurried back to the front, lest their visitor find it empty and conclude that they were closed.

He heard the door to the workroom close behind him, and sensed Balthazar's presence. He'd known his message would galvanize the older man into action. What he did not know was what direction that action might take. This was an unprecedented opportunity. While Ezra knew there was money to be made, he could not quite grasp whether it would be best to be on the side of the crazy man from the woods, or those who found him an outsider and laughingstock.

He moved aside as they reached the main counter, allowing Balthazar to step past him. Noah stood in the center of the shop. He paid no attention to the merchandise. He waited, and as Balthazar reached him, he spoke without preamble or emotion.

"I need information. I am told that you are the most likely to possess it."

Balthazar sized up his visitor in an instant. The two men had encountered one another over the years, but had never really spoken, or been close, despite their similarity in age. Two vastly different lifestyles colliding.

"Information is a thing that I have in great quantity," Balthazar replied. "Of course, it would be helpful to know the nature of the information you seek—the subject? I have histories, books written by Kabbalists and kings…"

"The information I seek is of a more practical nature," Noah said. "If I understand correctly, you have—over the course of many years—processed the remains of a great number of beasts. I am interested in information on the size of as many as you have encountered, as well as any information you have on their feed, or their habits."

"You are, perhaps, planning to open a menagerie?" Balthazar asked, smiling smoothly. "It would be a wonderful investment, though a great deal of work."

"My reasons are my own," Noah said. "I have been in contact with our Lord, my God. He has instructed me."

"Yes, yes, I have heard," Balthazar replied. "No details, of course, but there was something about a boat."

Noah ignored the obvious efforts to draw him into a discussion.

"Do you have what I seek?" he asked. "I am ready to pay, but my time is limited."

Balthazar changed tack with the agility of a seasoned sailor.

"Of course, of course. As it happens, I have been creating a journal that may be of interest. It involves much more than the information you seek, but it encompasses all that I have learned of the creatures of the world for the last, oh, three hundred years or so. I can't guarantee it to be complete. Every day it seems something new comes to light."

"I will take it," Noah said.

Balthazar fell silent. He was used to barter, to negotiation. He was also unprepared to set a price on something he'd been working on the greater part of his life. There was one copy.

"I am not certain it is for sale," he said at last.

"I thought the basis of such a business," Noah replied, glancing around the shop for the first time, "was that everything is for sale at the right price?"

"Normally that would be true," Balthazar replied. "However, there is one copy of my journal, and assuming that I have yet to reach the end of my longevity, it is incomplete. I would be willing to allow access to it. Such access could involve someone taking notes or copying verbatim... or merely studying the work. I cannot allow the only copy in existence to simply walk out the door. You must understand that it involves the work of my lifetime."

"And it would aid in the work of mine," Noah said. "Still, I understand. Perhaps I could send one of my sons. If I did, would you grant them full access? Assist if they had questions? The endeavor I am about to embark upon will not be a swift one, and the information I am seeking, I don't believe I would need it immediately. I could work with what could be garnered over time."

"I am certain that we can come to an arrangement," Balthazar replied. "We have workspace, and I'm certain arrangements that are mutually acceptable could be reached."

"It is well," Noah said. "I will send a messenger, then, and gold."

Without another word, he turned on his heel and stepped back into the street. Balthazar stood, one hand stretched out toward the retreating figure, an odd, puzzled expression on his face. Then he turned to Ezra.

"I am not certain what, exactly, just happened," he said. "It seems, though, that we are going to have to block off a section of my workroom and fit it with a table, lighting, and sufficient space for someone to study. I will leave those details to you.

When our new 'associate' arrives, you will be my eyes, ears, and voice. You will assist them in finding what they seek in the volumes of my journal, provide them with paper, quills, ink, whatever they need. We will be charging Noah a hefty fee for this service, so I expect it to be worth the price..."

Ezra stared at his master for a moment. He fought the urge to smile, because in some way he could not quite grasp, the tone of Noah's voice, and the serious, even gaze with which he'd met that of Master Balthazar, weighed upon him.

"As you say, Master," he replied. He hesitated a moment, then added, "Shall I spread the word? Knowledge of what is happening in the forest will be valuable soon. It could be good for business."

"Of course," Balthazar replied. "And I will count on you to engage whichever of Noah's children comes to our door. Become their friend. Become their confidante. I will expect regular reports. I will maintain my distance. My ways are too well known for subterfuge... but you? You may appear quite trustworthy."

Ezra considered his response for a moment before replying.

"I will take that as a compliment, Master," he said at last, "though I am uncertain that is how it was intended."

"Nor will you ever be," Balthazar said. He grinned, turned on his heel, and returned to his workroom. The door closed behind him with a decisive snap.

Chapter 4

Noah assigned his youngest son, Ham, to the work in the city. He could not spare Japheth, who was overseeing the workers and construction, or Shem, who had stepped up to deal with the merchants from the city, the supply trains, and the day-to-day operation of the compound, along with his mother, Na'amah, who was a genius at planning. Ham was the least necessary to the work at hand, and also the most inclined to books and history. It was an important gift, and Noah did not begrudge his son this passion, but at the same time, the hard work of the day and the organizing of laborers would suffer in his youngest son's control. Better to send him to the city, with stern warnings to avoid too close attention to the distractions—the women and the wine—not to mention Master Balthazar himself, with his potions and tinctures and odd ways.

None of his sons had seen a hundred years. He doubted that they could begin to comprehend the breadth of his life, or that the passage of so many years even felt real to them. There were others as old, some older, but they grew fewer and farther from their God. Sometimes it felt like his family, and his home beyond the city walls, occupied a different reality—a world that had only come to be since his children were born.

The information he needed from Balthazar was not deep or complex. His own memory, while good, was not perfect. He believed that he remembered the details of his vision—of his dialog with his Lord, but such visions were seldom specific. Dimensions, numbers of levels, cages, containments. Balthazar might be many things, most of them sinful, but he had spent a lifetime studying people and places, and if anyone knew the requirements for containing the beasts of the world, clean and unclean, it would be he. He was a historian, a scribe. He recorded what he saw, and what he learned.

Noah had drawn up preliminary plans with Japheth, but his mind remained troubled. There were some great and terrible creatures walking the Earth. Finding a way to entice them onto an ark, let alone containing and feeding them once there without risking the lives of his family and those of the other creatures, was the real task. That was the great task. He knew that his Lord would not present an impossible challenge, but the strain on his faith, and that of his family, would be very real.

Ham left early in the morning, grabbing food for himself from the kitchens and hitting the road before the others were up and about their various duties. He was excited at the opportunity to spend time in the city—a thing his father normally forbade. He was also happy to have an opportunity to prove himself, to perform an important task without supervision. As the youngest son, he was seldom granted such responsibility.

He felt the weight of his father's gaze as he reached the road. Noah rose before the sun every day. Ham did, as well, but had never interrupted what he understood to be an important time of meditation for his father. He had his own concerns, and the early hours of the day gave him the opportunity to pursue them without the ridicule, criticism, and general disdain of his siblings. It wasn't easy living in the one remaining house dedicated to the Lord's laws and works. It was even less easy bearing the brunt of the frustration such a life caused his older brothers and sisters as the temptations of the world confronted them.

The sun had only just risen, and the way was clear. It was early for merchants to be on the road. Traffic would not be heavy for another hour. The roads beyond the city were guarded by day, but there was still danger, and the farther one traveled, the greater that danger became. The forest where his family lived was protected by a series of hidden pits, traps, and snares. There were only a few roads leading into the compound. They were not as well protected as the city, but they were safe enough as long as they remained deep within the wood.

And there were the Nephilim. They inhabited the outer ring of the forest, keeping to themselves and almost never seen by any but Noah himself. They abhorred what had become of the cities, of the lives and loves and failings of man. They yearned for the kingdom of their Lord, but were bound by flesh, doomed to walk the Earth as long as it suited their father. They lent their protection to the small band of faithful that was Noah and his family, diverting the great creatures of the desert to other targets, and other meals.

Ham had seen them. He had seen his father commune with them, once, but was unable to hear, or, more precisely, to understand what was communicated. In some way, those towering ancient ones, too large to be exactly human, too beautiful, protected the family. Their home in the woods was not as secure as the city walls, but somehow felt safer. It wasn't dependent on a single point of failure, as his brother Japheth liked to say. Japheth was a builder. He understood how things worked, and often how they might work better.

And there was the giant, Og. Ham knew that Og was the child of one of the Nephilim and some forgotten woman. He towered over men, sometimes over the trees themselves. He could communicate, not with words, but with thought. He had been a part of Ham's life since he was born, an accepted mystery.

The road was a different story from the compound. It was guarded by men. Against most threats that was fine, but the great beasts, the truly dangerous ones, often tested those safeguards. There were flying creatures—not birds, but more like crocodiles—with great leathery wings. They could swoop down from hidden crevasses in the rocky outcroppings several miles distant and be on a traveler in moments. Bringing one down was next to impossible. It could be done, but the best defense was to find a place beyond their reach, out of sight, wait until they took another, and then run for it.

Ham's father said it was God's will, that those taken from the road were payment for the sins protected within the city walls, the wickedness that infected men and women throughout the streets and brothels, taverns, and squares. Ham preferred to believe in a God less vengeful. The world was a dangerous place. There were many choices—the choice between good and evil, between cautious and bold, and between life and death. A creator who provided such tests would not be satisfied by a herd of sheep-like followers. He would want to see those choices considered and acted upon.

As he wound on toward the city, Ham glanced from time to time at the rocks and cliffs, the higher dunes to either side. Nothing moved. There were no flitting shadows, and he felt no tremble in the ground. Faith was fine for most things, but only an idiot walked blindly into danger.

Whether by divine intervention or luck, the road remained clear. He entered the outer gates, hailed the guards, and entered the inner caged gate without incident. It felt as if he'd stepped between worlds.

Scents and sounds, music and laughter, assaulted him on all sides. Men, women, and children strolled and ran, laughed, and bustled up and down the streets. Carts lined the way, as well as vendors, open store fronts, a library, and a public bath, all within sight of the first cross-street he came to. Ham had been to the city before, but always with his father, always bundled into a cart, taken to whatever place of business they required, and then hustled back to the woods. He had never entered on his own, nor had any of his siblings, save Shem. Even Japheth was forbidden unless the family traveled together.

Noah had told them it was not their virtue he distrusted, but that of the city. That men—inherently Godless—would draw them in, corrupt them, and fill their minds with darkness. This translated easily in Ham's mind to "I do not trust you."

Faced by the full reality of what he'd been denied, he had to stop and close his eyes, letting it all wash over and through him before checking the small map his father had made for him and following it down the main street of the city.

He had the sensation that everyone was staring, but knew it was ridiculous. Few if any would recognize him at all, and there was nothing particularly interesting about him. His robes were plain, his sandals worn. He would not stand out in any crowd, unless it was to be the least interesting focal point. It changed nothing. He felt very alone and very vulnerable, and for a moment he hated his father for it. They lived so close to all of this—and also lived without it.

He bumped into a woman hurrying down the street with a basket on her arm, nearly bounced into the street, and sputtered his apology. He had been so concentrated on his map that he hadn't seen her coming.

"What's wrong with you?" she said crossly. "You act like you're lost."

"Actually," he said, blushing deeply, "I am. I am looking for Master Balthazar's shop, but it is my first time in the city…"

She stared at him. Took a step closer. Stared some more.

"You're one of his sons…Noah's sons."

Ham said nothing.

"I've heard what he's doing…heard what you're planning. He's crazy, you know."

"Perhaps," Ham said, "but what I do not know is how to reach Master Balthazar. Could you…?"

She stared at him for a long moment, shook her head, and pointed.

"Follow the main street," she said. "You'll find Balthazar's shop two doors before you reach the square, on the right."

Ham bowed slightly and turned to go.

"He's crazy," she repeated.

Ham did not turn back to acknowledge her.

Chapter 5

Japheth stood and watched as a huge tree was felled, dropping across the edge of the forest. The material to be used to construct the Ark would be taken from the outermost trees. The woods were the only true protection the family had, beyond that of the Nephilim, and the Ark would deplete that protection significantly before it was completed. It was best to control the borders. It would be more difficult to move the fallen timbers inward, and it would be more dangerous working near the tree line, but it would be safer for the family in the long run, and it would help to protect the work in progress.

Noah had hired a good number of artisans from the city, and along with that, the family employed their own contingent of guards. It was an uneasy alliance, because Noah did not want the workers, or the soldiers, near his family. The guards camped by the edge of the trees in a sturdy shelter that Noah had paid for. The workers, for the most part, traveled to and from the city daily, returning well before the sun dropped beyond the horizon. It shortened the workday, but it maintained the separation of the family from the city, and Japheth knew that this was nearly as important as the work itself. They would be taken aboard the Ark because they were Godly. If that changed, then the entire work would fail, and they would perish along with the rest of the world. Noah had not said this, but it seemed an unspoken truth.

It was a good thing that the workers and the guards believed his father to be crazy. If they had felt otherwise, the idea of protecting and building a giant boat in the middle of a desert that would take their employers to safety and leave them behind when the flood came might have posed a problem. As it was, they were happy for the work, and the job was a big one that would keep them in food and wine for many years to come.

The gathering of timber was progressing steadily. They had downed several trees, and a few of those logs had already been split and shaped, loaded on carts and rolled inward to the clearing they'd created for the construction of the Ark. The undertaking was huge—on the same scale as erecting a temple, or a great pyramid, though most of those were constructed of stone, not wood.

The sun slipped toward the horizon, and the day's work drew to a close. Already the workers who would return to the city were stowing tools and packing their belongings. The guards milled about, weary from the day's heat. It was a slow moment, everyone focused on the day's close and whatever plans they had for the next day.

A man approached slowly, and Japheth smiled. It was the foreman, Isaac. Isaac was not a Godly man, but neither was he profane. He was a worker—a craftsman—and he had done well in keeping the others on schedule and maintaining quality over long hours.

"A good day's work," Japheth said.

Isaac brushed the sweat from his brow with a sleeve, and turned, glancing over his shoulder at the workers behind him

Turning back, Isaac said, "Indeed. Progress is being made, but I have come to you with a proposition. Some of the men believe we can increase productivity."

Japheth frowned. He glanced back at the workers. He'd noticed no break in efficiency. He could see nothing obvious that would affect productivity in any serious way.

"In what way?" he asked.

"There is a crew in the city," Isaac said, "who have tamed several of the three-horned beasts. They are immensely powerful and would make shorter work of felling the trees, not to mention moving them into position to be shaped and finished."

Japheth shook his head. He knew how his father would react, how the family would react. The beasts were unclean. They were dangerous and not to be trusted.

"It's out of the question," Japheth said. "The work must be completed by men, using the skills that God has granted them."

"Some would say," Isaac countered, "that God must be the source of these men's ability to train what others see only as monsters. They are not meat eaters—they do not attack unless provoked. They are no more dangerous than a pet dog, but a lot more useful."

"Noah would not approve," Japheth said.

"Noah is not in control of this operation," Isaac said. "You are. This is a logistical decision, and it could ease the burdens of many of your workers. The cost of the beasts and their trainers are more than countered by the hours gained."

Japheth did not respond immediately. He knew that much of what Isaac said was true. They could save days, perhaps weeks, in the initial outfitting, if he acceded. Noah would not be pleased, but in the end, he believed his father would be won over by the progress. The seasons would change before long, and it was important that the keel and major supports of the Ark be in place before the weather grew colder. Much of the labor would cease during the winter months, at least at the tree line, but if enough of the structure was in place, they could spend those months doing more of the finishing work on the hull and frame.

"Contact these trainers," he said at last. "Tell them we will chance one beast, on a trial basis. If things go well, I will find a way to convince father to allow us to expand."

Isaac nodded. He wiped his brow again.

"We have already made progress, but this will put you ahead of schedule. You will not regret it."

Japheth frowned and watched the foreman turn and leave. He wondered what type of payment the man would receive for pushing the services of the great beasts. The work would cut into what there was for his own men, so it had to be a matter of personal gain. None of the workers, beyond collecting their pay, cared at all about the schedule, or the completion of the Ark. Despite his misgivings, he thought that if he could get the creature to the site without drawing his father's wrath, he'd be able to judge whether it was a worthwhile addition to his workforce, or a mistake. Japheth hated mistakes, particularly if they could be traced back to him.

He stood and watched as the workers trailed off down the road toward the city in the distance. He thought, perhaps, that he'd arrive earlier than usual the following morning. If he rose soon enough, he could be gone during Noah's quiet time. He could not be accused of failing to report his decision if no opportunity to do so presented itself.

The grounds were mostly clear. It had been a day of cutting, finishing, and loading, so when the beast arrived, there would be room for it to maneuver. Japheth scanned the tree line, working out the logistics. If he got the beast to the work site without drawing his father's immediate attention, he would have only a short time to get it started. He briefly considered snagging a couple of men to stay behind after hours to make initial cuts in a few of the taller trees. He knew that was how it would work. They would weaken the tree, and then, pressing from behind, the great beast would topple it. Once down, they would harness it to help in positioning the log for cutting and shaping. What it would take the men a week to do with a single tree could be done in a matter of a couple of days if things went well. He decided not to think about the ways that they might not.

Ham passed the workers on the road as they made their way toward the compound. By the time he'd found Balthazar's shop, it had been nearly midday. There had been time only to meet Ezra, who had shown him his workspace, and the books of diagrams, drawings, and text it would be his duty to sift through. The sheer volume of that work had overwhelmed him, and after sorting randomly through a few bound tomes, he'd settled for spending the afternoon organizing his supplies for the first full day's work the following day. Uncertain he'd have any more luck finding the gates again after he departed, he'd left early, carefully reversing his steps and grinning widely when he made the final turn and saw the road out of the city straight ahead.

He'd briefly considered wandering the streets for a while and taking in the sights, but he suppressed the urge. His father would know. He always knew. If he thought that the city was posing too much of a danger, he would lock Ham away in that forest and keep him there, then send someone else to do the work. Or, worse yet, he would find a way to do it himself, neglecting other duties.

By the time Ham passed the workers, who were just beginning the trek to the city, he was hot, tired, and glad that he'd not lingered. He would have an hour or two before dinner to prepare his thoughts, make some notes, and ready himself for an early start and a long day's work. He would report to his father, who would be able to find no fault in his plan, and he would rest. He thought, briefly, of the city, of its smells, the people he'd seen, the women, the laughing, playing children, the drunken men and the scents of food, drink, and incense. He was glad he'd left when he did, but he was also glad for the memories, and for the thought of the days to come.

Ham believed in God. He believed in his father, as well, but there were limits. He had been taught that man had been granted choices. Noah did not allow any such choices to his family. He denied them the world, and so, denied them the opportunity to live their own lives. Ham knew his father had their best interests in mind, but he couldn't help but wish there was more of a two-way trust involved—less control. Their family was a small monarchy with Noah as king.

He passed the work site and saw the trees that Japheth and the others had felled. He waved to one of the men leaving and smiled.

"A good day's work," he said.

"Wait for tomorrow," the man said. "We will double it. Just you wait for that beast."

Before Ham could question him further, the man slung his tools over his shoulder and took off after his fellows.

"Beast?" Ham said.

He turned again and stared at the fallen trees, troubled, though he did not know why. He trudged on down the road and followed the tracks of the wagons that had drawn the lumber and supplies inward. He thought he would ask Japheth what the man had meant, but by the time he'd reached his quarters and cleaned up for dinner, he'd forgotten the incident entirely.

Chapter 6

Noah sat, as he always did, facing into the desert. The sun was just peeking over the skyline. The forest was silent, and he relaxed, concentrating on his feet and his legs, then his sternum. He'd performed the same ritual every morning for so long that the years blurred, and it was difficult to remember its beginning. He relaxed himself one muscle at a time, reaching out to the world around him, and the heavens beyond.

But that relaxation eluded him. Something disturbed his thoughts, and though he concentrated and sought his state of inner peace, he did not find it. He opened his eyes and scanned the tree line, then expanded his search.

He still saw nothing, but the ground beneath him trembled. He frowned. There were occasional earth tremors, but this felt different—rhythmic. When the great unclean beasts skirted the edges of the forest, he sensed dissonance—they lunged and ran. They pounded their great claws on the sand and shook the trees. This was different. It was a plodding rhythm, as if great hammers were striking the earth.

He rose, turned, and started down through the trees. He was a couple of miles from the work site where Japheth was clearing trees. He did not know why, but he believed the sounds were coming from there. His usual calm had been replaced by nervous tension, exacerbated by the steadily pounding vibration beneath his feet, growing stronger every step he took closer to the forest's edge.

He heard the men's voices first. They sounded excited, more animated than he would have expected. It was almost as if they were cheering. Just before he breeched the clearing, the air exploded with a massive *CRACK!*

Time slowed. He started to step into the clearing, but something held him back. He waited. The cracking sound became a rending, violent roar. A moment later, he was nearly knocked from his feet by a massive crash. Something had hit the ground hard and fast. Right in front of him. He stood, very still, until the only sound was the roar of cheering voices. He took a deep breath and stepped into the clearing.

The beast towered over him. Its head was thrown back and, having felled the tree, it let loose a grunting roar of fetid breath and triumph, stomping its feet. It had three horns, one directly in the center of its snout, and the other two farther back on the skull, like the horns of a demon. Its eyes were huge and wild. Great chains bound it by the ankles and throat, but they seemed weak and insignificant. Noah stood his ground.

He turned his gaze up to the beast's face. One great, baleful eye glared back down at him. Every other sound in the clearing had died. Men pulled back, leaving Japheth and the men controlling the beast, if they actually had control, standing alone. Noah tore his gaze from the beast and found his son.

Without another glance at the monster still stamping by the fallen tree, Noah turned and strode across the clearing. He did not hurry, and he did not speak. He fought the urge to let his anger control him. Though the blood pounded through his veins and throbbed in his temple, he whispered a prayer and breathed deeply and slowly. A great number of things had converged in this moment. He needed these men to work. He needed his son to lead them. Despite that, he needed to assert his control and to vent his anger. His prayers shifted to appeals for strength.

By the time he reached his Japheth's side, the others had drawn back. The great beast, its task complete, had grown docile. Noah saw that the men fed it, and that it ate vegetation. There was no sign of carrion or flesh.

To his credit, Japheth stood his ground calmly. He met Noah's gaze steadily, though beads of sweat had formed on his brow and upper lip, and the morning was too cool to have caused it.

"What is this?" Noah asked, waving his hand to encompass

the clearing, the beast, the fallen tree, and the workers. "How has this come to be without my knowledge? What has possessed you that you believed I would agree?"

"I did not believe that." Japheth said simply. "I know how you feel about the beasts. But I also know that this task, this great quest you have set us upon, is extraordinary. This creature exists on plants and vegetation. It does not kill. It can—will—increase productivity tenfold. I was going to tell you today, after I had seen, and tested, what it could do."

Noah stood very still. His first instinct was to lash out, but Japheth was not a child. He had handed the management of this task to his son, and regardless of the outcome of the exchange to follow, he could not undermine that authority. The isolation he had imposed on his family tended to cloud his vision and his judgment at times, and he often spent quiet time searching for the inner peace to avoid conflict over his own need to protect and control his world. Stone and soil eroded slowly, but faith? Faith crumbled like dust in a strong breeze in the face of the temptations of the world.

He opened his eyes and met Japheth's gaze. He was proud to see the boy did not waver, only waited. The beast had grown docile, grazing near the fallen tree. The workers were still and silent, waiting to see how this confrontation would end.

"How long did it take?" he said. "The felling of the tree. How long did it take with the help of this beast, and how long would it have taken without?"

Japheth did not hesitate.

"It took less than an hour, Father," he said. "We scored the trunk near its base to weaken it on one side. The beast pushed from the far side. To cut this tree down by hand would have taken the better part of a week."

Noah turned to watch the great beast. He knew it was unclean. The scriptures were clear on what was and was not. He knew other such creatures would make short work of the men, women, his family, and the entire camp, but though he searched the great, liquid eyes of the creature before him, he detected no malice. He felt nothing wrong in its presence.

"Keep me informed of progress," he said. "Do not allow

another such beast on the site, for now. We will monitor progress, and we will assess the value. In the future, such decisions should be shared with me. I have entrusted you with this task, and I will not question your authority to complete it, but you know my opinion of such creatures."

"I do, and it shall be as you say, of course," Japheth said, obviously relieved. "As I said, this was but a test, though it has proved successful. Even with but one of these creatures assisting, we will have enough material to hold us through the winter months, shaping and finishing. If there is a requirement for more, I will consult with you, and give a full accounting of the care, behavior, and feeding of the beasts."

Noah nodded. "It is well. I would not be truthful if I told you this did not cause me some concern and dismay, but the work ahead of us is of such a nature that I cannot trust myself to manage every moment of it. I suspect that, as it rolls out, more and more of the day-to-day concerns will fall to the responsibility of others. You are my son, and I trust your judgment."

Japheth nodded. "You know that I respect you beyond measure, Father."

Noah nodded, stepped forward, and hugged his son tightly. Then, without a backward glance, he turned and slipped back into the trees. His morning ritual was lost, but the affairs of the day and the needs of his family remained.

Japheth watched him go. As soon as Noah was out of sight, he turned and gestured to the workers. Everyone seemed to breathe and move at once. The beast was led a bit farther off. A crew began scoring another tree, while others worked to remove the branches from the fallen trunk and ready it to be moved deeper into the forest. After only a few moments, it was as if the old man had never appeared.

Chapter 7

Ham stood for a long time on the road, poised between moving on toward the city and returning home. He heard the massive crash of a tree before he had even made it to the edge of the forest. As he broke into the open, where trees ended and the road began, he felt the tremors. He heard men shouting. There were no screams. He listened for more crashing, but it did not come, though there were tremors that rippled through the sand beneath his feet and sent shivers up his spine.

Something had changed. Something was happening at the work site, and he knew that once his father got wind of it and made an appearance, everything in their lives could change rapidly. In the end, that was what forced him on toward the city. If whatever Japheth had done brought Noah's anger down on them, this might be his last chance to visit the city. If not, he had work to do, and his best bet was to bring home something tangible.

He walked more quickly than he had the day before, nearly breaking into a run. Suddenly the notion of sitting in the back room of a shop that smelled of things he could only imagine, filled with sinful potions and blasphemous items, seemed like the finest thing he'd ever dreamed of, and he didn't want to waste a minute of it.

Ezra stood back and examined his handiwork. It had not been a heavy lift to clear a long table in the workroom, but the gathering of the notes, the organization of the journals and drawings, and providing light, ink, and quills had proved considerably more complicated. He didn't want their visitor to have any tales to take back to his notoriously vindictive father, or complaints to direct toward Balthazar. He thought he'd anticipated and provided for every contingency.

It didn't hurt that Ham was naive. The entire encounter was possibly the finest opportunity Ezra had ever encountered. He would have access to exclusive knowledge of what took place in Noah's forest. At the same time, he would have the opportunity to understand, possibly more than any other person in the city, what was happening, what this crazy project was all about, and how it would progress. It was certain to increase his popularity and status, and if it went well and was profitable, could improve his lot with Balthazar as well.

When Ham wandered up the street from the gates, unable to stop himself from staring at every window or perusing the contents of every street-side cart, Ezra was waiting.

He met the boy half a block from the shop.

"Ham!" he said brightly. "Welcome back to the city."

Ham, startled, turned and then grinned when he saw who it was. He was relieved to see a face he recognized, and to have returned to the shop without getting lost or distracted. He wanted a full day's work to report to his father. Above all else, the semblance of normalcy and propriety would be key to his continued presence in the city.

"I hope I'm not late," Ham said. "I got an early start, but there was something odd going on near my home."

Ezra smiled. "I heard," he said. "It seems your brother has hired one of the great beasts to aid in the felling and moving of trees. I suspect the commotion you heard would be related to that. I was a little surprised to hear your father would agree to it."

Ham stared. If Ezra was surprised, he himself was shocked. He thought back and realized it must be true—the loud crash, the trembling of the earth. Could Japheth be so foolish? Then he realized he was gaping at the other young man and snapped his mouth closed.

Ezra actually laughed.

"You didn't know?"

Ham hesitated, then shook his head.

"These are strange times," he said. "I am not certain that my father was aware of this new development, but I am certain that if I don't get a significant amount of work done this first day, he may reconsider my being here."

"Of course," Ezra said. "All has been readied. I have cleared a workspace and provided supplies. I will show you what I have done, and you can tell me if there is more that you require, or if something more would help."

Ham laughed. "I have no idea what I have gotten myself into," he said. "The task seems almost impossible."

"It is not going to be easy," Ezra agreed. "Master Balthazar's notes are meticulous, and very complete. There are illustrations and measurements. I believe, though, that they are organized well enough that pulling only the information required may prove simpler than it seems. I will help in any way that I can, as long as it does not pull me from my duties."

As they stepped through the door into Master Balthazar's shop, Ezra glanced out into the street. As expected, several groups had gathered to talk and whisper among themselves. They stared openly as he escorted Noah's youngest son out of sight, and he knew that, as soon as the day was completed and Ham was on his way back to the forest, he would find it difficult to pay for a drink. Strange times indeed.

Business was brisk. The shop filled early and remained that way throughout the day. Men and women stopped in for incense, medicines, cards and books, potions. Most of them were so distracted that it was clear they did not need any of the items they purchased. In fact, those things located nearest to the door leading into the rear chamber were in the greatest demand.

Ezra busied himself herding people away from the area as quickly and quietly as possible, fielding questions in hushed tones and doing his best to look wise. Once an hour he slipped into the back where Ham had several volumes open on the table, and a large parchment spread before him.

Before the work had begun, and before Ezra had opened the shop to the public, the two had organized the volumes of Balthazar's journals and laid out a plan of how the most important information could be categorized and recorded. Balthazar had recorded the creatures by type—those considered clean or unclean, those that slithered, those that climbed, those that flew, and those that swam. Some traveled in herds or packs, others were more likely to be alone, or in pairs, mated for life.

This categorization made Ham's job much simpler because similar creatures would require similar amounts of space, similar feed and care. Their habitats were recorded in the great books, often with careful illustrations.

As the afternoon ran toward its close, Ezra found Ham staring at the parchment, his brow furrowed.

"What's wrong," Ezra asked.

"Nothing specifically," Ham said. "It's just that I'm going to have to bring some things with me tomorrow. My father has what he believes to be very specific dimensions for this craft, this ark. For me to even begin to imagine how all of this..." he waved his arms to encompass the pile of journals sprawling across the workbench, "will be possible, I must have the diagrams side by side."

Ezra's heart sped a bit. This was perfect. The actual diagrams of the Ark would be incredibly interesting, and it seemed likely he would be the only citizen of the city to view them.

"You have diagrams?"

"Not exactly, but I have made rough sketches. I have the dimensions and instructions as my father recalls them from his vision. I will have to clarify them and do something more complete. Then I will have to calculate the numbers and dimensions required—at a minimum—to house the creatures."

Ham's gaze dropped to the parchment, and Ezra saw the sudden despair. He knew he should not care about this craziness, that it would never make the slightest difference how they arranged their great boat in the middle of a desert, but he felt a kinship with Ham. They both served demanding masters, and, truthfully, the challenge was intriguing.

"I will help," he said simply. "If you bring your drawings earlier, so that we have time before the shop opens, we can go over them together."

Ham glanced up in wonder.

"Why?"

Ezra shrugged. "Let's just say I don't want the drowning of many helpless animals on my conscience and leave it at that."

Ham grinned, stood, stretched, and capped the ink bottle.

"I have to get back to the forest," he said. "It is getting late, and I'll need time to work on those drawings. Also, I kind of want to find out what happened when my father learned they were using the beasts to fell trees."

They both laughed. Ezra walked him to the door and waved as Ham took off down the street toward the gates, the road, and home. Then he stepped quickly back inside, straightened his robes, and prepared for the sudden influx of customers he expected to follow.

Chapter 8

The family gathered at the table for dinner, as always, but there was no idle chatter. It was as still and silent as a tomb. Ham stared at his hands, clasped before him on the table, awaiting the blessing his father would eventually deliver. There had been whispered warnings and reports of the morning's encounter at the work site, but only Japheth had been present, of the family, and he had said little.

His father had not yet arrived. Noah ended his days as they began—alone, gazing out over the desert, and communing with the Lord. It would not matter how angry he might be, he would not break that routine, so there was nothing any of them could do but to wait and wonder.

Ham didn't care what kind of trouble his brother might have brought down on his own head, as long as that trouble did not extend to the research in the city. He was excited by the work, and despite the tension surrounding him, his mind spun with diagrams, dimensions, and the need to be past the meal and on to preparation for the coming day. It was almost more than he could stand to sit and wait.

The sound of approaching footsteps broke the silence and Noah strode into view. He did not appear angry, nor did he appear pleased. His features were placid, and that was more agitating than either of the other expressions might have been.

He stopped at the head of the table, his hands folded before him. He glanced once around, letting his gaze rest momentarily on each of those seated around him, before lowering his eyes, taking a deep breath, and beginning to speak.

"It has been said," he began, "that the ways of our Lord are mysterious. That we may not understand them, but only serve. It is also true that we are fond of setting our laws in stone, closing our minds, and walking a very narrow path, rather than considering options.

"Today has been a day of revelation. First, I realized that my children are not extensions of my own being, but individuals capable of right and wrong decisions. I have very often chosen to make important decisions that should rightly fall to others, and I blame this on my own pride. My faith. I see the world through a lens that is more like a spyglass—focused and blind to the vision of others.

"A great task has befallen us, and it is a burden I cannot bear alone. It will test every one of us, and only as a single force do we have any possibility of completing it. This morning, without consulting me, Japheth made a decision. He did so knowing it might anger me. He did so knowing it might be a disaster. He also did so knowing that, if it succeeded, our burden would be lightened. And he was correct.

"We are tasked with saving two each—a mated pair—of all unclean beasts. That includes the great ones, the dangerous ones, the evil ones. It seems that it will fall, at least in part, on those same beasts to assist in their own salvation."

No one at the table stirred. No one dared to meet Noah's gaze, lest they find a test there—a judgment—that his words did not appear to convey. Such an admission on his part was unheard of.

"Lord," Noah continued, "we thank you for all you provide. For the workmen and the beasts, for this food, and for the vision that will bring us safely through the coming flood. May we prove worthy. May we remain a family, under your care and guidance."

He fell silent, and then, raising his gaze to sweep the length of the table, he took his seat. At first, there was no sound. No one moved to take food onto their plates. No one wanted to be the first to whisper, or to clear their throat. Noah, as if nothing out of the ordinary had transpired, reached for a plate of bread, and dropped a chunk onto his plate. He passed it down the table and poured a glass of wine.

That was all it took. Whispers rippled up and down the length of the table. Bowls and plates were passed, voices rose, fell, and rose again. The family came to life, and Ham breathed a sigh of relief. He was not the current focus of his father's attention, and there was no wash of anger, as he'd feared. He immediately began going over the numbers and the designs for the Ark in his head. Very suddenly, though he was hungry, he wanted nothing but his papers, his quills, some ink, and a quiet space to work. He knew he'd have to speak to Noah before he returned to the city, but suddenly that seemed a good thing, rather than a disaster in the making.

As soon as it was possible, he excused himself and slipped away.

"So," Noah said, leaning close to examine one of the larger diagrams Ham had sketched, "you recommend, thus far, that we stagger the levels, not setting each to a single height, but varying to prevent the necessity of predators and prey existing side by side."

Ham nodded. "I believe we are going to have to look into potions that will make the animals docile, or even sleep. Many will be easy to handle, but others are unmanageable under normal conditions. Considering the balance of the craft, and the limits of integrity possible in the structure, I think it prudent not to depend entirely on our Lord to control them. Also, the placement of the heavier beasts will act as ballast, keeping us upright."

Noah grew silent at this, and Ham held his breath. He knew such a statement was dangerous, but felt it was also important. It was hard to imagine reaching a point where they were actually loading all the expected beasts onto a great Ark, but harder still to imagine doing that if those beasts were aware at full strength and energy.

"I believe you are correct," Noah said. "See if Master Balthazar can recommend a variety of such concoctions. I assume that the various creatures will have different traits, resistances to certain things, and weaknesses to others. It will serve no purpose to load them and lose half of them to violent ends, or, worse yet, to put our family in more danger than necessary. It is easy to get caught up in the vision, to forget that our virtue is earned. I believe this is as much a test of our intellect, and our resolve, as it is of faith."

Ham stared at his father. It was rare that the two spoke as equals. Rarer still that his father hinted at any lack of confidence on his own part, or intimated respect on the part of his son's.

He lowered his eyes to the diagrams, biting his lip hard to prevent an embarrassing tear.

"We will meet nightly," Noah said. "You will show me what you have learned, and we will plan accordingly. This is important work—possibly the most important work before us. I have chosen well."

Noah leaned in and hugged Ham tightly, then rose.

"It has been a long day," he said. "A day filled with surprises, lessons, and remarkable events. I am going to bed early, and suggest you do the same. The morning will be upon us before we realize it."

Ham began rolling his scrolls up and stowing his gear.

"Yes, Father," he said.

He watched as Noah disappeared into the shadows.

Chapter 9

Ham reached Master Balthazar's shop shortly after sunup. He'd risen early, taken his morning meal in solitude, and hurried off. On the road, he'd passed the great beast and its handlers. Despite its size, it did not appear to offer any threat. Its movements were ponderous and slow, but it seemed content. After a moment's hesitation to watch it pass, Ham turned his attention to the city.

He had not shaken the odd sense of empowerment his father's words of encouragement had brought. He was thrilled to be considered vital, and he was determined not to prove a disappointment. He was also determined not to lose his newfound independence. There were so many things he hoped to see, and to learn, as his work continued.

He passed through the gates without incident and hurried up the street. The city was quiet, not yet fully awake, and in that silence, he found it less imposing. He was able to take in the storefronts, the carts, the general sense of the backbone that would bear the weight of animals and carts, men and women, laughing children. It was much less overwhelming than his first visit, or even the second.

Ezra was waiting outside the door and smiled as he approached. They came from different worlds, but Ham believed he felt a kinship with the other young man. There were certain similarities between Balthazar and Noah. The distinctions were obvious, but it still made Ezra easier to understand.

"You are early," Ezra said.

"I did not want to get caught in the crowds. Also, as you know, my brother has brought in one of the great beasts to help with the felling and moving of trees. I wanted to be on the road early enough to watch its passing."

"They are magnificent," Ezra said. "The few that suffer our control have changed our lives."

"I was concerned that my father would not approve, and that things might change," Ham said. "It seems I underestimated him. I think he wanted to object, but something changed. I don't know how to explain it. It's as if this vision has widened his perspective. Things he would have found sinful a few weeks in the past are acceptable now, as long as they support that vision."

"It's true, isn't it?" Ezra asked. "He believes the world—as we know it—will be wiped out in a flood. So much water that every living thing drowns or is washed away."

Ham didn't say anything at first. Then, lowering his eyes, he nodded.

"Of course. I would not be here if he did not believe in the vision. We would not be designing an ark capable of carrying so many diverse creatures if he were not certain we were protecting them from extinction."

"And no other men—or women—will be allowed on board?" Ezra asked.

Ham shook his head again. He did not speak.

"I have to say then," Ezra continued, his tone neither accusatory nor angry, "that I hope he is wrong. I think it will be a grand project. I believe this ark will be one of the wonders we see in our long lives, but I hope it never rises to the top of the waves. I hope there is no flood. I am sorry to say, I would rather see your father laughed out of the streets of the city than die by drowning. I hope you understand."

Ham didn't even hesitate.

"There is no way that I could blame you for that," he said, "nor do I wish to see any die in a flood. I have seen things in my life that lead me to believe in my father's visions, but he is a man. I will do as I am bid, and I will hope that when all is said and done, I can abide the consequences."

Before Ezra could comment, a huge bellowing roar sounded, far too close. Men and women shouted and screamed, and the earth shook.

Ham rose, alarmed, backing toward the nearest wall. "What...?"

Ezra only grinned. He turned toward the street and beckoned for Ham to follow. Then he took off at a run for the front door. After only a moment, Ham followed.

The streets were filled with people. Overflowing. They spilled out of doors, off of side streets, and lined the main avenue. All of them stared down toward the main gates of the city.

"What is it?" Ham asked, grabbing Ezra by the shoulder. "I thought I heard—"

"You did," Ezra said. "It is one of the beasts. I'm not an expert, Master Balthazar would know for certain, but I believe it is a Mace Tail!"

Ham's thoughts reeled. He knew the creature in question. It was heavily armored, low to the ground, but with a deadly mace-like tail that could be used as a devastating weapon. They ate plants but had been known to take down large predatory beasts, and to kill groups of hunters and soldiers too close and incautious.

"But—" he said.

"Just watch," Ezra said.

Ham did. The crowds had all carefully backed off from the center of the street. They pressed to the walls, holding one another and laughing. He saw a sort of manic quality in their eyes, felt something a little off in their laughter. They were excited, but they were frightened as well.

Those in the street, carts, horses, pedestrians, all of them parted and pressed as close to the walls of the shops and buildings as possible. There was a sense of near-panic that Ham had never experienced.

The ground beneath his feet, and even the air, vibrated. The approaching creature was huge, much larger than the road had been designed to contain. Dust rose from the street, and rivulets of sand and silt slithered down the walls from the roofs of the buildings.

"Why is it in the street?" Ham asked.

"This *is* why," Ezra said. "Look around you. If you wanted to get people fired up to watch a battle, what better way? Frighten them. Bring the danger close, then take it away safely."

"What if it's not taken safely?"

"That's the point, isn't it? Life is not certain. Moments like this, they remind you."

Ham craned his neck to stare down the street toward the gates. Finally, as the surging crowd cried out and pressed even more tightly to the store fronts, the beast's great head came into view. It was muzzled with thick bands of leather. Its eyes were not crazed, but they were huge. They stared, flicking left, then right, taking in the crowds. Its neck was short and powerful, and despite the handlers moving it slowly up the street, it swung its great head back and forth. Each time it did so, men and women ran and squealed.

Then the body came into sight, followed by the great tail. They had secured the latter with cables and a wooden structure that prevented it from swinging freely. The device seemed functional, but also frail. The sense that the creature could burst its bonds and create havoc was close to the surface.

The handlers scrambled about the beast's legs. They made a great show of ducking and crying out, but it had a theatrical feel to it, as if it were orchestrated for effect. Despite being aware of this, Ham found his heartbeat racing. It was a thrill. The nearness of something he'd been conditioned to fear all his life was impossible to ignore.

Then the creature spun its head, and for just a moment, Ham met its gaze directly. There was a connection, and his stomach churned. It was wrong. Something was wrong. The beast's motions were not just orchestrated, they were sluggish. The expression on its face—Ham knew there could not be emotion behind it, and yet, it was there. Pain. Loss. Something broken.

Ham thought of slaves he'd seen, chained, and forced to labor that would drive them toward early death. Suddenly the thrill of the moment darkened and churned in his stomach, and he turned away. Staggering to a wall, he fought back the urge to vomit on the wall. He staggered back toward the shop, the silence, the books.

Ezra caught him just as he reached the door, placing a hand on his shoulder.

"It's a lot to take in," Ezra said.

"It's wrong," Ham nearly choked as he forced the words out. "Can't you see it? Why are they doing it? What is the purpose?"

Ezra stepped back. "What do you mean?"

Ham stood, his face pale, and pointed after the creature, at the men and women scurrying into the street in its wake, laughing and screaming and remaining just far enough behind to not be in any real danger.

"That," he said. "What did the creature do?"

"Do?" Ezra asked. "Why it, I mean, I'm sure they captured it near the road."

"It attacked?"

Ezra frowned. He turned and glanced after the beast, then back.

"I don't think so. The Mace Tails eat plants. They are dangerous, but…"

"Then why is it here?" Ham asked. His color was returning, and his anger growing. "Why is it chained and dragged through the streets? Why are they laughing?"

"To fight," Ezra said simply. "It will fight another beast in the arena. There will be ale, concessions, and vendors. Gladiators will fight as well, possibly thieves, or prisoners. Everyone in the city will be there."

"I will not," Ham said. He turned back and re-entered the store.

Ezra took one last long look after the passing crowd, then followed Ham.

"What is wrong with you?" he said, as he entered the store. "It's a beast. It's a dangerous creature. They fight for sport, for entertainment."

Ham met Ezra's gaze levelly.

"And you see no problem with that? You find nothing wrong in pitting one living creature against another to be maimed, or killed, for entertainment? And prisoners? You'd take a man who likely stole bread to feed his family, and watch him fight to the death against a creature whose sin was eating a tree too close to a road, while you got drunk and cheered? This is who you are—who…" Ham waved his arms… "all of you *are*?"

Ezra just stared. He started to speak, then clamped his jaws shut. He wanted to lash out. He wanted to tell this righteous bumpkin to grow up, that there were things he needed to understand, and to learn, but every time he started to put the thoughts together, the words dissolved.

He could not form an argument that did not make him seem exactly as Ham had labeled him. He could not explain, he suddenly realized, the arena or the battles, the reasons behind it all. They involved money and greed. They would end in drunken brawls and gambling debts... to be repeated a few days later.

"I—"

Ham turned away. He returned to the shop, the table, and the books, and pretended to work, but it was obvious his heart wasn't in it. Ezra took a seat at the far end of the bench.

"I don't have answers to all the sins of the city," he said at last. "I will admit, I never considered the questions you have asked. I never had a reason to. The battles, the arena, you can't tell me—even as isolated as you are with your father—that you did not know they existed."

Ham looked up. "I have heard, but words and experience are different things. I am sorry. I did not mean to accuse you, or to judge. It's not my place. I did not expect to react so—"

"Compassionately?" Ezra said softly. "Let's see if we can't get some more of this work done and take your mind off it. You've certainly given me things to think about."

As the day progressed, the two worked steadily, cataloging beasts, studying feeding cycles, sizes, mating cycles—and ignoring all that passed on the street. They were so intent on the work that they nearly missed the time for Ham to return home.

"Safe trip," Ezra said. Maybe tomorrow I'll be able to find something to show you that shines a better light on our lives here."

"I'd enjoy that," Ham said. "As much as my father sets us apart from the rest of the world, we have more in common than it seems. Something you said earlier keeps coming back to me. He does believe that the world will be swept away, and that only our family will survive it, and knowing that, he continues. He calls that faith—and there is no doubt that it *is* faith—but it's also horrifying in the same sort of way those beasts being led to the arena were. He's willing to watch as an entire world is swept away."

"Maybe he'll just get a big boat," Ezra said, "and everyone will be fine."

"I almost wish I believed that," Ham said. He turned, then, and stepped into the street, hurrying toward the gates and the road home.

Chapter 10

Shem stood at the end of the main trail leading through the forest. He watched as a caravan made slow progress across the desert from the city. The compound received supplies twice weekly from the city, and he knew they would not arrive for the better part of an hour, but he couldn't help wanting to be early. There would be meat, fruit, vegetables from the gardens within the city walls, and various other items necessary for the maintenance and upkeep of the family, the guards, the workers while they were on site, and the forest defenses. He had a scroll in one hand, and he glanced at it disinterestedly. He knew the numbers by heart. It was all routine, and he was good at routine. It was how he managed his world and his life. Numbers, warehouses, cattle, and labor. None of those things were on his mind.

The supply train had approached their forest at exactly the same time, as it had for years. The past two years, however, there had been something different. Something special. A girl. At first, he'd only noticed her in passing, pulling her weight in unloading supplies, carefully annotating what she delivered. He'd seen that others respected her, and as time passed, even deferred to her decisions and suggestions. Her name was Sedeqetelebab, and he had been unable to stop thinking about her. He'd decided that this was the day he would approach her father, Eliakim, and make known his intention of proposing marriage. Eliakim was a son of Methuselah, so ancient that there were songs sung about him. Shem had spoken to his father for his blessing. He would soon reach his hundredth year—his youth was waning. It was time he considered marriage, and even had it *not* been time, he could not get Sedeqetelebab out of his mind.

The closer the supply train drew, the faster his heart beat. There was a rustling in the trees off to the right side of the road, and he glanced over and up. Nothing was clear, but he knew one of the watchers was there. Probably Og. The giants patrolled the perimeter of the trees, diverting the great beasts and protecting the family. They confused Shem. They should not have existed, and they represented a break in the faith that was the core of his existence. If an angel could be tempted by the flesh, an abomination be born of that union. Then that abomination protected the faithful, and it added layers to his universe that he could not comprehend. He'd spent hours, entire days in prayer seeking understanding, but he was no closer than he'd ever been to achieving it. When the supplies arrived, the watchers were always vigilant. It was a moment of vulnerability, and their presence, while unsettling, added a touch of comfort that was hard to ignore.

He turned back to the approaching caravan. With the construction crews working full shifts, he'd had to completely re-evaluate storage, the quantities and quality of food, materials, and the scheduling of deliveries. He loved the work, and the fact his father entrusted such important details to his control threatened him with the sin of pride.

He closed his eyes, offered a short prayer, and sorted his thoughts. There were construction supplies in this supply train that went far beyond any similar orders in the past, and he knew he had to be on his guard. Those in the city were not beyond shorting orders or sending materials of a lower quality than he had requested. It all had to be inventoried, inspected, and probably haggled over before it could be accepted, before payment could be arranged.

Something in the distance caught his eye. He stood still, staring, then ran to the edge of the forest and began to scream, waving his arms impotently as the supply train wound its way slowly across the sand. Behind them, launched from beyond a large rock outcropping surrounded by dunes, a vast winged shape had lifted into the air. It was too far away for any sound to carry, but Shem had heard the creatures before. By the time that sound broke the silence, flight was impossible. They were vast, as large as some of the worst of the land beasts, with leathery wings and beaked jaws that could rend and tear the flesh of men, pack animals, or other beasts with terrifying strength and speed.

He knew there was little chance that those in the supply train could see him, or, if they did, that they would know he was trying to warn them, but he had shed all pretense of caring about the supplies, or even the men and beasts carrying them. All he could think of was that Sedeqetelebab was in danger. With a last glance over his shoulder, he turned and started running down the road, into the open, his robes flying about him crazily.

He was a good quarter of mile from the front of the small caravan, and he wasn't a swift runner. He was, however, fit. He spent his life in motion, both mentally and physically, and fear for another drove him to greater effort. Still, he was no match for the beast. It rose with heavy bursts of power, wings driving down and catching the air in loud, slamming beats until it reached a great height, just beneath the clouds.

Shem saw it at that peak, sunlight glaring off its wings, shining through the leathery skin and glinting off its eyes. In that moment, it seemed an avenging demon, formed of fire and light. He nearly stumbled, then, averting his eyes, increased his speed once again, barreling down the road toward those approaching. Whether from his frantic efforts to warn them, or because they'd heard its scream or seen its shadow, the caravan had increased its speed. He saw horsemen breaking off to the sides but knew they could not possibly carry weapons adequate to fend off the coming disaster.

In the forest behind Shem, among the taller trees, a form stepped from the shadows. It was huge, half the height of the trees themselves, but quick. Deceptively agile. Og had seen the winged beast before Shem, had heard its cry, despite the distance. He'd held his ground, because the threat was to the supply train and not the forest. Then the son of Noah had fled into the desert, and everything had changed.

They were far away, but Og was prepared. He pulled a great sling from his belt. The giant reached to a pocket of the hide tunic he wore and pulled free a stone. It was the span of a bull's head. He tucked it into the pocket of the sling and crouched. Despite the necessity to act, he did not wish to be seen. The protections he and other watchers provided to Noah and his family would be less effective if they were out in the open. Noah was a devout and faithful man, but there were prophecies and omens. Og was careful to draw no attention to his presence.

This situation required action. He watched the beast carefully. As it reached the apex of its climb, he began, very slowly, to swing the sling in a circle, speeding its motion with each rotation, but controlled. There would be one chance. The only thing in his favor was that the beast was predictable. It attacked in a single manner, over and over, confident in its success. Og had the advantage of experience and years of quiet vigilance.

He glanced to the road. Shem was about three quarters of the way to the front of the caravan, but, rather than helping, it was obvious that he'd caught the beast's attention. The supply train's defenses were weak, but the separated prey was always preferred. The beast diverted its dive, just slightly, aiming for the lone man running at what must have seemed to it to be the pace of a snail.

Og took a deep breath. Despite the pointlessness of the action, he mouthed a silent prayer in a language rarely spoken in those latter times, and with a huge roar, he loosed the stone.

Shem was never quite certain what happened next. He told the story many times, but it never seemed quite the same as he remembered. He was close enough to see the faces of the first of the merchants. He saw the circling riders, great crossbows at the ready, aimed to the heavens. He thought, but was never certain, that he saw Sedeqetelebab, her eyes wide and her hands outstretched toward him. He saw the great shadow turn, saw how it angled down across the road toward him.

And then, like a clap of thunder, something struck the beast head on. There was an awful scream and a crushing, blasting explosion. Blood, skin, and gore rained down, plummeting toward him at incredible speed. The gore struck him full on, driving him from his feet. He was buried in a hot, sticky wash, drowned in its stench. Just before he passed out from the impact and the lack of air, he wondered briefly why he did not feel talons rending his flesh. The last thing he saw was the sun, blazing overhead. The last thing he heard, beyond the last splatters of the great beast dropping around him, were the cries of the merchants and the pounding of hooves.

He vaguely remembered being lifted from the sand, and the swaying, bumping roll of a wagon beneath his back. His next memory was waking in his own bed, his mother by his side. He'd tried to rise, but found he was weak, and thought better of it.

"You're awake," she said.

Without thinking about the consequences, Shem said, "Sedeqetelebab, is she…?"

His mother smiled. "She is fine, and she is outside. The supplies have been delivered and inventoried. There were no injuries, other than your own. They are calling you a hero for warning them."

"But I did nothing," Shem said. "The beast, it—"

"I know," his mother said. "But you must listen to them. They believe that you called upon our Lord, and that he saved you."

"But…"

"They cannot know the truth," his mother said. "You know this, Shem. You know what your father will say. The Watchers—they are not trusted. Those in the city are as frightened of them as they are of the beasts."

"I heard him," Shem said. "In the trees. I think it was Og."

"Never speak of it."

Shem shook his head. "Of course. It's true, really. I prayed as I ran, and the Lord provided."

His mother patted him on the head.

"When you feel you can stand," she said, "there is a young woman who would like to speak with you. It seems that she refused to return with the wagons. She is very concerned."

Shem's face grew red, and he said nothing.

"Your father would like to meet her. He has asked me to provide her accommodations."

Shem glanced up.

"Temporary, for now," his mother said.

Shem smiled and reached up to rub a tender spot on his head. It was a day he was unlikely to forget, and he thought that, soon, he would have to make his way into the trees and offer thanks. He hoped that the proper ears, as well as those of his Lord, would hear.

Chapter 11

Ezra had thought his most difficult duties would involve organizing files and juggling his work in the shop against his assistance to Ham in the workroom. As it turned out, he had seriously underestimated the value and quality of the gossip he'd been entrusted with. The shop had never had more business, and everyone bought something, even if they didn't need it. No one wanted to appear curious, but everyone had questions. He could not simply sell a tincture or a potion. He had to endure countless efforts at small talk from citizens who had never given him the time of day, all intent on coaxing some new tidbit of information from him before he took their money, and they had no excuse for tarrying.

He had originally believed that this would be his moment, his chance to make acquaintances and contacts, but since the incident with the beast in the street, he had developed a protective attitude. He did not want to barter his new friend's life, or that of his family, for favor with those who would forget him in a second if they no longer believed he could provide them with new stories. Ham, on the other hand, appeared to honestly like him and to enjoy his company. Weighing the one against the other, he had slowly found himself becoming reticent in the passing of gossip, short with customers he felt were pushing for information, and protective of his new friend.

There were limits, though. The girls were his undoing. He could not simply dismiss their praise or their questions. And it wasn't just him they were interested in. He knew that Ham would be worried if he knew, that Noah would pull him from the work, and from the city, if any inkling of impropriety should surface, but Ezra was ill-equipped to handle the situation. After careful consideration, he realized that the only honest way forward (which had never been a priority for him) was to simply explain the situation to Ham and allow him to make his own decisions.

That morning, as he waited near the front of the shop for Ham's arrival, he noted that the crowds were larger than normal. Groups of citizens were gathered, speaking animatedly, and waving their hands. Something had happened, something important, and he wanted to go out and ask what it had been. He also knew that if he did so, Master Balthazar would have his head. There would be time. Customers would come to the shop, and he would eventually get the news.

Then a new commotion began down the street, toward the gate. He turned just as Ham burst free of a crowd, clutching an armload of scrolls, and running at a full sprint. Those he passed called out to him to stop, reached out as if to stop him. Ezra hurried to Ham's side and got behind him, forming a very thin, very inadequate shield.

"Is it true?" a man cried.

"A miracle?" a woman said.

Within moments, amid a cacophony of voices, shouts, and pounding feet, they entered the shop. Ezra spun, just managing to close and lock the door before the crowd swelled against it. He turned back, put his back against the door (as if that would make a difference if the crowd really wanted in), and stared at Ham.

"What," he said, "was that?"

Ham, who had been sprinting since entering the gate and catching sight of the waiting crowds, squatted for a moment, catching his breath. He rose shakily after a few seconds.

"Shem," he said. "It was Shem."

Ezra stared, waiting.

"*What* was Shem?"

Ham settled a bit, shook his head to clear his thoughts, and told the story as he'd heard it. He knew it wasn't the truth, or at least he didn't believe it was the truth. He was fairly sure this would mark the first time that his father had, while not exactly asking him to lie, laid down a falsehood as the truth and made it crystal clear that he would broach no discussion or argument.

"There was a supply train," Ham said. "It was nearing the line of trees surrounding our compound when one of the great winged beasts appeared. My brother, Shem, has lost his heart to a girl who was with the caravan. When he saw the beast, he ran out into the desert, trying to warn them. The beast turned and went after him, but before it could strike, it was struck dead by a bolt from the heavens. It exploded, bits and pieces everywhere. No one was hurt, and they are saying that Shem prayed and was answered."

"Exploded?"

"As if lightning flashed and struck it mid-flight," Ham said. "Except, there was no storm, and no one saw lighting. One man claimed he saw a dark shape flash across the sky. Everyone's eyes were on the creature, fearing for their lives."

"And you believe this?" Ezra asked.

Ham averted his eyes, just for a second. "I have no idea what to believe, but I know what my father told me, and what he believes. He believes the Lord intervened, that the prophecy states that he and his family will board the Ark."

Ezra started to ask more but stopped. Something in Ham's eyes told him it would be best to let it go.

"Well," he said, "that explains the crowd. I have no idea how we're going to get you out of here at the end of the day. We'll have to explain to Master Balthazar when he arrives. I'm sure he'll know what is going on before he makes it to the shop. He will know what to do. I hope."

"I hope so, too," Ham said. "I almost didn't come today. I did not want to let my father down, but I knew that once the supply train returned to the city, word would spread. I had no idea how far, or how fast. I think if you had not come out to get me, they might have torn me to shreds trying to get me to talk."

"They might have at that," Ezra said. He grinned. "You are welcome for your life, Ham, son of Noah."

Ham laughed. "I almost forgot," he said. "I brought you something. Actually, I brought you something and other things you can give to Master Balthazar. I have no idea if they are of any use, but on my way from the forest, instead of coming straight here, I wanted to see the site where Shem was attacked. The caravan apparently moved on very quickly, and my family would have no use for such things, but I found these."

He pulled a pouch from his pocket, untied the strap that bound it, and poured the contents out onto the main counter. There were teeth and bones, quite a number of them. There was still flesh attached to many, but it had dried in the desert sun.

Ezra stepped forward, picking through them slowly and smiling. "Oh, Master Balthazar will be pleased, but I think, before he arrives—"

He quickly picked out four teeth and slid them into his pocket.

"What are those for?" Ham asked.

"Look outside," Ezra said. "Look at that crowd. Remember why they want to speak to you, probably touch you, maybe steal your clothing. As far as they know there was an actual miracle, and that creature was the recipient of God's wrath. They may not truly believe in that miracle, but to own a piece of it? Something they could wear, or display in their homes, talk about at a party? This might as well be a small bag of pure gold."

Ham blinked, turned to stare out the door, and then turned back. He grinned. "Maybe," he said, "you should give this batch to Balthazar. I will stop on the way home, and again on the way back tomorrow, and bring you more. You have been a great help to me."

"I will tell you why I took four teeth," Ezra said. "I have come to consider you a friend. Maybe the closest I have in the city. I don't get out of the shop often. I am going to drill holes in them and suspend them from leather. One for you, one for me, and one each for the girls we meet and decide to spend our lives with. I meant to speak with you today. You have a number of admirers, and it won't be long before they begin to go out of their way to make this known. I know your father and your family, so I am going to prevent them as long as is possible, but you are not too young to choose a bride. You might want to consider that. Considering the amount of attention your presence is drawing, your best, and possibly only defense, is going to be matrimony."

Ham's jaw dropped. He stared but had no idea how to react, or what to say.

Ezra laughed. "Not today, my friend. I just want you to be aware. I will help in any way that I can, but you are no longer a boy, and, though I am not the best judge, I do not believe you are unattractive. You may even be what the local girls would call a perfect match. Add to that, if your father is not crazy, whoever you marry will survive a coming flood, and you can see why you might want to start paying attention to those around us."

At that moment, the door flew open, and Master Balthazar entered in a rush. He quickly turned and locked the door again.

When he returned his gaze to the two young men, he was smiling broadly.

"Well, well," he said. "I am not sure what has brought such luck to the doors of my humble establishment, but I must say, when I first spoke with your father, I never anticipated anything like this..."

"I am sorry," Ham said. "I did not mean to bring such chaos to—"

Balthazar laughed long and hard. It was infectious, and within moments all three of them were clutching their stomachs with tears streaming down their cheeks, though Ham was not certain why it was funny. It was impossible not to share in such uncontrolled mirth.

Ezra recovered first. He grabbed Balthazar by his arm and turned him to the table, where all but the four teeth he'd pocketed rested on the counter.

"It's better than you think," he said. "These are the remnants of the beast, the creature that was destroyed. Ham brought them to you, thinking they might be of some use."

Balthazar fell silent. He stepped forward, picked up one of the teeth and examined it carefully. He held it as if it was a holy object.

"You will find this creature," he said, "in my journals. They are like the lizards in the desert, but they fly. Their wings are tough, like leather, and they can grow to the size of a large bull. I have never heard of anyone surviving such an attack. As I listened to the stories, I was certain it was an exaggeration, a tale that would enhance your father's odd reputation. I thought it would help me barter your presence into gold. But this?"

He turned and held the tooth up in the light. There are tens of thousands of men and women in this city. Many of them are as wealthy as kings. Every single one of them will want one of these more than they want success for their unborn children. This," he spread his hands out over the pile on the counter, "is wealth beyond measure. Very seldom am I at a loss for words, and I am certain Ezra will back me on this. But I thank you, and I will adjust your father's debt accordingly."

"No!" Ham cried, then turned away, red cheeked. "I mean, please don't do that. He has no idea that I brought that here, and he would most certainly not approve. Could you, perhaps, tell people that Ezra went out to that site and collected them? I did not bring them with the hope of profit, only as thanks for the help you, and Ezra, have provided."

Balthazar stared at him thoughtfully, and then nodded. "As you wish," he said. "I admit I've grown fond of having you here. It's been good for business, and whether or not your father is crazy, his money is good, as is his word. Now, I believe that if you hope to have anything new to show him this day, you'd better get yourself hidden away in back. Ezra and I will handle that mob, sell them things they don't know that they need, and send them on their way with... what? What shall I tell them?"

"My father is saying it is a miracle," Ham said. "You can tell them that I passed on his words... that Shem prayed, and the Lord answered."

"You don't seem so certain," Balthazar said, narrowing his eyes.

"It is not mine to question," Ham said, lowering his gaze a bit.

"A miracle it is, then," Balthazar chuckled. "Miracles are always good for business."

Chapter 12

What had begun as a daunting task had transformed into a quest for Ham. The key had been his drawings of the designs for the Ark. The only thing his father's vision had provided were the dimensions. The interior and the logistics were a puzzle, and the more of Balthazar's journals he skimmed, with Ezra's help, the clearer it became that there would be a pattern. Some creatures would need to be transported before maturity, possibly even in eggs that could be cared for carefully. The assumption was that the Lord would prevent aggression or violence, but the reality was that a plan that minimized the possibility, since the ability to formulate such a plan was granted to men, was the wiser course.

He had created a space with the exact dimensions provided. He had divided it into levels, originally, but then had realized that his uninformed decisions would cause problems. They arranged each creature by size, aggression, feeding habits, and rate of growth. There were correlations between predators and prey, cooperative species, and natural enemies. There were special considerations for juvenile creatures, those that had not hatched or been born. Every space, every location, and every interaction had to be taken into consideration, weighed, and a decision made.

It had almost become a game, finding the potential problems first and applying solutions. It seemed an impossible task. The number of creatures that required space, and the available boarding area were opponents in a game of strategy, and the data all supported the overwhelming numbers and opposed the available space. It was a scenario designed to demoralize,

consistent, in Ham's experience, with other prophetic pro-
nouncements. It was a difficult task, but it was not insurmount-
able. The further he and Ezra pushed their inquiries, the more
certain he became that they could find a solution. There would
be a mathematically sound arrangement for the creatures being
transported, and for those who would have to care for the cargo
and survive the journey.

He was also aware that there was not another in his family
who could solve it. He even believed, secretly, that his father had
come to understand this as well. He provided nightly reports,
and his father paid scrupulous attention, often asking important questions that led to new solutions. What had seemed like
an unsolvable puzzle had become an elegant design. Ham knew
that Ezra did not share Noah's faith, but he was as much a part
of this process as Ham himself. He felt like a lost brother, the
friend he'd never been able to have because of his isolation. They
spent time together in the shop, even when neither of them was
concentrating on the project. Sometimes Ham helped out in the
shop, if things got too busy, and there were others he met, and
liked, people who spoke to him about his father's ark, of course,
but over time, about other things. And there were the girls.

Ham held no illusions. He knew that he would marry, and
he knew that either his father would choose his bride, or that his
father would have to approve. Most of the girls that frequented
Balthazar's shop would fall short in one way or another. It was
not their fault—Ham understood that now in ways he'd never
considered. Life was vast and complicated. It was one thing to
be devout in a small family group. It was quite another to deal
with all of the intricacies of society and not slip up. He had come
to understand that his father's retreat from the city, and other
families, was a defense mechanism. It was not a testament to
strength; it was fear of weakness. It broadened his understanding, but it also brought new questions.

Thankfully, the work occupied his thoughts, and he was
able, with an effort, to concentrate on it. Mostly. There was one
girl who had caught his eye. She came in often, but she rarely
spoke. Those that did seemed flamboyant, their surface more
of an illusion than a representation of their thoughts. Ham had

little experience with others his own age, but rather than being a handicap, it gave him the opportunity to study them, and to make comparisons that might not have been possible if they'd grown up together.

Just like with the Ark, there were patterns. Groups of people patterned themselves after the most popular among them, and the more they seemed to be mirror images, the more obvious it became that they were putting up a false front. Those who were more honest spoke less often. They did not want to draw attention to the ways that they didn't match up with their peers.

The girl Ham could not seem to erase from his thoughts was named Naḥlab, daughter of a man named Marib. She rarely spoke when she was in the shop, but he'd caught her watching him. He did not speak to her, because he sensed her desire not to be the center of attention when there was a crowd. For weeks Ham tried to find a way to spend a moment alone with her, but it was simply beyond his means. He was in the shop for a purpose. If he was out front, helping, it was because there was a crowd. He had begun to despair that he might never get a private word with her. He was worrying over this when Ezra entered the room, watched him for a moment, waved his hand with no response and started laughing.

"Who is she?" Ezra asked.

Ham blinked and sat up straight. He pretended, just for a moment, to be scribbling notes on the paper in front of him but stopped. He took a deep breath.

"How did you know?" he asked.

"We are not so different, you and I," Ezra said. "Very few things can distract you from this work, even if it proves to be the creation of a madman, a ship in the desert that never floats. I see the look in your eyes. I have seen that same expression in the mirror more than once. So, who is she?"

"Naḥlab," Ham said. "I can't stop thinking about her, but I can't seem to find a moment to ask if she feels the same. I know nothing about her. I have no idea if my father would approve."

"I can arrange for you to speak with her," Ezra said. "There is something more, something that might be in your favor, though might also upset you."

Ham raised an eyebrow.

"Her father owns the business that captures and houses the beasts for the arena. She is one of his younger children, not high in standing. I happen to know that she works in the arena. She has housed, fed, and cared for the creatures. I also know that she hates what happens to them."

"How do you know so much about her?" Ham asked, suspicious.

"Simple," Ezra said. "She is my cousin."

Ham's eyes widened, and Ezra laughed. "Distant cousin, but close enough that we've met at family gatherings. I will talk to her."

Ham started to say something. He knew he should not agree. He knew he should go to his father first but the smile on Ezra's face was too much for him.

"Okay," he said. "I would like to meet her, but you cannot make it seem as if—"

"I know, I know," Ezra said. "It cannot be unseemly. Just two people meeting and talking. I will bring her in to consult on the plans for housing and caring for the beasts. I am actually certain she will be useful. That will give you a chance to meet her, and to see what you think, with no pressure."

"Thank you," Ham said. "You are a good friend."

"I think the same," Ezra said. "For the son of a crazy man, you are surprisingly interesting."

They both laughed.

"Let's hope that Naḥlab agrees."

They chatted a few moments longer, and then returned to the work at hand. Business in the shop was brisk, but Ezra still managed to find time to review the notes and details Ham discovered, and to make suggestions. The routine was comfortable, and they fell into it easily. Ham almost managed not to be distracted by thoughts of Naḥlab and worry over explaining those thoughts to his father.

Chapter 13

There were three of the great beasts now, and a crew of ten men to tend them and keep them working steadily. Japheth watched, unable to prevent a smile. They were felling and preparing trees for construction at a rate nearly ten times that of any previous period. He'd diverted the workers who would have been performing these tasks to cutting and shaping the logs into the various pieces and parts of the Ark. At the rate things were progressing, he'd have enough material to see them through the winter months. He hoped to have the keel and the "ribs" of the Ark in place and to begin work on the hull. There was a lot of work that the family could handle once they got a good portion of the exterior in place.

Japheth was both surprised and grateful at the quality of the work Ham had accomplished. The plans he'd already provided would give them a good start on the basic layout of the craft's interior. It made the logistics of shaping timbers, cutting the right lengths and widths, a simpler task, and would decrease the amount of time necessary to outfit the interior of the Ark significantly. Ham had always shown an aptitude for math and art, but had never before found a way to bring those skills to bear in any useful way. It seemed they were all growing up, very suddenly, shouldering responsibilities they had never anticipated.

And the least likely of all to show signs of growth, his father, had changed as well. When the Ark had first been announced, the great work they would dedicate their lives to, everyone had expected Noah to transform into an even harsher taskmaster, to manage every small detail and drive them to exhaustion and beyond. What they had witnessed, instead, was a man who had a vision that he knew he could not realize alone. A prophecy that included many soldiers and messengers, and not just one, old and wise as he might be.

The beasts were also a revelation. Though he'd heard stories about them all his life, most of those stories had come from his father. Rumors stated that there were as many and varied beasts as there were men and women. Some were vicious killers, others subsisted on plants. Some were prone to attack, and others were docile, even friendly to men. Now he'd seen this in person, the reality that men and beasts could live and work in partnership. There had been times in the not-so-distant past where he'd thought that his family and other humans could not manage that.

He was finding it necessary to re-evaluate nearly everything he had been taught to believe over the past hundred years. He wondered about the city, where all of his workers lived, loved, and labored. He wondered about the shop where Ham was doing the work that was going to make their project possible. He thought about his wife and her family. All of it had taken on a surreal aspect from the moment he had been told and believed that the world as they knew it was going to cease to exist. That the God they prayed to, sacrificed to, and denied themselves for would send a flood, cleansing the Earth of all but a chosen few. He also had spent a lot of time in prayer, trying to understand what it was about himself that numbered him among the survivors.

What made it hardest were his flaws. His father's flaws, his brothers', his mother's, and sisters'. They were righteous people. They believed, and they lived their lives according to the commandments. Except, no man could fully live up to that standard. He had been told most of his adult life that the city would corrupt him, but he found enough corruption in himself to believe he could find righteous men inside those walls, as well. Perhaps he was naive. Perhaps he and his family *were* the closest to Godly men and women. Who was he to judge? It was a lot to live up to, and the implications to humanity as a whole were troubling, at best.

Japheth made his way around the perimeter of the area they'd cleared to where the workmen handled the beasts. Each of the creatures wore a massive collar that was attached to a chain nearly the girth of a full-grown man. Despite the incredible weight of that chain, it seemed useless and fragile in comparison to the huge, muscled Three Horns. They were working in shifts. One crew worked at a fresh tree, cutting it so it would fall into the open area, away from workers and equipment. A second group, with another Three Horn, was positioning a fallen log to be cut into different lengths, then shaped into timbers that could be transported to where the Ark itself would be built.

The last of the creatures stood idly by, munching vegetation and small branches from a large wagon that had been hauled in for that purpose. They cycled through the various jobs and periods of rest, making it possible to keep a steady flow of progress without tiring or angering the beasts. It was efficient, and Japheth saw that at least the old man who supervised the operation had developed a singular rapport with the Three Horns. Japheth had seen him climb one of the creature's sides and sit atop it while it ate, and he often called out to the creatures, as did his men, in low, deep tones that formed a crude communication. It was thrilling and fascinating, but like most things that had not begun with his family or their isolated home, that fascination was a concern. It was too easy to get caught up in the majesty of the beasts and the mastery over them that the men had gained, and to forget the important work it was all supporting.

Still, he thought, it would be a wondrous thing to climb atop one, just once, and to see the world from that height, sharing the vision with the giants. He scanned the trees and stopped, standing very still. A huge, shadowy form rose nearly to the height of the tallest branches. It stood very still and silent.

"Og," Japheth said softly. He watched, and slowly, very slowly, the huge figure moved closer to the cart where one of the three beasts was chewing slowly at a pile of small branches and leaves. The beast stopped. Not suddenly, but very casually. It chewed more slowly. Japheth glanced up and saw a long, muscled arm slip slowly from the trees. It moved so slowly he had to concentrate to be certain that he saw it at all. None of the workers had noticed. No one was attending the beast while it fed. Japheth held his breath. If Og frightened that creature, his fears about the strength of the chains would be put to the test.

There was no reaction at all. Og's huge hand brushed the beast's neck. Like a man petting a tamed wolf or a cat. The creature resumed its chewing. Japheth watched, uncertain how to feel, and then glanced up. Og was looking directly at him. He'd rarely seen the giant, had at times wondered if he existed at all. Japheth had heard the stories from Noah, the fallen, the women they'd interacted with—and their children, the Nephilim. There had always been more than just the trees protecting his home. This was the first moment where he not only took that in as a solid, real-world fact, but also understood that there was so much more to it that he did not understand that he might never be able to reconcile it.

Then Og slowly melted back into the trees, and Japheth took the breath he'd been holding. He knew he should tell his father what had happened, but after hearing Shem talk about his encounter in the desert, and his belief the giant had saved him, it seemed like it would be a betrayal of sorts. He wasn't ready to shoulder that, so he turned and walked on past the placid beast. There was work to do, and it was his responsibility to make certain it went smoothly. That responsibility had grown, but something inside him had grown as well. Something he was not entirely comfortable with but felt was important.

And it was a private thing. He could not discuss it with his father or his brothers. He might be able to tell his wife, if he could find the words, but though she loved him, she would not be pleased. She would tell him to listen to his father, to protect their family. She was part of the family, but only through their marriage, and he knew she believed. She believed she had been chosen to survive. If he voiced any doubts or gave any indication anything might have changed in his own faith, she would react badly. She might even choose his family over his love. She might tell his father, and then his own failure to admit his doubts would become that much worse.

He stood still for a moment. He cleared his mind and offered a silent prayer that whatever it was that was changing inside him was growth. That it was insight from the Lord and would strengthen him, not weaken his efforts. Too much of what was to come rested on his shoulders for him to falter. If the Ark were not completed, all of them would perish along with the city, the beasts, the animals. He opened his eyes and glanced once more into the trees. There was no sign of the giant, and the handlers were in the process of changing the beasts, leaving another to feed, while they led the other back to its labor.

It was going to be a long day, and there would be many more to come.

Chapter 14

Ezra led Ham down the street, pointing out sites and establishments as they went. It was the hour they would normally have taken a break to eat, but this day Ezra had packed food they could eat while walking. There was nothing scheduled at the arena for several days, and he had arranged for them to meet with Naḥlab. On the surface, they were visiting to take notes about the housing, handling, feeding, and needs of the great beasts. When he'd made the arrangements, he'd noticed a quick blush in Naḥlab's cheeks. It was only momentary, and he forced himself not to smile.

"Do you think she will want to talk to me?" Ham asked.

"About the beasts?"

Ham glared, and Ezra laughed.

"I'm a pretty good judge of people," he said. "I deal with them every day, read what they want, what they need, sell them things that are neither. I don't have to sell you to Naḥlab. She tried to hide it, but I think she wants to talk to you as much as you do to her."

"Because of my father," Ham said.

"No," Ezra said. "Because I told her what you said the day you saw the beast being led to the arena. Because she has seen and watched you in the shop. Because of you, my friend."

Ham glanced at Ezra. He knew they were friends, and every time he was reminded of it there was a catch in his chest. It reminded him that the very nature of the work they shared meant that they would be separated, violently, and that only one of them would survive. He didn't want to think about it, so, of course, it was the only thing he could think of. That and Naḥlab.

"You told her that? I would think she would laugh at me."

"I have learned," Ezra said, "that your thoughts on the beasts, and the way they are captured, treated, and slain, are not uncommon. There is an entire movement in the city working to try and end the spectacle. They have no chance of success, of course. A small percentage of the citizens control the majority of wealth, and the arena is the most valuable business enterprise in the city. There are the ticket sales, certainly, but so much more. Food, wine, hard drink, gambling, souvenirs. There are artists who sketch, or paint portraits posed with the creatures. The flow of money is endless. One thing your father is right about, for certain. Those wealthy are the heart of this city, and the heart is rotten to the core."

"So Nahlab cares for the beasts," Ham said, "but does not condone their deaths?"

"Something like that," Ezra said. "I believe she would set them free if she could."

They rounded a corner, and off to the right, not too far away, the walls of the arena rose above the rooftops. They were formed of huge stone blocks. They did not rise as far as Ham had expected, though, and he stopped, staring.

"Surely that is not tall enough to contain so many men and women, and the beasts."

"It extends below the ground," Ezra explained. Considering the dangers involved with handling the creatures, it was deemed prudent to keep all of it well below the ground where the likelihood of an incident would be minimized. Plus, it is easier to dig and support such an arena than it is to build it up from the Earth. There is a land, I'm told, where they build huge stone structures, wide at the base and coming to a point at the apex, but even those would not serve this purpose.

"So, they dug it deep, like a dish. They used the bedrock beneath the city to carve the tiers of seats, creating levels of halls and paths. It is one of the greatest achievements of the city, though it was built by the blood, sweat, and lives of men and women who never enjoyed it. Slaves, indentured servants, the armies, and families of fallen enemies. The more I look at the entire enterprise through that first new perspective you provided, the more it seems like a vast, dark construct I can barely remember enjoying."

"Where do they keep the beasts?" Ham asked.

"On the lowest levels. They have vast chambers with high ceilings, cells and stalls carved into the stone. All of their food is brought in by wagons. The only light is from torches. They are not well cared for. The owners of the arena want them angry and hungry. Even though many of them don't eat meat, if they are healthy and happy, they might not fight."

Ham frowned, and he hesitated, just for a moment.

"I know," Ezra said. "There is nothing we can do, we two, this day. Maybe, though, there will be. Knowing the situation is important, yes? And for some reason I am absolutely certain you must meet and speak with Nahlab. For many reasons. For instance, have you given any thought to the fact that some of the creatures will have to be young? Not eggs, because you could never be certain two would survive, or that they would be a mated pair. I believe you are going to have to build a menagerie of some sort, a place to learn the care, feeding, and raising of creatures you know only from pictures in a book. If your father is right, they will begin to come to you. It will take years to create that ark, but many of the animals you hope to save do not exist here. They will have to travel, be carried, herded. They will have to find their way to you, and when they do, you will need a place for them—and others who understand how that can be accomplished.

"The more I think about this entire prophecy, the greater the responsibility feels, the more widespread and impossible the accomplishment of it all appears. At the same time, the longer I know you, and the more we work on the plans and the notes, the more I believe you *will* find a way."

"Then why would you help me?" Ham asked. "You know what it will mean for you, for your family and friends, Master Balthazar and his shop…"

"If I believed," Ezra said, "as your father believes, I would know that the Lord has decreed this cleansing. I would understand that it has been brought about by our own actions, the way we live our lives for ourselves, and ignore his will, and his commandments. If I believed that he was a loving God, I might think it is my destiny to help you as I can, and to accept my fate."

"We will find a way through this," Ham said. "I swear this to you in this moment. I don't know why I believe this, or how it might happen, but I do. I am no prophet, but from the moment you became my friend, even before I realized you had done so, I have felt we have a great deal more to accomplish together."

"That's enough of that," Ezra said. He turned away, and Ham thought perhaps it was to hide emotion his friend did not want him to see. "Let's get to the arena. Naḥlab is waiting for us at the entrance to the lower levels, and we will have to return to the shop before long. We can take extra time if we tell Balthazar the reason for the visit—the creatures and their care, because it's important. Possibly important enough for him to request a bonus from your father. But we can't take all day."

They started walking then, not talking, just glancing at the shops as they passed. It only took a few minutes to reach their goal, and without hesitation, Ezra led Ham through the huge gates of the arena and down a set of stairs to the right that led into flickering torchlight and dancing shadows.

The stairs leading downward seemed endless. As they passed each level, Ham glanced down long passageways with doors opening to who knew what. Wagons rolled up and down underground roads, and groups of men, merchants, soldiers, guards, and others milled about, bartered, laughed, and went about a business Ham could not even begin to sort out. It was too vast. The scale was out of his range of comprehension.

Eventually, the stairs steepened. He felt his ears tighten, almost in pain. Then there was a soft pop, and they cleared. He held his hands to the sides of his head, and Ezra smiled. "The pressure of the air," he said. It happens when you climb a mountain. At least, that is what Master Balthazar says. There are men for whom it does not happen, and they have to return to the surface, or something inside their ears bursts, and they either lose their hearing or sometimes die.

Ham rubbed his ears and glanced around once more. They

stepped down onto the road at the bottom. The air was dank, and there was a heavy scent of manure in the air. It was almost overwhelming, and both boys held their arms up across their noses as they proceeded.

"Augh," Ham said. "How could anything survive like this?"

"You learn to live with it." The voice came from their left, and both boys turned to find Naḥlab smiling at them. "As bad as it is for the caretakers, it is infinitely worse for the creatures we care for."

Both boys removed their arms from their noses, though it brought tears to their eyes. Naḥlab wore a cloth wrap that covered her face beneath her eyes. She held out a cloth to each of them. Ham took one and wrapped it around his face. The scent of eucalyptus cleared his breath, and he sighed with relief. He took a deep breath, coughed a little at the unfamiliar scent. His eyes watered, but he could breathe.

"I am sorry," he said. "I did not mean to say it was in any way the fault of the beasts. They did not choose to be confined here."

"They did not," Naḥlab agreed. "They actually handle this better than we do, but it is impossible to know how they feel, how deeply it might upset them. It is even more difficult to know the state of their health, particularly the largest, because they are kept in a constantly drugged state."

"That's horrible," Ham said.

"It is, but they are alive," she said. "I always hope I'll find a way to get them all, or a few, back to freedom. Since I have not found a way, I feed them, I take care of any wounds they might have, I study them."

"It must be hard," Ezra said, cutting in. "I knew that you worked here, but, as Ham and I have been discussing, the actuality of what happens here, the senseless killing and mistreatment. I am not sure I could do what you do."

"Someone has to," she said.

"I'm glad to meet you," Ham said. "I have seen you in Balthazar's shop."

"I saw you as well," Naḥlab said. "When Ezra told me your reaction to the 'games' in the arena—"

"I just don't see how anyone could find it entertaining," Ham said. "With all of the wondrous things this city and this world have to offer, why would men and women cheer as any creature fought another to the death? It sickens me. This place, the incredible size and depth and rot. My father has always told me that the city is beyond redemption. I don't believe that the city and the people who live within its walls are synonymous, but the city itself is dark. This place is like a symbol of all that is wrong."

"Come," Nahlab said. "Let me show you my work, the creatures. I know your time is short."

Ham fell silent and nodded. "I am sorry," he said. "I did not mean to launch into a speech."

Nahlab smiled. "I was happy to hear it, but I don't want your time here to end without a complete understanding. I am not the only one here who shares your views. Many of us would release the beasts and lead them to freedom if there was any hope of success, or if doing so would make the slightest difference. It would not. They would never reach the city walls, and even if they did, they would not be released. They would be hunted, taken down, probably killed, but certainly brought back here, under worse conditions than before."

She started off from the bottom of the stairs, her steps hurried. Ezra and Ham followed, glancing to either side as they passed through the shadows. There were sounds, some scuffling, some like large huffing breaths. Occasionally something stomped, and it shivered through the stone beneath their feet. The first time he heard this, Ham glanced up, suddenly aware of all the floors above them, all the stone and earth. He caught his breath, closed his eyes, just for a moment, and cleared his thoughts.

Ezra caught his expression and nodded. "It's immense," he said. "There are men and women who can't even walk here for fear of it, but it's stood the test of centuries. It wasn't always this big, or this deep, but it's not going anywhere this day."

Ham nodded. "I'm fine," he said. "Just needed a moment to take it all in. This place is so much more than I'd thought."

A side passage opened on their right, and Nahlab turned into it. They followed. The air was heavier in that passage, and the scents of sweat and manure were stronger. There were gates, spread several yards apart, and Naḥlab stopped at the first, waiting for them to catch up. They stared through the bars at a shadowy figure near the rear of what turned out to be a deep-cut stone stall.

"Not too close," Naḥlab said. "There are a lot of beasts here. Some are docile, at least until riled. Some eat plants, trees, but others—"

At that moment something charged from the rear of the pen. Three somethings, in fact. They struck the far side of the bars, claws slipping through the grates and scrabbling to get through. Ezra and Ham cried out and leaped back. Naḥlab stepped back but made no sound. Elongated, yellow eyes fixed on them. Deep, hissing growls emanated from the far side of the bars. Very carefully, fascinated, Ham stepped forward. What he saw were three creatures similar in form to the great toothed beast that had nearly caught him at the gates. The scale was much smaller, but they were fast. Their arms, rather than being short parodies of useful limbs, were proportionate. Their eyes held an intelligence and malevolence that chilled his heart.

"They fight in packs," Naḥlab said. "They are fast, smart, and can take down a much larger creature with ease. Only the largest and fiercest of the others can stand against them. We call them Tooth Devils. I do not believe men have ever defeated them."

"Men?" Ham said, turning sharply.

She nodded. "Of course. Prisoners, slaves, it's not only the beasts who are sent to the arena. Sometimes they fight against other men. Sometimes they fight in groups against one of the great beasts. Sometimes, they are simply hunted. These are hunters, and they are the best. I wanted you to see them first. I wanted you to know that, in spite of what I have just told you, keeping them here is no better than keeping the gentle giants, or the men. It's an abomination. There are times I wish I could find a way to release them without dying in the process, and just let them roam these halls until they were cleansed."

Ham was shaken. He'd not expected this, and he'd not expected such insight from Naḥlab. He turned away.

"Show me," he said.

Without a word, Naḥlab led them down the passage, stopping here and there to point out one of the beasts, and to speak of its properties, its diet. Ham listened, and watched her, realizing how dedicated she was to all of them, to her work. At the same time, part of his mind wondered how they would safely transport the killers he'd just seen. He felt overwhelmed by the size and scope of what she showed them, insignificant and totally unprepared.

"Do you know why I'm here?" he asked at last.

Naḥlab smiled. "Well, Ezra told me that you wished to speak with me, so, I hope that is at least a part of it. Still, everyone is aware of your father's prophecy, of the coming flood, and of the Ark."

"Then you know," Ham said, ignoring the first part of her answer, "that I am tasked with designing the interior in such a manner that we will be able to house, feed, care for—and survive—mated pairs of every creature. You have shown us a small portion of the beasts in your care, and I feel…"

"Overwhelmed?" she asked.

Ham nodded. "Exactly that. How could we survive creatures like the first you showed us, or transport beasts so vast they could glance in over the bow of the Ark and watch us as we stood on the deck?"

"You are not looking at it properly," she said. "Every living thing on the Earth has stages. Birth, death, life, growth. Your father is either a prophet, or he is not. If he *is*, then there is an answer. A pattern, like the pieces in a child's puzzle, pressed together to create a final whole. I assume that is why you need my help."

"And you offer it?" Ham asked.

"I do, but there will be a price," Naḥlab said.

Ham watched her but did not speak.

"I want to be a part of your planning," she said. "This work does not take all of my time. My father is wealthy, and I work here because I feel it is important, because I don't trust the creatures to the others in his employ. I can spare time to be in the city, in the workshop. I can help you to answer the questions you have. I believe that Ezra has already mentioned that you will require a menagerie. I suspect the two of us could devise a proposal to present to your father that would convince him."

Ham stared openly. "You... you want to work with me?"

"Would that be so bad?" she asked.

"I, no, of course not. But..."

"Then it is settled," Naḥlab said. "I will come to the shop early enough tomorrow that I can be in the back room before anyone knows I am there. Ezra can help us to prevent others from noticing. I can move in and out of the shop when there are no customers, and when we are ready, you can present the work to your father."

Ham closed his eyes again and tried to clear his thoughts. When he did so, all he saw was her face, the bright intelligence of her eyes, and heard the passion in her voice. He opened his eyes.

"It will be as you say," he said. "And I hope that the work is not all that we will share. I have dreamed of you. I am telling you this because I am a young man. I have no experience with women. I have only one friend, and that is Ezra, who I met—I thought—by chance. I no longer believe that. Every time the work set for me seems beyond my abilities, an answer is offered. You are such an answer. I feel as if there is more to all of this than any of us comprehends, and I would be happy for your help, and your insight."

Then he stood, waiting for the others to laugh. He felt as if he'd bared some part of himself that he should have protected, as if he'd dropped walls that were there to protect him. He had given all he had to this moment, so he waited. A moment later, both Naḥlab and Ezra stepped forward and embraced him. It was only a quick circle, but something passed between them. Something more than just emotion. Then they pulled apart.

"We need to get back to the shop," Ezra said. "But we will see you tomorrow?"

Naḥlab nodded.

Unable to trust himself to speech, Ham turned and started back the way they'd come. Ezra followed. Naḥlab stood alone in the shadows, watching them disappear.

Chapter 15

Ezra had been uncertain about bringing Naḥlab into the shop. Everything they had discussed made perfect sense when he discussed it with Ham, or when he went over it in his mind, but his own thoughts and those of Master Balthazar did not always travel the same roads. He'd arrived early, and, true to her word, Naḥlab had been waiting outside, sipping tea. Now the two of them were ensconced in the rear of the shop at Ham's table, poring over the journals and their diagrams.

The door jangled, and Ezra knew that the time of reckoning, one way or the other, was upon him. He stepped away from the table and into the main shop. Balthazar stood in the doorway, as he often did, staring out into the city and watching the crowds. Ezra had seen him do this time and again, turn, and tell him what to display and what to hide, as if the streets were a parchment he could decipher with some mystic key. This day, he simply turned into the shop, and stopped.

"Is someone here?" he asked. "Surely Ham has not come so far, so early?"

"It is not Ham," Ezra said. "He...we have brought in a consultant. Someone with first-hand experience caring for the beasts."

Balthazar stepped past him without speaking. Ezra hurried to follow, but he was too late. Balthazar loomed over Naḥlab, glaring at his journal, wide open on the table, and at the drawing she was scribbling notes on. Ezra started to speak, but Balthazar held up a hand. He leaned in close and studied what Naḥlab was doing. He made an odd sound, half gasp, half grunt. He leaned in closer.

"You have seen this?" he asked without preamble.

Nahlab glanced up. "I have, many times. Your drawings, and your notes, are very complete. I have made additions, but not, of course, to the journals themselves. I have worked beneath the arena for most of my life. My father believed, as did you, that the Tooth Devils were simply smaller versions of the great dragons, but they are so much more. They move and think as a single unit in the arena. They have killed those caring for them by setting elaborate traps. They plan, and they wait—and they hate."

"You call them Tooth Devils?"

Nahlab nodded.

"When you release them into the arena," Balthazar asked, "how do you return them to captivity? If men cannot defeat them?"

"Men cannot defeat them in battle," she said. "We have a potion that renders them unconscious for a time. It is delivered in a mist. When they kill, they eat. Always. At that time, they can be recaptured. It happens very quickly, and men have been lost, but we always have a pack in waiting. There is no show in the arena that draws a larger crowd."

"And you have many beasts," Balthazar mused. "Different species?"

"We have held and cataloged over a hundred and fifty species, that I know of," Nahlab replied. "We have, I believe, forty now."

"I have long thought that I might approach your father," Balthazar said. "I would truly love the opportunity to study those creatures, and I believe there is business to be made in souvenirs from the fallen."

Ezra saw a shadow pass over Nahlab's features and he held his breath. She recovered quickly.

"I am sure I could arrange a meeting," she said. "What we have learned from close association with the beasts could only be enhanced by the knowledge you have recorded. There are creatures in your journal I've not only not seen, but never heard of. If you know where some could be obtained, I am sure you and my father will be fast friends."

Balthazar stepped back. He was smiling, deep in thought, and had clearly forgotten whatever it was he'd been about to say when he'd entered the room. Ezra, counting his blessings, held his silence. It was then that the door jangled again. Ham passed Balthazar on his way into the room, caught sight of Naḥlab, and turned to watch Balthazar's retreat. Then he spun back to Ezra who held up his hands.

"I will admit that I did not plan this perfectly," he said. "But I am starting to believe in your idea that this is somehow destined. I say this because Balthazar broke into this room ready to kick us all to the street, and believe me, I've seen that expression. I know what he was thinking. He left entranced, ready to give me a raise and form a business partnership with Naḥlab's father. I don't even believe he saw you when he passed you."

"He did seem focused," Ham said. He glanced down at the drawings and the notes, and slid into the seat beside Naḥlab. He ran his finger down the lines of text, studying them, and then glancing at the larger diagrams he and Ezra had already worked on. "This is important," he said. "I understand why Balthazar is excited, but beyond that. These are the kinds of details that could mean the difference between surviving the flood and being consumed by the very creatures we intend to preserve."

"What you are attempting to do," Naḥlab said, "is near to madness. I am not even certain it can be done, but if it can, there can be no detail left to chance. Every single creature is as important as all the rest combined. One miscalculation, one enclosure that cannot hold the creature it is intended to hold, one breach of separation or lack of the proper care and food, and some will die."

"And that is not acceptable," Ham said. "We need to annotate what I already have presented to my father with your information and explain the necessity for a menagerie. If possible, it seems to me, when the Ark begins to be constructed, some of the creatures might need to be housed in the body of the construction itself to test the strength of the enclosures, or the methods of feeding and care."

Naḥlab smiled. "Exactly," she said. "So, shall we get to work?"

Ham smiled. "Yes, but do not believe that this will be the easy part of this task. We have to prepare the work in a manner that will not only convince my father that we need the menagerie, but that he must let you be a part of it."

There was a moment of silence. Then Naḥlab said, "I am not the only qualified person for that task. In fact, there are men with years of experience beyond my own."

"Yes," Ham said, smiling. "But I do not intend to introduce any of them to my father, because I do not intend to request his permission to spend more time with them."

Naḥlab blushed, but her smile did not fade. "My father will be equally difficult to convince," she said. "He believes your father to be crazy, after all."

"Perhaps he is," Ham said. "I'm becoming increasingly unable to believe it, though." He turned to Ezra. "By the way," he said, "I wanted to mention to you, and I say this without any brotherly bias, I have a sister I would love for you to meet, if we can get this menagerie off the ground. I assume my father will allow us all to work on the project, once he approves it."

Ezra stared at Ham for what seemed an eternity. Then, very suddenly, he started laughing. It was contagious, and the three of them only fought against their mirth when Master Balthazar poked his head into the room and glared at them. Once they were under control, they set to work with increased energy. They did not stop until it was time for Ham to make his way out of the city, and when he did, they accompanied him to the gate.

"I will speak to my father in the morning," he said. "When I come to the shop tomorrow, I will know more."

They all embraced once more. It felt like more than friends parting. It felt oddly like a family.

Chapter 16

Noah stood off in the trees, watching as Japheth, having taken time away from supervising the gathering of lumber, worked with Ham and his crew to lay out the foundations for the menagerie. So much had changed. Rather than cutting himself off further from the city, and its people, he found them encroaching on his life and his family.

There was no denying this work was necessary, or that the Lord had brought it about. There were simply too many people in that city for Ham to have accidentally run across the proper knowledge, skills, men and women, and resources to conceive this plan. It was ambitious. The boy had foreseen building walls, cages, and pens. It would have eaten into the resources they were gathering for the Ark, and it would have slowed things too much. Thankfully, this was the area where Japheth shone.

When the plan had been unfolded, Japheth had listened closely. When Balthazar's assistant, Ezra, had explained the method used to create the great arena, information that Noah possessed, but had not considered important, he had come to Noah with a proposition. They too could dig into the bedrock of the desert. They would not be able to share that work with those from the city, and they would be hard-pressed to explain how they accomplished it, but it could be done. Og, working under the cover of darkness, could make short work of such a project.

It was also obvious that, though Ham appeared to have weathered the lure of the city's sinful ways, he had developed deep feelings for the girl, Naḥlab, and the boy, Ezra. It was also apparent that Ham had gone out of his way to involve his sister, Yalith, in the planning, despite the fact she had nothing specific to offer. Noah felt the Lord had brought these young people together, and he knew, though he detested the notion of being manipulated, that he would support a match between Ham and Naḥlab. He suspected there would be a similar budding romance between Ezra and his daughter. He did not like the influence the two would bring to his family, but he was not naive. Without their help, no matter how hard he, his sons, his wife, Na'amah, and even the Nephilim had tried, they would have been lost trying to house, feed, separate, and care for the legacy they had been bequeathed. Clearly, he should have expected his Lord to provide the means to accomplish his task, but it still felt strange to welcome members of the society he had left behind, the sinful lifestyle he believed to be the cause of the coming flood into his home. Into his family. There were levels to this prophecy he was only beginning to comprehend. It had become his way to look down upon other men, and other families, and he was coming to see how narrow that view had been, how arrogant, and how dangerous.

He had been chosen to survive the coming cleansing. It could have been Balthazar. It could have been Ezra's family, or Naḥlab's. He had been chosen, and it was a very human thing to feel pride in that. The truth was that it was an incredible responsibility. It came with guilt beyond anything he'd ever experienced. If he could have maintained his distance from the city, it might not have been so bad. Now the reality was sinking in. When the flood came, and the Ark floated, everyone he had ever known in centuries of life would be dead. He would have his wife, his sons, his daughter, and their spouses. He would have the animals left to his care. He would also have a weight no man had ever borne—that of being the chosen among all the men of the Earth. The responsibility to be the source, along with his family, of those who would populate the world when the waters receded. The necessity of passing his faith on to his children, and his children's children, to prevent a second cleansing. The ancient phrase "fear of God" was so much stronger.

He found it difficult to interact with merchants and workers. He left this to his sons whenever possible, and then felt guilty for his weakness. He knew none of them actually believed in his vision. It changed nothing. Naḥlab had valuable information and experience. Ezra showed great promise as a planner and leader, and even Balthazar, for all his pointed remarks about how he was working to support his own death, had provided supplies, insights, and unexpected moments of connection. Those were the worst. Noah had his faith and his family, but he had not had anyone he called friend in centuries. He barely remembered a time when he was a part of the world, and not just his own world. There was an ache in these moments that bit into his heart. He avoided them as much as possible.

He knew that he had to. There were things he could not share with any of the newcomers, or with Balthazar. He could share them with his family, but only after the fact. Only after there was no chance that secrets would be shared. He could also not be present when the questions came. This was going to be one of them. He stood out of sight until the workers cleared and returned to the city. He waited until Ham had gone to dinner, knowing that the family would await his arrival. The sun was setting when he finally stepped into the cleared area where the menagerie would be built.

He felt the vibration of Og's footsteps. He watched as the trees parted slightly, and the great form of the giant became visible in the shadows. Noah stepped closer and raised his eyes. He could not make out the rugged, worn features, but he knew them as well as he did those of his sons or his wife.

"You know what must be done?" he asked.

There was a rustle of leaves, but no answer.

"You must not be seen," Noah said. "The basic work must be completed this night."

There was motion in the shadow. A huge hand reached out and down. Noah watched it and waited. Og's fingers gently brushed the top of his head. Then they were gone. Without a word, the giant turned toward the clearing. It was all the answer he would make, and all that Noah needed. He owed much to this creature, born of the fallen and mortal women, abandoned to the shadows. He knew he should feel no compassion. He knew what had happened greatly angered his Lord, but without the help of Og and the other Nephilim, his life of righteous separation would have been impossible. They would have been destroyed by the beasts. They would have died, or given up and moved back to the city, become ensnared in the very things that would cost the world everything.

As he made his way back through the trees toward his home and the dinner table, he heard the sound of some great tool attacking the Earth. He felt the thud as displaced soil dropped away to the side. He stopped, just for a moment, and spoke a silent prayer that he was doing the right thing, that he was being led to the proper actions, and not being seduced by the simplicity of allowing sinners to do the work he had been set. He hurried his steps and left those thoughts behind. He intended to enjoy his evening meal. He knew the next day would be filled with turmoil and questions.

He had explained away a lot of things over the years, but even he was going to be hard-pressed to explain the miracle of a great pit appearing overnight. Ham would suspect, or, more likely, he would simply know. Japheth would not be surprised but he would hold his tongue. The simple truth was, after reading and absorbing all the information that had been gathered, Noah had come to understand that they did not have time for men to excavate the pit, and even with the help of some of the beasts, it would take years. If Ezra's and Ham's calculations were correct on the time it would take to gather the creatures that they'd been directed to save was even close to correct, those animals would begin, by one means or another, to appear soon, and would continue to do so over the months and years of construction. They would need to be housed, fed, cared for, and studied. No other course of action seemed viable, so he had heeded Japheth's advice, again, and turned to Og. He knew others would be involved. He knew the Nephilim who helped to keep his home and family safe would in some way assist. He did not want to know the nature of that assistance. He did not feel worthy to know. He knew they would be destroyed as surely as the city and other cities beyond, and that he would survive. He also knew he would have to live with the weight of that for the rest of his days.

In that moment he was thankful that his Lord had told him

men's lives would be shortened to no more than one hundred and fifty years. No other would have to bear the weight of all he had seen and known, loved and despised. He entered the main camp and made his way toward the dining hall. He had little appetite, but knew he would eat, talk, and laugh. Then, before he slept, he would retreat from it all, and he would pray.

Ham stood on the edge of the chasm and stared into the depths. He could not see the bottom, though he was able to make out steps and angled trails leading downward. It was immense, even grander than they'd planned. It was impossible, and yet, he knew that it was not. He glanced off into the trees, wondering if Og, or even his father, was watching.

The sun was rising, and he knew that soon the workers and supply trains would roll out from the city and bring the workers, Ezra, Nahlab, and the rest. He tried to think of what he would say, and, just for a moment, he considered walking back to his room and closing the door, climbing into his bed, and waiting for the day to end. Of course, he did not. Things were going to have to happen very quickly. It seemed that responsibility he was not prepared for had just landed on his shoulders. He thought of Nahlab, and that thought calmed him. He turned and walked away from the site. He needed to find his father. He needed permission to wed, and he needed to get the promise of a dowry to be paid to her father. Immediately. He thought Ezra might feel the same. There was no way they could fully contain this, but it would be disastrous to send them back to the city with this story and no real answers. They were going to need to meet and form a plan.

They could no longer just bring in whoever was available to work on the menagerie. They would have to choose carefully, and even then, stories were going to be leaked. People would whisper, and then talk. It would be more difficult to work in Balthazar's shop, and he wondered if it might be possible to arrange to move the journals closer, for a time. His mind whirled and he fought to focus. The next few hours would change every aspect of his life, and he needed to be certain that the changes were positive.

He knew where he would find his father, and he hurried his steps. He had never interrupted Noah's quiet time in the morning, and he was uncertain what would happen when he did so now, but he could imagine no other course of action. They had to expand their family and tighten their security. Things they took for granted, that were not known to those in the city, were dangerously close to being revealed.

He thought of Og, and of the arena in the city. He knew that, while some would be in awe and share his amazement at the giant's existence, others would see nothing but profit and stop at nothing to exploit such knowledge. No other could have dug that pit, and he felt that even Og must have had help. It was that help that frightened him the most. The Nephilim served God. Even unbelievers and sinners knew that, whether it meant anything to them or not. If they were here, and involved, then the creation of an ark to escape the end of the world could take on a darker aspect. If those in the city began to believe, that would, ironically, be the worst possible outcome. They would not want to die. Ham didn't want them to. He understood almost nothing about prophecy, and he trusted his father, but this seemed like the most selfish endeavor he'd ever embarked upon. He had always been taught that the Lord had given men the gift of choice. It seemed strange to offer that choice, and then destroy any who did not make the one expected of them.

It was complicated. He saw the evil in the city. He saw the erosion of morals, the greed, the sickness, and the debauchery. He knew these things were wrong, knew they were ungodly. Even when he saw the good in men walking those streets, he felt the rot, deep beneath their feet and seeping up through the sand and stone. He could not imagine a way to reverse that corrosive darkness, but that knowledge did nothing to ease his personal sense of inadequacy and guilt. If someone asked him why he and his family had been chosen, he would be hard-pressed to give any answer other than it was the Lord's will, and he knew how he felt when that answer was offered to him.

He found his father seated, staring out into the desert. Glancing over Noah's shoulder, he saw the caravans moving out from the city, winding their way closer. For a long quiet moment, he stood, watching. Then his father turned and met his gaze.

"I have been waiting for you," Noah said.

"You know why I'm here?" Ham said.

"I believe that I do. I share your concerns. I would have consulted you before summoning Og, but I wanted you to rest well. I knew that this day would be long and arduous. Perhaps impossible. There are times when you know what you must do, but not how it will turn out. You understand that there will be consequences, and all you can do is trust that, whatever they may be, they are right and just.

"I will visit the city today. I will visit Master Balthazar, and I will visit the girl's father as well."

"She has a name," Ham said, raising his eyes.

Noah's features hardened for an almost imperceptible moment. Then he nodded. "I will visit Naḥlab's father, and I will make the necessary arrangements. I have seen how you watch her, and I have seen, as well, how she smiles when she watches you. She will be a great asset to you, and to our Lord."

"I am not certain we will be able to contain this," Ham said. "We have a crew who has been working on the menagerie. If we pull them off it suddenly, they will talk. Some will try to sneak close and figure out why. If we retain them, I have no idea how we can prevent them spreading stories."

"I have spoken with Shem. He is already arranging for tents, a kitchen. We will offer what we can—food, more pay for the work—if those involved in the menagerie will stay here until it is finished. I suspect there will be issues. Some will want to return home to pack, others will want to consult with their families. If we can, we will handle this for them, and we will convince them that the benefits offered outweigh the difficulties, and hardships. It is only a matter of time until stories leak, but the longer we contain them, the more possible an alternate explanation will seem. The more people will be focused back on the crazy old man building a boat in the desert."

"When you first told us of the Ark," Ham said, "I was half convinced that was the case. I know you are a man of faith. I know you have shown me things, and done things, that I cannot explain, unless what you believe is true. When you sent me to the city, I had no idea what to expect.

"Then I met Ezra and Master Balthazar. I saw the knowledge they held, and how it fit perfectly with your prophecy. I saw a great beast being led through the city, probably to die, for men's pleasure, and it sickened me. Because of that, I met Naḥlab, who felt the same, but more than that, another piece of knowledge, another part of the same great puzzle. I know, had that not happened, we would have failed. It is possible, of course, that the Lord would have provided some alternative, that a door would shut while another opened, but I don't really believe that. I believe we are being swept along in something we barely understand, and I actually feel that I have a part to play in it—that I'm important."

"And I," Noah said, "have learned that I am not a single prophet, but a part of a bigger prophecy. All of my life I have depended on myself and my Lord. I have ordered, directed, and demanded, but seldom listened. First Japheth, with the men and the beasts, preparing the construction. Then you, alone in a place I considered nothing more than a den of iniquity, manage to return with absolutely essential knowledge, a friend who, had you asked, I would have said would lead you to sin, and a woman who cares for you who is as integral to the prophecy as any other. Then Shem, organizing it all, the supplies and the food."

"He nearly got eaten by a flying beast," Ham noted.

"And that brings me to the thing I find the hardest to reconcile. Og. I have been arrogant, I know. I have taken for granted the things the Lord has provided, the protection of the Nephilim, the services Og has provided. No one has said it, but we both know that, while I believe the Lord watches over us, the giant was the instrument of Shem's salvation. He has been here so long; I can barely remember a time when he was not. And now he works to provide us safe passage from a world where he is destined to die."

Ham was silent for a long moment. Then he spoke.

"I will never be able to reconcile my life after the death of so many. I will never understand the Lord's determination that we are somehow chosen, but no one else. I understand sin, for we have been taught of it from birth. I understand faith. This prophecy, though, bears a guilt, and a weight, that should not be ours."

"Such matters are beyond our understanding," Noah said. "If we did not survive, possibly no one would survive. If all the people of the world died away, it would not be a better thing than if we survive. We have been granted life. We have been given a world filled with great beauty and incredible evil. It is what we have made it."

"I have the feeling," Ham said, "that this is not the last time we will speak of guilt, faith, and prophecy. For now, I will meet the workers at the road. If I can find Shem, I will ask him to accompany me. I assume he will know what to say, what has been planned while I slept. It will be best if we do not approach the workers with different stories. Not that it will have the slightest effect on those that travel back to the city."

"It will," Noah said. "The more different stories that eventually make their way to the city, the more it becomes gossip, and not fact. No one will know exactly *what* to believe, and that will buy us the time to complete the work."

"I hope," Ham said, "that the work is worth the deception. It doesn't feel wrong, exactly, but…"

"The Lord will lead us, if we let Him," Noah said. "Now hurry. Find your brother and set things in motion. You should be excited. Unless I have read the girl wrong, you will be betrothed by nightfall."

Ham turned away, hoping he managed to do so before his father caught the flush in his cheeks, or the smile that split his face. He hurried back into the trees and took off for the main road at a trot.

Chapter 17

In the end, like so many other facets of the prophecy, things simply worked out. The workers were happy to accept higher wages to remain on site. Many of them probably figured that a detailed account later on would be worth much more than rumors in the present. It wasn't like the Ark would material-ize overnight. Or the menagerie. Initially, there were a lot of questions. Ham and Shem did their best to answer indirectly, to never really provide a "lie," while avoiding the truth.

Despite all of this, for Ham, it was a magical time. His father had visited Master Balthazar, and Ham did not know what had come to pass during that interaction, but Ezra, the journals, Naḥlab, all had moved to the compound. He thought he would miss the variety, the color, and the interaction of the city, but he found that he did not. He was lost in an amazing period of interaction with his friend, and, after only a short wait, his wife. They worked long hours, but it did not seem like work. He was fascinated by the creatures, and by the structures necessary to house and control them. Their diets. Their idiosyncrasies.

Ezra also seemed in his element. Master Balthazar made regular trips to check on their status, and to meet with Noah. The journals and the diagrams for both the Ark and the menag-erie were housed far from the actual site. He never got close enough to grow genuinely curious, and, probably by accident, he had provided the answer to explaining away work that seemed impossible or completed too quickly.

Folklore spoke of a book that had belonged to Adam, a gift from the Lord, with all the knowledge of the Earth, its crea-tures, and its mysteries. It had been passed from father to son, through Enoch and Methuselah, and then lost. Balthazar, in jest, suggested that Uriel himself must have been sent with that very book to aid Noah in his labors. A single payment in sapphires to one of the merchants, handled by Shem, was all it had taken to cement the rumor in the imagination of the city. The legends claimed that the covers of Adam's book were crusted in sapphires. Balthazar had lived a long time, and he was well-versed in legends, scriptures, and folklore. He was also the merchant paid in sapphires and knew the value those stones would command if they were accompanied by the proper provenance.

Between the remnants of the flying creature Og had destroyed, the sapphires, and the notoriety that accompanied having his apprentice marrying into Noah's family, he was becoming even more wealthy and influential than he'd been before. It came, of course, with the nagging sense that he was contributing to his own death, but Balthazar was not young. He and Noah were among the oldest men still walking the Earth. There was little he had not done, and done several times. He'd married, had children, seen them grow and leave. Some had died. He lived alone, save for a small army of servants, and the only entertainment in his life, until recently, had been small traffic in gossip, and the work—his journals. He was not afraid to die, and he was even less inclined to try bartering boredom for a longer life.

And then there was the last thing. It was a small thing, and though he was as aware as any that the sin of pride was the one most likely to bring a righteous man down, it was important to him. Maybe the most important thing in in his nearly six hundred years of life. He'd been explaining to Ezra, Ham, Yalith, and Naḥlab about the fabled book that Adam had been presented by the Lord, and that had been used by Enoch to learn all of the mysteries and secrets of the Earth. When he'd finished his story, which they had all listened to attentively, Ham had glanced up at him, his hand resting on an open volume of Balthazar's journal.

"Has it occurred to you," Ham said, "that fables and prophecies often seem to find unlikely ways to express themselves? These journals, the ones you've worked on for so many generations, and that have filled your days and nights, may not be encrusted in sapphires, but are as close to containing all of the secrets and mysteries of the creatures of the Earth as any source. I have seen how unlikely the bearers of secrets and answers can be in myself. I was granted, first, access to your books, then to Ezra and Naḥlab. Perhaps *you* are the book. Before things were written and recorded, they were passed down from father to son, from priest to supplicant. Perhaps we are all books, books of flesh and blood, and you have done something so remarkable—recorded so much, in such detail—that your work became the prophecy."

None had spoken after that. Balthazar had risen in silence and left the tent where they were working. He'd walked to the edge of the trees, where the road entered, and caught a ride with the next merchant leaving for the city. He returned to his shop, where the volumes of his journal that had already been studied remained. He closed the doors of the shop and locked them, lit a candle, and sat, flipping slowly through the pages, remembering passages and reliving the memories of where he'd found the information, what he had collected in each instance, and what it had been used for. Tears streamed down his face, and he had to stop several times, unable to quite breathe. He poured a mug of wine and sat there through the night. The next day, he did not return to Noah's encampment, but he sent a package to Ham.

Inside was a leather bookmark with a prayer burned into it. At the top, embedded deeply, was a single, brilliant sapphire. There was a note included.

"So that you can find your place in the book, and so that you can remember the gift you have given me."

It was many days before he made his way back across the desert, and when he did, he made no mention of that gift. He caught Ham looking at him now and then, though, and Ezra. It was the first time in centuries that he'd felt his existence might be making a difference.

Chapter 18

Ezra and Yalith, and Naḥlab and and Ham were wedded in a small ceremony near the edge of the trees. Balthazar was there for Ezra. He had come to Balthazar as an orphan at a young age and had no idea who or where his parents might be, so the old merchant was there for him. Naḥlab's mother, Sara, and father, Thaddeus, attended, with a small entourage of their own. They seemed distracted, as if just the notion of being outside the city, combined with being within the confines of a man they had been taught was mad, was simply too much to comprehend. They did not ask for a tour. They did not ask to see the progress on the Ark. They stared into the trees, watched every shadow, as if convinced they would either be smitten by Noah's Lord or dragged into the trees by demons.

The young people paid them no mind. It was a genuinely happy time, and Noah, despite his reputation, clearly surprised his visitors by enjoying himself immensely. There was music and some dancing. It did not last long, because those who were visiting were anxious to make their way back over the road to the safety of the city. In his own way, Noah was anxious to have them go. The less interaction between strangers and his family, the better, and the fewer areas of the compound those visitors saw during that interaction, the better.

Og had continued to work during the nights, helping to shape the levels of the menagerie to the specifications that Naḥlab and Ham laid out for him. His work allowed the day crews to concentrate on gates, locks, and installing feeding systems and intricate means of providing water into the enclosures. Many of the beasts would be dangerous. Handling them directly would be far too dangerous and time consuming, so, with Naḥlab's help, they installed means of automating this— tall funnels through which food and water could be released in measured amounts. It was all beyond Noah's understanding, though each bit and piece that came together made perfect sense, once in place and understood. Yalith, who had no real experience with beasts, but who was a practical girl, had conceived a mechanism that would allow them to have floors in some of the enclosures that could be slid out beneath the bars that would contain the creatures, allowing them to be kept clean with very little human contact.

Noah did not interfere, but he'd kept close tabs on all of this. Ham did not know it, but his sister, Yalith, had passed on his observation about the books, and the way the prophecy seemed to be a living thing, not a single book of secrets, but a web of knowledge that led down disparate and unlikely threads to the next important bit of understanding. He wondered what Balthazar had thought, but he knew he would never ask. To bring into the open a prophecy of his own salvation and the other man's death would seem prideful, even if it were not and could end in no positive understanding. Still, from the way Yalith presented the tale and her description of the old merchant, he believed his son had managed something that six hundred years had not. He had gotten through to Balthazar, given him evidence of a part he played in something grand. The simple truth was that Noah had far underestimated his son, and probably all three of them. More likely, he had overestimated himself.

As the sun lowered on the horizon, the visitors made their farewells, last-minute gifts were exchanged, and there was a general sense of urgency as many who had rarely left the confines of the city felt the urge to bolt for safety, bundling themselves in robes and blankets that would be of no help in the face of an actual attack, and hunkering down in the wagons as they rolled out onto the road and passed beyond the tree line. Noah stood out of sight. He had greeted those he knew, or those he felt would feel insulted if he did not. He had been gracious with parents and cousins, curious uncles, and friends, and then he'd pulled back. He wanted to watch them leave. Their presence made him nervous, and he seldom knew how to respond to their attempts at conversation.

He stood as the shadows lengthened and watched them wind across the sand. He prayed for safe passage, for nothing that could be blamed on him, or his family, to befall those making the transit. It was that vantage point that allowed him to witness one of the strangest things he had ever encountered. He blinked to be certain his vision was clear. Not on the road, but parallel to it, a straggling line of possibly a dozen creatures drew nearer to his camp. This wouldn't be notable, except, they progressed in a group, and he could make out at least two small creatures, three wolves, and, unless his vision had failed him, a pair of lions, a horse, and two goats. None of them showed the slightest inclination to attack or devour the others. He also noted that the stragglers leaving for the city had seen the odd companions and where they were headed.

Noah turned and hurried back into camp in search of Ham. He hated to interrupt his son on the day of his wedding, but he had the feeling that this was not only a turning point, but possibly the beginning of something they were in no way fully prepared for. He only hoped they could reach the road before the creatures did, because, despite how they were ignoring one another and moving as a single unit, it was not certain how they were going to react when confronted by men, particularly if the first men and women they met were not aware of them and ready to get them settled.

Ham and Nahlab, thankfully caught before they'd retired from the remnant of the day's festivities, rushed to where the road met the trees. Not far behind were Ezra and Yalith. Nahlab had run to the menagerie first and grabbed several ropes with loops at the end. She'd passed them out to others along the road, but none of them felt particularly anxious to drop one of those loops over the head of a lion. If it had not been for Nahlab's confidence and Ham's absolute trust in her, they might have lacked the courage.

As they neared the edge of the trees, they slowed. The sun

had dipped the rest of the way below the horizon. Others followed them with torches, but they stood at the edge of the flickering pool of light. It reflected in the eyes of the creatures that faced them, large and small. Two of the beasts, a lion and lioness, stepped forward. There was a rumbling sound, but it did not appear to be a warning. Naḥlab stepped forward, and both lions lowered themselves to the ground. There was no sign of aggression, and the other creatures, as if in fealty, also dropped to the ground. She reached out tentatively with the loop of rope, and then let it drop to her side. She took two quick strides forward and held out her hand to the lioness. The creature met her gaze steadily, and then, very gently lifted her head and licked the offered hand.

Naḥlab turned to Ham, her eyes wide. He stepped forward beside her, offered a quick shrug, and spoke.

"Come."

The lions rose and shook, dust billowing around them. They had clearly come a long way, and some of the other creatures looked hungry and dehydrated. Ham took Naḥlab by the hand and turned, heading down the road toward the trail leading to the menagerie.

"We should send workers ahead," Naḥlab said. "None of the pens are prepared. We need straw, water, food..."

"We cannot," Ham said softly. "There are things I was unable to share with you before now, reasons why we never use torches and work by night. This task is ours. Yours and mine. I do not even want Ezra there, if we can help it, though if he is, Yalith must come as well."

"What are you talking about?"

"It is a thing I can only show you," Ham said. "Now we must hurry. These animals need care, and they have come to us expecting it. We must not let them down."

She did not question him further. They walked, and the animals followed in a line, as if they were children being led off to class or prayer. Ham did not look back. He also tried to ignore the stares of those they passed. He knew some of the workers would see, and he prayed they would not follow once he turned down the path toward the menagerie. It was forbidden, but the existence of rules seemed the surest method of insuring they were broken. He saw Shem standing beside the path and beckoned to him.

"What...?" Shem asked.

"Not now," Ham said. "Please, brother. Once we have passed, close the path to the menagerie. There is work going on this night, as every night." Shem's features shifted and his eyes widened. He nodded. "I will see to it," he said.

Naḥlab glanced at him as Shem hurried away. Ham ignored her. He was trying to sort out the next hour or so of his life in his mind and figure out a way that it would not end badly. The sun was setting. There had been no work on the menagerie pit that day due to the celebrations. He glanced down at his clothes, his finest, and sighed. They were sure to be ruined.

They rounded the last corner and the relatively flat, two-story structure stood silhouetted against the trees in the last dying light of the sun. There was a glimmer of light showing through the crack where the main door stood slightly ajar. Naḥlab stopped.

"There is someone in there," she said. "There should be no work going on at this hour. Everyone was at the celebration."

"Come with me," Ham said. "There are secrets, and then, there are sacred trusts. I have waited to show you what I'm about to show you for so long, and I am hoping you will forgive me for waiting."

He didn't wait for her to answer. He started forward, and she followed. The animals fell in behind them, the lions in the lead. Ham drew the door open wide and followed a passageway to the right that angled downward, into the pits. He knew that the only pens that were remotely ready for occupancy were near the center, where they had established a sort of base, halfway from the depths, where the larger, cooler containments were located, to the surface where they expected to house birds and creatures that would require periods of fresher air. There were pens and fenced areas outside. He wasn't certain these creatures would remain in the central area, but he knew they needed to be there for now, and he needed to be that far in to find what he needed to show Naḥlab.

They descended slowly. Ham had stopped inside the front door. A torch burned, hanging from a sconce on the wall. He grabbed it and carried it, lighting others as they went. The lions balked at first, not trusting the fire, but after a few moments they followed him into the depths. Ahead, a heavy scraping sound echoed through the passages, followed each time by a heavy thump.

"Ham," Naḥlab said. "What is that? What is happening."

"I know you understand that there is no way that our workers could have created this place in the time it has taken to complete," Ham said, raising his torch high. "I have no idea the years it took to excavate your father's arena, but it has been only weeks since we began. I know you have wanted to question me many times, and I have held my breath, uncertain how I would answer if you did. Tonight, you will have that answer."

They descended another level, and Ham turned toward the center of the menagerie. They had designed it so that, from this point on, there was a ledge, with a carefully designed railing for safety, a place from which you could see down into the lower levels. It was intended to allow them to see when or if a problem developed with the larger beasts before they actually had to address it. This night, it provided a different view.

Ham stopped and held his torch high. Naḥlab stepped up beside him. Far below, a huge pickax in his gnarled hands, the giant, Og, grew still, and turned his great visage upward, perfectly centered in the light from the torch. No one spoke. For a long moment, those above and below held that gaze, then Og turned, and resumed his labors, cutting huge chunks of rock and soil from the lower walls.

Ham turned and studied Naḥlab's face. She was staring. She did not seem horrified or angry. She looked astonished, but a smile twisted the corners of her mouth.

"Nephilim," she breathed softly.

Ham nodded. "His name is Og. He has been known to my father for longer than I have been alive. I do not know or begin to understand why he serves us, but he does. He dug this pit. He protects us. When Shem was on the road—"

"He slew the flying beast," Naḥlab said.

Ham nodded. "He did. No one can know. No one can even suspect. They would try to capture him. They would put him in the arena if he did not kill them. He is my friend, though I'm uncertain that term really applies. He has served my father for a very long time."

"But," Naḥlab said, "the Nephilim are unclean. They are monsters. Is that not true? If the stories are to be believed, they are born of angels and mortals, and they have forsaken the Lord."

Ham nodded. "All of that is true, and I have no answer for you. My father, like Master Balthazar, is old. Even he has trouble remembering the early days of his life. Other Nephilim are near, as well. It is why we don't fear the great beasts. They are denied entry."

Naḥlab turned to the animals, who had stopped behind them.

"We have to care for them," she said. "There will be time for questions, and for answers, but we have not time for them now."

They hurried down the passage until they reached a single, large enclosure. Ham opened the gate that sealed it and turned. He gazed at the lions. They hesitated, just for a moment, then the two slunk through the gate and into the interior of the pen. He closed the door behind them. Before they moved on, he spoke. It felt strange, but it seemed important, so he ignored the self-conscious sensation of trying to converse with animals.

"We will return soon," he said. "We will bring food and water. We will bring straw for you to rest. We have to care for the others as well, but I want you to know that we are here for you. We will *be* here for you. I am certain you have reason to believe you cannot trust us. I am here to tell you we are different. This is different. I will protect you with my life."

The lioness watched him, her eyes glittering, but the male strode slowly forward. He stood just beyond the gate, and without really knowing why, Ham slid his hand through, into the interior. There was a rumble, not a growl, but a low vibration that emanated from deep inside the creature. It pressed its head, just for a moment, into his hand, then turned back and returned to the lioness's side.

"I think he understood me," Ham said.

"We'd better hope so," Nahlab said. "Come. We have many more to tend to, and you may have forgotten, but it is our wedding night. I do not expect you to complete your chores and fall away into sleep."

Ham blushed and laughed. It was a beautiful sound, one he felt he could never grow tired of.

It took them the greater part of two hours, but they managed to house all of the creatures who had come to them, and to provide at least a small degree of comfort and sustenance. When they finally made their way to the surface, Ham left some of the torches burning. He did not want to plunge the animals into darkness in an unfamiliar place, and it occurred to him that they needed to find better ways of providing fresh air and adequate light. It was a problem for the daylight.

Their final stop was the pen where they had left the lions. Ham pulled a heavy cart. It was loaded with straw, there was a jug of water to pour into the trough in the pen, and one other rather large package. It was that package that made him most uneasy. They had returned to the main camp and returned with half of a slaughtered calf. The meat had been meant for the family meal the next day. Ham did not hesitate to claim it. This was the prophecy. This was the first of probably thousands of sacrifices to come.

He opened the door to the pen. The lion and lioness reclined near the rear of the pen. He moved directly to the two troughs. In the first, he dumped the meat. He stepped back quickly and helped Nahlab to carry the jug of water and pour it into the second. The lions, smelling the fresh blood, moved forward. He saw that they moved low to the ground, and he caught a glitter in their eyes that had not been there previously. They were hungry.

He backed away, and without reserve, the two great cats attacked the meat, tearing off great chunks and swallowing it so quickly that it hardly seemed possible. The scent of fresh blood filled the air and Ham's pulse quickened. He turned back to the wagon quickly, and Nahlab joined him. They moved the straw, large armloads at a time, to the far side of the pen. It was difficult to focus on the work, because behind them the sound of ripping flesh had grown louder and clearer, but they took their time. They arranged the straw so that there would be a good-sized space for the two cats to rest.

"We will have to bring in a box with sand," Naḥlab said. "They will need a place to defecate, and we will need to be able to clean it. Perhaps we can use one of Yalith's removable floor trays."

Ham turned and stared, amazed she was concentrating on other details while the two lions fed so close behind them. They finished their work, rolled the cart back out of the pen, and closed the gate. Ham glanced at the lions, and the male turned, just for a moment. Their gazes locked. There was no animosity. There was acceptance. Ham turned before that could change, grabbed the handle, and began dragging the much lighter cart up and out of the menagerie. Naḥlab walked at his side. Behind them, far below, the sound of a great pickax driving into stone rang out and echoed.

Chapter 19

Naḥlab was not sure what had awoken her. She'd seen Ham sleeping soundly, had slipped from beneath the linen sheets, careful not to wake him. She drew water, washed herself quickly, and dressed. It was strange. She wanted very badly to be in bed when Ham woke, but it was as if she were compelled to rise, and to move. She left her new home for the first time, and immediately heard voices in the distance, crying out. She took off at a run.

She saw the creatures from a distance and increased her speed. She remembered how things had been the night before. There had not been a crowd, and Ham had been at her side. The situation had been calmer, strange, but somehow controlled. What she saw this morning was a ragged, hungry line of beasts with too many people gathered around them, staring and chattering as if it were some sort of show for their benefit. Eventually, they were going to startle or threaten one of the creatures, and she knew it was going to be up to her to prevent it. She and Ham had foolishly slept, believing that the first group of creatures arriving had been a sign they were doing the right thing, rather than the opening of a literal floodgate.

As she ran, she processed what she saw. Wolves, a bull, a small group of rabbits, and two of the hunting creatures she'd cared for at the arena, but younger, and separated from their parents. They were the biggest threat. If they felt they were in danger, they would lash out. They were intelligent and dangerous, young or not.

As she drew near to the crowd, she began waving her hands and calling out to the crowd.

"Get back," she said. "There is no magic protecting you. Don't startle them. Please, go and let me get them settled—"

Some of those gathered listened, and stepped back, but most stood their ground and simply stared. Some were the workers assigned to the menagerie. Others were simply laborers, or Noah's family, or servants. None of them was going to listen to a girl only one day a member of Noah's family. She wished she had awakened Ham, but at the same time, it angered her. How could people be stupid enough to stand beside wolves and expect to be safe?

She reached the rear of the grouped animals and was relieved to see two workers she both recognized and trusted. Ezekiel and Hannah saw her approaching and she read the relief in their expressions.

"We have to get them inside," she called out. "We brought in others last night. The pens near the center are ready. Help me get them inside, and then we can bring them food, straw, and water."

Ezekiel moved first. He withdrew to the doors of the menagerie and pulled them open. Hannah was only a step behind, and Nahlab pushed her way through the crowds to the left of the trail to join them.

"They will follow us in," she said. "I don't know why, but I know that it's true. We have to get them away from the crowd."

The two did not question her. They opened the gates while Nahlab placed herself between the creatures and the crowd. More of them moved back, but there were still stragglers who would not be put off. The nearness of the creatures drew them, and there were too many for her to confront one at a time. The best she could do was to move along the line of animals and try to slip between them and whoever moved too close.

Then it happened. A man broke free of the crowd. He was fixated on the young Tooth Devils. They were not like the great beasts everyone feared, barely larger than a dog at this point. The man appeared, even at that early hour, to be drunk, and he staggered closer, reaching out a hand. The closest of the Tooth Devils half-turned and cocked its head to the side. Nahlab had seen that move a thousand times. She cried out and dove forward. The creature was incredibly fast, head down low to the ground but turned to the side for a better grip on a leg or a hand. She closed her eyes, just for a second, and breathed a single word of prayer.

"Please," she whispered.

At the very moment she dove between the attacking beast and the suddenly startled man, a voice rang out, strong and clear. All motion slowed, and then, miraculously, stopped. The Tooth Devil shuffled back in line beside the others. The man turned and staggered off through the crowd. Nahlab turned and stared.

Noah strode down the path. His eyes were dark, and those gathered parted before him as if *he* were the dangerous beast. As if he might smite them where they stood if they did not back away. And they did, slowly at first, then in waves, rolling back and rushing down the trail toward jobs, meals, anything and anywhere else. Within a few moments, Noah, Nahlab, and the small line of animals stood alone. Hannah and Ezekiel stood inside the gates, waiting. Neither seemed inclined to step into the open. They moved aside as Noah stepped closer to Nahlab.

"What is happening here, daughter?" Noah said.

Those words melted her tension. "We were not vigilant," she said. "When the first group showed up last night, we thought it was a sign. Just that. It did not occur to us that it was a signal that our true work had begun. We..."

"It was your wedding night," Noah said, "and those gathered should have known better. I will see to it that guards are stationed, and a watch. If this is to be a progression, then we must guide and protect them. Are we ready for these?"

"We are," Nahlab replied. We will get them settled. If you had not shown up, though, these two," she gestured at the Tooth Devils, would have caused a rift that would be difficult to heal. If the creatures do not appear to be safe and controlled, there will be trouble with the workers, maybe from the city. They are small, I know, but believe me when I tell you—they would have dismembered that man in a matter of moments. Once started, they would have been difficult to control."

"I do believe you, as does my son. I am happy to welcome

you, personally, to our family. Is there anything I can do here to help?"

Footsteps pounded on the trail, and they both looked up to find Ham, hair wild about his head and eyes wide, rushing toward them. He stopped, took a second to catch his breath, and began to speak.

"I could not break through the crowd," he said. "I was afraid they had done or caused something awful, that they were running from—"

"It is fine," Noah said. "Naḥlab saved the one fool who got too close."

"And they fled when your…when Father arrived," Naḥlab said, glancing up at Noah. He smiled in return.

"It would appear," Noah said, "that we have reached a landmark in our prophecy. We were just discussing guards and guides for new arrivals. We are also going to have to find others we can trust. The two of you must sleep, and if other creatures appear in the night, we have to be ready to greet them."

Ham stared, just for a moment, then nodded. "There are some we trust," he said. "Clearly there is Ezra, and if you can spare her, we can teach Yalith. She has already shown an affinity for the animals and their care, and she is very quick to learn. We will have to set a schedule, and now it will need to include cleaning, feeding, and care for those who have already arrived. I am glad we have worked as hard as we have because we are barely ready."

"Almost," Noah said, smiling and placing a hand on each of their shoulders, "as if it was going according to a plan."

He turned then and started back down the path. "Ham, I will expect a report tonight, and every night."

"Of course," Ham said. He was not sure his father had heard him, but it didn't matter. He spun toward the gates to the menagerie, and Naḥlab joined him. They slipped in past Hannah and Ezekiel, and the small troupe followed them. Once all had passed inside, Ham sealed the door behind them.

Chapter 20

Life in and around Noah's compound had become a blur. The gigantic framework of the Ark itself rose like the skeleton of some dead beast, decaying in reverse, coming to life one plank, one level at a time. Japheth and Ham had slowly become a single unit, the menagerie being built, maintained, and filled at a pace barely ahead of the arrival of the birds and beasts, predators, and prey. Lessons were learned, changes were made, and as that happened, Ham, Ezra, and Japheth adapted the design of the vessel to incorporate them. The crew handling the beasts had grown very slowly. Trust was imperative and had to be earned. Any lapse in concentration or judgment could endanger both the animals and the other workers, and the pace of the work, while not exactly brutal, was relentless. There were so many new creatures, so many different routines, feeding schedules, exercise periods, and they not only had to be followed and executed, but also documented, studied, and modified for efficiency.

It was fascinating, and for those who left the city to become a part of it, it brought purpose and a sense of accomplishment that was sometimes difficult to explain. There were always the two swords dangling over their heads. If Noah was a prophet, they were working toward their own deaths. If he was simply crazy, they were working on a monumental folly. That would have been fine, because work was work, but the fact that the creatures continued to arrive in odd, misaligned groups was difficult to ignore. There was also the fact that impossible amounts of work took place in the menagerie itself—new levels, larger containments, new passages, all when no one seemed to be doing anything at all. When something appeared ready to collapse, or go horribly wrong, something else prevented it. As the months passed, it grew increasingly difficult to explain it all away as the ravings of a crazy old man.

It didn't seem to matter. The animals needed care, and it was impossible to work with them seriously over any length of time without forging a bond. There were more than two of each. In many cases it was clear that adults would be long dead before the Ark was complete. They were in the same situation as the workers, and the fact they had come to this place and submitted themselves to captivity, and even study, felt like a second bond. They appeared to be aware of the sacrifices they were making and were willing. Even the beasts, though there were not many of them yet. The Tooth Devils had grown, and they were the most difficult to control, but even they were docile compared to those in the arena. Nahlab had told stories that were chilling, and at the same time inspiring, to Ham and the others. The Tooth Devils were perfect predators. Fast, intelligent, hunting in teams, and yet they had killed nothing since their arrival, despite growing steadily. They were a mated pair, and despite the danger, everyone involved waited expectantly for eggs and young.

While all this work continued, Shem had become the lifeline for both of his brothers' operations. The Nephilim, who had always looked out for them, had provided him with a steady supply of gemstones. He did not question where they'd been found. He had also, after a few conversations with Balthazar, come to understand that there was a certain value on anything associated with the Ark or the prophecy. He did not go as far as creating souvenirs or offering tours, but he took his meals with the workers, the traders, and the supply drivers, and he listened. When someone mentioned a thing they admired, or something their family or friends asked about, Shem worked out ways to provide bits and pieces, like Ham had done with the bones from the flying beast. It might have seemed wrong, but the workers were sincere, concerned, and interested. He thought there was little harm in sharing things that might, at the very least, allow them to feel connected to the work.

The money allowed him to keep adequate feed and supplies flowing to the menagerie, and to keep the workers on at long hours building the Ark. He was aware, at times, that it seemed too easy. Deals he believed would fall through went forward without complication, often with better terms than he'd imagined possible, but he did not question it. He also did not kid himself into believing he was responsible. They were all a part of something greater than any individual. Even his father had changed, a man who had been so overbearing and imperious for most of Shem's life that it was easier to fear him than to love him.

The hardest part was remaining clear of the machinations of the merchants and the workers—ignoring the opportunities to work a "better deal" or to turn a profit. His work brought him in contact with a great many merchants, and most of them, as was their way, spent more time trying to strike a better bargain, or find an angle to better situate themselves than their peers, than they did in providing services or quality products. To them it was a game to be won, and it was hard not to be sucked into it. Particularly when he began to realize that his situation gave him an advantage. He managed to keep his distance, but he paid strict attention. He heard others talking when they did not believe he was listening. He saw men gathered in the shadows, and he made note of who spoke with whom, correlating this information to the things he heard.

He was aware that not everyone in the city approved of his father. Those who were not working on the project gossiped about it. The merchants not doing business with Shem were jealous of those who were. Balthazar, old and powerful as he was, did not own the only shop of charms, magic, or oddities, and some of the others were into darker things. Sorcery, necromancy, and who knew what other madness. Such things were not easy to prove or disprove, but Shem was not naive enough to believe his family had the favor of the city. When they had been isolated, they had been an oddity. Now they had everyone's attention. Families talked about them over evening meals. There would be trouble before all was said and done, and Shem knew he was in the best position to spot and deal with it.

He'd considered consulting Balthazar, but though they had dealings on a regular basis, he had no real connection with the man and did not fully trust him. Ham would be the one, if that route needed to be followed, and Ezra, now his brother. Shem liked Ezra more than he had expected. The young man came from the city, where the iniquity and sin were literally bringing about the end of the world. That had been an easy concept when there was little contact with the city, and all they had was Noah's word on what was happening beyond those distant walls. Now it was not so simple. Those Shem had dealt with were good, bad, wicked, or not, but human. Just that, and nothing more. He had not met many who he would call righteous, but it was getting harder to think the lack of that was a reason to destroy the world.

And the rub was, it came down to faith. If he were to present these thoughts to his father, he knew it would result in less responsibility. He would be cut off from the city in some way, handled as a child, as if questioning the prophecy was somehow the worst sin of all. As if adherence to the old laws meant more than living or being a man. All teachings led back to the Garden, to Adam and Eve, a choice between ignorance, or the knowledge of good and evil. In all scripture it was pointed out that the greatest gift to man had been the freedom of choice. What always seemed to be ignored was that if that choice was between absolute servitude to a Lord that they had little or no contact with, and who seemed almost petulant in his responses to their actions, or living their lives by making *actual* choices and being forsaken—it was not really a choice at all.

Similarly, there was the plight of the giant, Og. His father had been an angel. His mother, a human. Because the angels made their own choices, they, and their offspring, would be destroyed along with mankind. The scriptures claimed them all to be wicked, but Shem had known Og all of his life. There was no "friendship" with the creature, but neither did he seem wicked. He had saved Shem's life. He had done all Noah had asked, and much that he had not, and other Nephilim had protected their family. Though many drawings were rendered in black and white, the world was painted in bright, brilliant color, and it felt wrong, in some way, to restrict it.

Noah was his father, and it was impossible to ignore how the prophecy itself continued to play out as if it had been written in a scroll. That did not make any of it easier to reconcile or to understand.

Chapter 21

On one of the darker streets of the city, two blocks over from the arena at the end of an alley, there was a shop. There was not much foot traffic there, clients learned of the location by word of mouth and visited by invitation. There were no browsers, and the windows had been shrouded with dark curtains to prevent anyone who, by whatever unhappy accident, wandered too close from glancing in the window and growing curious.

The shop belonged to a man named Onan, who had been the proprietor for nearly three hundred years. Onan specialized in charms, spells, and business dealings that could not be pursued by the light of day or in public venues. That was on the surface. Those were the things citizens would say if asked about Onan or his work. They would also admit, after a bit of thought, that it was odd how well off the man was. The shop was not remarkable, and though he had a reputation for certain skills and products, none of that would account for serious wealth.

The back of Onan's shop opened onto a single large room. It was locked and inaccessible without several keys, the last of which would not work if the holder did not know the proper incantation. There was a symbol burned into that door, but you could not see it without removing a framed painting of one of the great beasts. Only a handful of men had access to that space, and they never entered alone, with the exception of Onan himself.

This night, Onan sat alone, but candles lined the table, sending shadows sweeping back across the floor and up the walls. There was a loud creak as the door was pushed open and two men entered. One was slight and swarthy with eyes so dark they stood out against the shadows. The second was tall and thin, bending slightly to enter. He wore a dark turban settled over bushy eyebrows and bright, inquisitive brown eyes. A few moments later a third and a fourth entered, twins, rotund and hurried. They took seats between the candles but did not speak. A final figure slipped in through the door and pressed it closed. He was taller and broader than the others. His hair was long, dark, and wavy, and he wore a leather breastplate. A saber slapped against his leg lightly when he moved. He pressed his hand against the inside of the door and spoke several words in quick succession. The others could not hear him, but they mouthed the syllables. A flicker of light rippled along the crack surrounding the door. The man turned, made his way to the table, and took one of the empty seats.

"Did you bring it?" Onan said.

The man nodded. He drew a drawstring-tied bag from his pocket. He untied the straps and dumped a small pile of objects onto the table. He was too far from the others for them to make out the details. One at a time, he handed them around toward Onan. Those in between passed them across the table, examining each for a few seconds before moving it along. Eventually Onan studied a small semicircle of items that, under most circumstances, would be of little interest. There was a tooth. There were three crystals of varying color. There was a lock of hair, tied in silk. The last object was a strip of parchment with a line of symbols etched across it. And there was a long, slender blade. The hilt had once born some sort of leather padding but had been stripped to base metal. Onan picked this up, and, using the tip, slid the other objects around, arranging them one way and then another, until he was satisfied.

"It is good," he said. He tapped the hilt of the blade on the table three times. There was a rustling in the shadows behind him. Soft footsteps padded close, and a silver bowl was placed on the table before him. The bearer of that bowl slipped back to the shadows before anyone could make out any details, or even be certain there had been details. The figure might have been carved from solid shadow.

The bowl was filled about three quarters with clear water.

The rim was etched with letters and symbols, but the interior was polished to a mirror finish. Onan used the blade to slide the remaining objects into position around the bowl's exterior. Each time he placed one, he drew the blade back quickly and exhaled a word. Closest to him, he placed the tooth. It was from the beast that had been slain attacking Noah's son, Shem. He'd had it procured for him in secret from Balthazar. The old merchant would never have allowed him to possess it directly but was becoming incautious as his notoriety grew. Onan closed his eyes and with a quick, precise stroke, drove the point of the blade down in the center of the bowl. He released it, but it did not fall. Instead, it began to rotate, very slowly. The water flickered, and a deep, greenish glow began at the blade's tip and swirled out toward the edges. The rotation bent the light so that it crossed over itself and formed patterns that grew more distinct as the rotation sped. Onan leaned over the bowl and waited. The others watched him in silence but made no move. No one wanted to distract his concentration. There would be time for questions when the ritual was complete.

The surface of the water in the bowl shimmered, and as the blades spinning became a blur, images formed. Onan saw the road leading out toward Noah's complex. The images flickered, and the menagerie came into focus. There was a line of animals outside the door, and several workers were leading them toward a squat building. Onan knew there had to be more to that place because there was simply no way so many creatures could be housed in a one-, or even two-story structure. Something very strange was happening there.

Then he was staring at a hulking structure. The frame of a great boat rose toward the treetops. Most of the hull was in place, and a great door opened down from one side, accessible by a ramp. He saw workers carting supplies and planks up that ramp. Then the image shifted a final time. He was staring at the trees beyond the Ark. They were tall, dark shadows, like sentinels, watching over the workers. One of them, though, was oddly shaped. Onan thought he saw huge, sloping shoulders. Just for a moment he believed deep, burning eyes gazed back at him. Not only were they looking in his direction, but he felt them, felt their attention, and knew that whoever, or whatever, it was, was aware of his presence.

He pushed back from the table with a startled cry. As he did so, the blade tilted, ceased its spinning, and flipped out of the bowl. He narrowly avoided it as it flew past his cheek. Had he remained still, it would have pierced his eye. The sound of the metal dropping onto the wooden floor had an odd quality, hollow and echoing loudly. Onan turned and saw that the blade had buried itself halfway to its hilt in the floor.

The last man who had entered stood slowly and backed away from the table. His hand went to the hilt of his sword, and he studied the room carefully, scanning the shadows.

Onan turned to him. "It is done," he said. "I did not expect resistance."

The twins who had entered, Akeem and Akbar, spoke almost in unison.

"Resistance?" They glanced at one another, and Akbar, the darker of the two, frowned. Akeem fell silent, and Akbar continued. "It would seem there was a bit more than simple resistance. What happened? What did you see?"

They all turned toward Onan then, eyes bright.

"I saw the Ark," Onan said. "I saw a building that I knew, somehow, to be the menagerie—where the animals and beasts are housed, but it was too small, barely two stories, and squat. But there was something else. In the trees. Something huge. I don't know how it is possible, but whatever that was, it felt me. It may have seen me. I had to break the connection."

The tall man with the saber, Ehsan, stepped around the table and walked to where the blade protruded from the floor. He stared down at it.

"I don't believe it was you who broke the connection," he said. "I believe you barely made it out with your life. But," he spun to face Onan, "it's true, then? What we have heard? A giant? Nephilim?"

Onan's features shifted through several expressions, as if he were weighing how much to tell them. Then he nodded. "I don't know what else it could be."

The last two at the table were named Ghazalan and Hashir.

They had been leaning together whispering. Hashir raised his head. "Sit," he said. "Please. We have much to discuss. The ritual did not go exactly as planned, but we have the information we sought. We must form a plan. If what you say is true—if this Nephilim has seen you, or knows you were there, our time may be limited. We may be in danger if we do not act in accordance with our plan, and swiftly."

Onan nodded. Ehsan hesitated, then returned to his seat. The room fell silent for a long moment while they collected their thoughts.

"It is going to take something very powerful to control this creature," Onan said. "Something beyond anything we have attempted. Something we may not even be able to find."

"There is always a way," Ghazalan said. "But I will say, for myself, that if we are to continue this night, it would be well to have something strong to drink, and more light. Shadows are fine for rituals, but I believe a fire would help to ease our minds and fuel our imaginations. I believe we will need both before this night is done."

Onan rose again, as did the others. They moved about, gathering goblets and bottles, placing kindling and wood in the fireplace and lighting lanterns. Outside the shop, the streets were dark and deserted. There were hours before daylight, and these were men accustomed to darkness. Of many kinds. It would be long before any of them dropped away to sleep.

Just beyond the menagerie, deep in the shadows of the trees, Og stood very still. He stared off across the desert toward the city, and his normally placid, expressionless face was twisted in a scowl. The greater part of his life and those of his brethren was spent in maintaining secrecy. It had been years, possibly more than a decade, since there had been an instance where one of those who remained close to Noah had been exposed, and that had been ignored as madness or drunken visions. This was different.

Whoever had watched him had power. Not immense power, but power born of knowledge. It was a danger, and he knew that he would have to deal with it. Noah and the others would have to know about this. The connection had been too short for him to pinpoint a source. The giant closed his eyes. Then, very slowly, he raised his pickax over his head and ducked in through the great double doors leading to the interior of the menagerie and his work. There would be time for other concerns after the sun had risen and the labor was completed. He sensed that something different was coming, something larger, and more dangerous. The work could not be ignored.

Chapter 22

Noah sat, watching the sunrise, as always. There had been no new message, no visitation, but his routine never varied. He knew if he ignored his prayers, if he did not present himself, that something would be missed. He was not certain how he knew this, but he was a righteous man, and a part of that was a desire for strict adherence to rules. It didn't matter that it was his own rule. The morning silence was important to him for many reasons. It provided a short escape from the day, from the endless machinations of those from the city, and the unending labor the prophecy had brought upon his family.

He was not prepared when a rustling sound behind him, deep in the shadows of the trees, disturbed the silence. He knew who was there. It was the timing that was unprecedented, and he felt a sudden chill pass through his veins as his mind raced over possible reasons for such a breach of boundaries.

He never actually spoke with Og. The giant knew his thoughts if he allowed it. What he sensed was an urgent request for such a sharing. That urgency also chilled him, because there had never been an instance when the Nephilim had made such an approach. Not in the centuries of their acquaintance. Noah turned to the desert and cleared his mind, just for a moment. He needed to know if his Lord would offer an explanation or a warning, any form of guidance. There was nothing forthcoming, so, with a deep breath, he turned back to the trees and opened his mind.

What passed was not conversation. It was a series of images, often blurred. He saw a shadowed room. There was some sort of silver bowl and a dagger. The scene shifted from the Ark to the room, to the menagerie, to the trees. Silhouetted in those trees he saw the shadowed figure of Og. The link to the bowl and the dagger and the room broke with a snap and a last flickering glimpse of the blade, flying from the bowl toward a shadowed face.

And then it was gone. All of it. He sensed no presence. He saw nothing in the trees. His skin felt wet and clammy, and his heart hammered in his chest. He knew what he'd seen. The city was rife with sorcery, and someone was watching him. Someone was watching his family, and now they knew Og existed. It was what he'd feared most from the moment he received the prophecy. The Lord was unknowable, but men were all too predictable.

Noah rose, all thoughts of prayer or communion with his Lord forgotten. He needed to speak with his sons and others. It was strange that he immediately knew that the extended family he'd inherited since the prophecy had taken over his life would be important. He'd spent a lifetime being told he was special, protecting his reputation and his faith, turning away from the world, friends, and other branches of his own family. Now, rather than the noble patriarch who should be listened to and obeyed, he felt, for the first time, as if he were a part of something greater, something beyond his control. It should have frightened him. It should have filled him with dread and insecurity, but it did not. His boys had matured into competent, good young men. They had married well.

After the morning meal, Noah asked Ham, Nahlab, Yalith, Ezra, Shem, and Sedeqetelebab to meet with him. They walked together to the menagerie, where Ham had created a workspace that housed Balthazar's journals, his own notes, the drawings, and the records they were keeping as they took in each new creature and cared for it. It was a large space, well lit, with several benches and shelves lining the walls. Noah glanced around and the sight of it eased his mind. Trouble would come, there was no denying it, but he was also certain they would stand against it.

When they were all seated, he spoke, quickly, and without

hesitation. The others remained silent and listened.

"There are men in the city," he said, "who bear us ill will. They are aware that something is strange about this structure, the menagerie, and they are aware, though I am uncertain exactly how, of Og and the other Nephilim. I do not believe that they think my prophecy to be true, but they will come. They will try to turn others against us. They will try to find and bind Og, possibly force him to their arena."

Noah turned then and glanced at Naḥlab. "I don't believe your father is involved, or even aware. I don't know him as well as you, so I don't know how he might react if someone brought him such a suggestion."

"I wish I thought he would turn them away," Naḥlab said, "but you are correct to worry. And it sounds as though whoever is watching has turned to dark arts. There is far too much of that in the city, and in particular near the arena."

"I will speak with Balthazar," Ezra said. "He would have nothing to do with something like this, but he has a lot of contacts. If he can get us a name, or names, we should be able to plan more carefully."

"That makes sense," Noah said. "As it stands, anyone who comes here could be involved in this. We'll have to be more watchful. Spread the word through those you trust the most to be aware of any odd behavior, new workers, anything at all out of place. I know you are all working long hours with little rest, and this is one more burden. I don't know how to avoid it. Og has to continue his work, or we will fall behind and have more creatures to care for than resources. If we come out directly and try to find out who is watching us, we have to admit to knowledge of sorcery, and possibly to the existence of the Nephilim. The only course I know, the one I've followed most of my life, is to believe that the prophecy will work itself out if we remain strong in our faith. Despite that, it seems to me that the knowledge Og imparted is part of the prophecy as well—a test or a warning. I have lived a long life. There are parts of that time that are gray to me, that I barely recall. There are lessons I've learned and forgotten, faces that haunt me more like ghosts than memories. The thing that has kept me sane is my faith.

"You would not know this, and I barely remember it myself, but I was not born… normal. I have vague memories of being told I was unique. There were other prophecies, and the longer we work to build this ark, the more those memories return. I wish there were records. In those times, when I was a child, we did not record things on tablets or scrolls. We passed them from father to son, from mother to daughter, and we remembered. I have never mentioned this to anyone, but I will tell you now, because we are bound. We are all part of one greater whole.

"The prophecy said that there would be a child born who did not require circumcision. He would have a light that was impossible to explain. His coming would precede a great flood, a cleansing. I was that child. My grandfather, Methuselah, consulted with Enoch himself to know why I was different, and this is what he was told. That memory remained buried, and even when my Lord spoke to me of the Ark, it did not surface. Now, slowly, I am remembering.

"Ezra…when you speak with Balthazar, ask him if he knows this story. Ask him if there are any records, even written long after the fact. He is nearly as old as I, and he may have a better or different set of memories. If there is anything we can learn, any other part of that prophecy that has been remembered or recorded, it could be important."

"I will go to the city today," Ezra said.

"I will go with you," Naḥlab said. "I will speak with my father, and I will check around the arena. I can spend some of the time-sharing things we have learned with those who care for the beasts and ask about any new developments. I was not the only one who cared for the creatures. There are others who will watch for us and report."

"Are you sure?" Ham said. "I don't like the idea of you being in danger."

"We are all in danger," Naḥlab said. "I will do what I can, and you must watch the menagerie and the workers. They love you. They talk about you all of the time when you are not there."

Ham stared at her. He wasn't certain if she was trying to make him feel better, or if it was true. He understood that she was not going to take no for an answer, though, so he just smiled.

"I will be eager to hear what you learn," he said.

Naḥlab smiled.

"I believe it is time we go about our day," Noah said, rising. "I saw a group of animals arriving earlier, and I'm sure there will be questions and special needs."

Chapter 23

When the bell at the door of his shop rang, Balthazar glanced up and actually smiled. Ezra had entered, glancing around slowly, taking in the changes since he'd moved across the desert to Noah's compound. The place was less tidy, but overall, not much different.

"I suppose I'll have to find a new apprentice," Balthazar said. "I'm not as spry as I was, say, three hundred years ago."

"You'll live forever," Ezra said. He crossed the room, Balthazar rose, and the two embraced.

"It is good to see you. Business is brisk, but it still feels rather empty."

"I may have something to interest you," Ezra said. "Something that could help to ease the boredom."

"Oh?"

"It seems that Noah has drawn some dangerous attention," Ezra said. "Someone performed a seeing. They were gathering information about the compound, the menagerie, and they saw something else. Something I'm not at liberty to speak of, but that I believe has put everyone out there in danger."

"A seeing you say?" Balthazar said. "That would be a fairly narrow group, given the distance. Probably even smaller given the type of information you have mentioned and the possible gain it might bring. No one performs magic in this city unless there is money or power involved."

"That much I know," Ezra said. "And personally, I know only a very few with the knowledge and experience to pull such a thing off."

"You would be surprised," Balthazar said. "This is an old

city, and one thing about Noah's prophecy is absolutely true. The men and women here have fallen to sinful ways. There are more who practice dark arts than attend any temple, and even those temples are filled with priests of a very different nature than originally intended. It wasn't always thus, but now? There are many who could perform such a seeing. What I must do is ask a few subtle questions to see if I can find out the *why* of it. That will lead straight to the who in short order."

"There is more," Ezra said. "A special request from Noah to you personally."

Balthazar raised an eyebrow.

"He told us this morning of a prophecy," Ezra said. "It was ancient and passed down from Enoch himself, if it's to be believed. He says that there has always been a prophecy of a deluge—of a great cleansing. The prophecy foretold the coming of a man who was more than a man. A man who, from birth, did not require circumcision."

"And he told you that he is that man," Balthazar said, returning to his seat.

"He did."

Balthazar pressed his hand into his forehead and sat very still, then he rose, moved behind the counter, and drew out a flask and two mugs. He poured a generous portion into each and handed one to Ezra, who stared in astonishment. He'd worked with Balthazar most of his life, but they had never shared a drink. They had never, really, spoken as friends.

"Oh, take it and enjoy it," Balthazar said. "You are going to need it when I tell you what I am about to, and possibly more. This is a very old story, and one I have wondered about myself since Noah announced his vision."

Ezra sat and took a sip. It was a dark liquor, sweet, but not too sweet, and it burned like fire as it ran down his throat."

"That drink is a century old," Balthazar said. "It is one of the finest things I ever acquired."

Ezra set down the cup, afraid he'd been drinking too fast.

Balthazar burst into laughter.

"I didn't say it was scarce or expensive," he said. "You know how I operate. I bought barrels of the stuff from a merchant who had no real idea of its worth, and I have stored it all these years. It simply gets better with time. Now listen. I don't want to have to tell this twice, and it is a tale so old that it is not recorded, as far as I know, in any journal or history."

Ezra grinned, took another sip, and sat back.

"You know," Balthazar said, "that Noah is the grandson of Methuselah. As old as I am, Methuselah lived another three centuries. It is said that when Noah was born, there was something too perfect about him. He seemed to glow with inner light, he was a beautiful child, and, as you have said, he did not require the ritual of circumcision. They went to Enoch himself to inquire of the boy and what he might be, and that is when Enoch prophesied the deluge, a great destruction. In those days, they did not call him Noah at all, but Menahem. It was thought, and your story seems to bear it out, that men had become too wicked, and that calling him by his true name might give too much power to those given to sorcery and magic. When I met him, he was called Menahem, and I can't recall when or why that changed. In those times, only Methuselah called him Noah. I suppose, over time this was overheard and repeated, despite Enoch's warning.

"The thing is, men have never been wise. Like the warning about the name, the prophecy of a great destruction was largely ignored in favor of debauchery and sin. Men had other things on their mind than faith, and belief in danger from a vengeful Lord seemed mythical and very distant. Over time, it was forgotten. Now there is a man in the desert, building a boat to save his family, and only a handful of us left who might remember that we were warned so long ago. I find it ironic that you have come to me for this story, while at the same time reminding me that I could, at any time in the last five hundred years, have changed. I might have preached to those in the city, led them from sin."

"You do not believe that." Ezra said, surprising himself. He thought it must be the drink. "You have lived the life you wanted to live. Of all the lessons you've taught me, that is the one I am most fond of. My own road has diverged from yours, but the lesson is sound. And now you are doing what you can.

You are enjoying life, making bargains and deals, drinking," Ezra's smile widened, "'one of the finest things you have ever acquired,' and watching it all unfurl. I believe you are a good man. I believe, also, that you are a wise man. But you are a man of this city—you helped to build it. You know it better than most."

"Wise? That is certainly in question. I am old, though, and you are right that I understand this city. I will make inquiries about this 'seeing'. How did you come to know of it?"

"In the end it was detected," Ezra said. "The connection was broken."

For a second time, Balthazar seemed surprised. "By someone in the compound? That is interesting, indeed. I do not know of any particular prayer that could manage that. Does Noah have an angel on staff? A demon?"

Ezra very carefully kept his features still. "I cannot tell you what you want to know," he said. "But I believe that if you bring Noah the information he requires, he might. He has come to trust you, and the two of you share more years than any others that I know of. I believe, though he will not vary from the prophecy, that he would enjoy your counsel and company."

"Tell Noah," Balthazar said, "that I will come with tomorrow's supply train. I will bring some of this," he lifted his glass. "He can share, or I will drink, and he can watch as we talk. I can't promise I will end the threat, but I should be able to define it."

Ezra finished his drink and stood. He walked over, and Balthazar rose once more. They embraced a second time, and the old man held him at arm's length.

"There is no reason that he would listen to me," he said, "but may you go with the grace of the Lord. I will see you tomorrow."

Ezra nodded. "I am off to the arena, then," he said. "Naḥlab is there, trying to gather rumors, and sharing information she has learned about caring for the creatures. I promised Ham that I would keep her safe."

"Tell that young man," Balthazar said, "that he has chosen well."

"I will," Ezra said. Then, before the conversation could grow awkward, he turned and hurried out the door.

Balthazar watched him go and smiled. Then he shook his head.

"Strange days, indeed," he said softly. He turned and poured another mug of the liquor, returning to his seat and contemplating who he would approach first.

Nahlab entered the gates leading to the pens beneath the arena slowly. She'd passed that way so many times it should have felt like routine, but somehow it felt entirely different. She saw familiar faces, waved at friends, but there were already others—men and women she'd never seen before—bustling about their daily business. She moved deeper into the passageways and started down. Just before she reached the pen where the Tooth Devils were housed, a familiar smiling face melted out of the shadows.

"Nahlab! You have returned to us."

A smiling young man, younger than Nahlab herself, bowed slightly, unable to contain his pleasure. "We thought you had left us forever!"

"And I have, in a sense," Nahlab replied. "My duties to family and my husband are many. Still, I have missed this place, and all of you. Who is here today?"

"The usual crew," Assan said. "There are a few new faces, but not much changes here. Hard work is not popular with the youth of the city, as well you know."

Nahlab laughed. "I do," she said. "And," she lowered her voice in case they were not actually alone, "you are always welcome to come out and work with us. We have more beasts than we can care for, and so few with real experience."

"I will keep that in mind," Assan said. "But what brings you here alone?"

"There are strange things happening in the city," Nahlab said. Then she laughed. "Okay, stranger than usual. Someone is gathering information they have no right to on the compound and the menagerie. Someone in the city is planning something, and I just have a feeling that it leads, at some point, to the arena. I would ask my father, but one of two things is true. He knows, in which case he'd never tell me, or he does not know, but would be worried for me if he did.

"I'm looking for rumors, anything odd, new faces or voices talking about events. There is sorcery involved, so it's dangerous."

"I will keep my eyes and ears open," Assan said. "I have long wanted to visit your menagerie, so I will make you a deal. If I hear anything of significance, I will make the journey out to visit. There is always something new in play, but I have heard nothing in the past few days. They are bringing in another Mace Tail, but it's smaller than the last, and not likely to do well in the arena. They have a batch of slaves from a recent battle, warriors that may create a spectacle if properly armed, and not immediately overmatched. None of it is unique."

"What I am looking for will be more than unique," Naḥlab said. "I can't explain it, but if I am correct in what I believe, they will think it is the greatest show ever to be considered. It will cause more than a small ripple. I will leave your name with those who watch the road, so if you come, they will bring you straight to myself, or to Ham. And I appreciate this."

"You would do the same," Assan said. "Probably more."

Naḥlab stepped forward and gave the boy a quick hug. "I would. I'm happy that you understand that. I don't know how to explain what is happening at that compound. I don't have words to express the wonders I've seen, or the doubts that accompany them. I am happy. Ham is a good man, and you know Ezra; he is there as well."

"Yes," Assan said. "I have known Ezra almost as long as I've known you. It has become much harder to get good gossip in the city since his departure. Master Balthazar is much less talkative."

Naḥlab laughed. "Ezra is visiting him now," she said. "I expect him to meet me here."

"Would you like to see the new acquisitions?" Assan asked. "We have something new, like a Tooth Devil, but larger. Ezra nearly got eaten by one of them not so long ago, if memory serves. Master Balthazar is still peddling teeth from that one. What we have is juvenile but growing very quickly. It's strange that I never noticed it before, but this creature, and the Tooth Devils, resemble another creature we care for regularly. I have actually meant to mention it to Balthazar, now that, as it grows, there is a new detail to add. They are like great, giant chickens. The resemblance fades as they age, but this juvenile beast actually has feathers."

"Feathers? Seriously?"

Assan nodded. "Come, I will show you."

She followed him into the lower levels, glancing now and then into the pens, spotting creatures that were familiar, others she knew were new, and finally coming to a halt before a huge gate. The lower section of it was solid planking, and the upper was constructed of iron bars. Assan opened a sliding portal at eye level, not large enough for an exit, and also barred, and she stepped forward.

At first, she saw nothing. Then, near the rear of the pen, a dark shape peeled free of the shadows. She caught the glint of torchlight off yellow eyes. It was tall—three times the size of one of the Tooth Devils—and Assan had said it was young. It was the height of a man and much broader. It moved quickly, head tilted, and its arms, as they came into focus, were small, like they had not fully formed. They were disproportionate to the head, which, now that Assan had mentioned it, darted this way and that in the same manner as a chicken, or as a hawk might. Even the way it walked, the huge, clawed feet, the way it bobbed its neck. She had heard Balthazar say that birds move their heads in that manner to keep things in focus, that the position of their eyes required the motion to improve their vision.

"How big will it get?"

"She," Assan said. "If the creature that nearly killed Ezra is a good example," Assan said, "as tall as a house, and with teeth large enough to tear the head off a long-neck with only a few bites. I don't know that we have anything that can stand before it, though it is possible that a large enough pack of Tooth Devils might pull it off. This one does not exhibit their intelligence and does not seem to desire a 'pack'."

"It will be magnificent," Naḥlab said.

"Yes, and likely dead within a couple of years, at the most.

Not to mention all of the men and beasts it will devour in the meantime."

Naḥlab fell silent. She pressed her hand against the gate. The creature minced closer, slowly, watching the open window. Then, very suddenly and with enormous force, it rushed the gate, crashing into it without regard for its own safety. The entire structure shook, and Naḥlab fell back with a cry."

"We should go," Assan said. "It's not getting out of there, but I don't want to upset it further. Are you okay?"

Naḥlab nodded. "I'm fine. But... it is so angry. So hungry. This one should not be kept in a pen. Something horrible is going to happen."

"I fear that you are right, but what can I do?"

They turned and started back up the passage toward the surface and the streets.

At the top, they found Ezra, just arriving. He smiled, but his expression turned serious when he saw Naḥlab's face.

"What is it? What has happened?"

"Nothing," Naḥlab said. "It really is nothing. At least, it's nothing we can do anything about. Just had a bad experience below."

"I am sorry to hear that," Ezra said. "I have had a good talk with Balthazar. Have you finished what you needed to do here?"

Naḥlab turned to Assan. "I have," she said. "Assan is going to watch for us. If there are rumors or something strange happens, he will come to us."

"I appreciate that," Ezra said. "And I would love a chance to sit and talk. I know it's only been a short time, but it seems like an eternity since I caught up on what is happening here."

"Nothing compared to what is happening out there, I believe," Assan said, "but I will come soon, regardless of what I learn."

"Thank you," Naḥlab said. "Now, we must be going. There is just enough time to safely cross back over the desert, and after what I've just seen—"

"I understand," Assan said. "We will talk soon."

Naḥlab gave him another quick hug, and then she and Ezra hurried off down the street and out of the city. They had a cart waiting, and they could tell as they climbed aboard that the driver was concerned by the late hour.

"Do we have time?" Ezra asked him.

"We will make it."

Ezra nodded. He leaned back, and Naḥlab sat beside him. As they rolled across the desert, pulled by a small pack of Reem, their massive horns swaying side to side, they shared the findings of the day. They both scanned the sides of the roads, the rocks and crags. There would be much to discuss when they reached the compound, and they wanted to be sure they had everything straight. The ride passed quickly, and before the sun could set, they rolled through the gates of the compound. Naḥlab noticed that there was a small pack of animals just ahead of them, entering slowly. She smiled. It was the best thing that could have greeted her, the work that filled her heart.

Chapter 24

Balthazar closed shop early and turned toward downtown and the arena. He'd sent a messenger ahead and knew that Thaddeus would be expecting him. The two had never been close, but since the weddings at Noah's compound, they had spoken several times. They'd developed a kinship, between Ezra and Naḥlab and the shared family ties, however weak. Balthazar was not a parent, only a guardian, but Ezra had been with him from a young age. The strangeness of visiting Noah for any reason, the animals they'd seen, the prophecy. All of it had formed an odd bond that Balthazar was hoping to take advantage of. For once, he didn't seek that advantage for himself, and that alone was worthy of the two bottles that hung heavy in the pouch at his waist.

He carried two bottles of the liquor he'd shared with Ezra, and he hoped that it would help him to form an alliance. The information Ezra sought would not be easy to come by. The fact was, if he were correct, and there was something Noah was hiding that could bring money and prestige to the arena, it would be widely sought after. Thaddeus might not be involved, but if it were presented to him, there could be pressure from many sources to make whatever that sensation was a reality.

It could only end badly. The city was a dark place. There were good people and happy people, but for every good one there was a greedy man, a thief, a woman using her wiles to warp the future of a family or another woman's husband. He couldn't pinpoint when it had passed over the line that set the prophecy in motion. But he believed, now. He did not believe it would be soon, but he believed the deluge would come, and he had made his peace with it

Ezra had told him that part of Noah's vision was that men would no longer live so long that they forgot what a gift life could be. No more than 150 years, he'd said. Such a short time compared to his own life, and yet, he only remembered fragments of his early years. He thought that long-lived as men had been, 150 years was probably a good reckoning of how much life one's mind retained with clarity, and each time that hourglass was turned, it grew a little emptier, filled with less wonder and burdened by cynicism. Thaddeus was not as old as he or Noah, but he was more than four hundred years and might be at a point where he could appreciate this new way of looking at things.

Either way, it concerned his daughter, and Balthazar was counting on that to mean something. It was another risk. Men in the city did not consult their women as they might. They preferred sons to daughters, and bartered daughters for wealth or power. In most houses, using the fate of a daughter as a playing piece in a larger game would be a mistake. Naḥlab was special, though. She had been a big part of the arena's success, had stepped up in a family where there was but one son, who seemed more or less content to enjoy life until such time he inherited his father's businesses and holdings. Balthazar was betting on Thaddeus to be very fond of Naḥlab. Strange times called for strange alliances.

Thaddeus had chambers one reached from the ground floor through a guarded doorway and a steep set of stairs that Balthazar was not looking forward to. There was a room where Thaddeus conducted business, and if there was anything happening in the arena, another set of stairs led to a box seat with a wonderful view of the action below. Balthazar had been invited one time to view a battle from those seats, and it had been breathtaking. Now, thinking back on it, something marred the memory. Something that he could not put his finger on, exactly, but that, nonetheless, made him queasy when he thought back on it.

The battle had been between several of the Tooth Devils and a small squad of warriors captured in battle. The men had been fully armed, armored, and were clearly well trained. None of that had mattered. As they moved carefully about the arena, forming lines and using carefully placed obstacles as shields, the creatures arrayed against them had picked them off. At first it was one at a time, a feint here, a lightning strike there, but as the battle progressed the creatures learned. They reacted more quickly and attacked more viciously. In the end, all of the men were slaughtered, and Balthazar remembered one of the Tooth Devils had turned its head at the end. It lifted its bloody muzzle to the sky and screamed, and, just for a second, it had made eye contact.

In that gaze, Balthazar saw rage and pain. He felt the thing's frustration at being captured and confined. There was no remorse for the fallen—it had been kill or be killed, and the creatures had killed. But it was wrong. To send those men to their certain death was wrong. To hate the creatures was possibly not such an evil thing, but to share in that evil for sport?

A shiver ran up his spine, just as he reached the doorway he sought. The guard stepped in front of the door and Balthazar smiled.

"Thaddeus is expecting me," he said. "If you need to send word of my arrival, I am happy to wait."

The guard stepped aside.

"We were informed of your visit, Master Balthazar," the man said. "I wish you a good evening."

"And you as well," Balthazar said. He reached into his pouch. He'd brought a third bottle, just for such a moment. It was nothing like what he intended to share with Thaddeus, but it was likely levels beyond what the salary of a guard would purchase. He handed it to the man. "Share this with your fellows, when you are off duty."

The man took the bottle and smiled. "I thank you," he said. "Thirst is a constant in these times."

"And the work you do is important," Balthazar said. "I am certain that Thaddeus appreciates it."

The guard said nothing but offered a quick salute. Balthazar entered the doorway and started up the stairs. It never hurt to have friends in the right places, and he'd learned that a kind word, backed by an expensive gift, could turn the tide in many a dangerous situation. You never knew when you might need a friend.

Thaddeus looked up as Balthazar entered. He rose and offered his hand. His smile felt genuine, and Balthazar returned it.

"Welcome," Thaddeus said. "I was a bit surprised to hear you had asked to see me, but I admit to being glad that you did. Your shop has long been a subject of conversation, and I personally own several of the wonders you've managed to collect over the years."

"And I have attended a great number of entertainments in this arena," Balthazar replied. "You may recall that I joined you in your private box for one such, a few years back."

"I do," Thaddeus said. "I have to say, I wish it had been any battle but that one. The Tooth Devils are a big draw, though betting is not as profitable. They never lose. I have tried every beast that has come my way, hardened squads of warriors. If there is more than one Tooth Devil in the arena, they win."

"But why would you not wish me to witness that?" Balthazar asked. "I will add that I was not particularly taken with the show, for similar reasons, but now I'd like to hear yours."

"There is no sport in it," Thaddeus said. "To fight them is a death sentence, and there is something about those creatures, about their eyes, and the expressions they manage, that speaks of greater intelligence than the other beasts we've encountered. There is the sense they are biding their time, and that some form of vengeance is in store. It's a silly thing, I know, but I sometimes wish we'd never encountered them. I am not a fan of any contest that is not, at least at its base, fair. I don't like sending men, even slaves, to their deaths. I would not do it, but it's not always my decision. The crowds, the elders of the city, the rich, they will have their entertainment, and if not from me, well…"

"I understand," Balthazar said. "We all have to balance our desires against those of the rich and powerful. In a way, that is exactly why I am here this evening, but before we get to that, I have brought a gift."

He pulled the two bottles out of his pouch and placed them on the table between them.

"One of these is for you," he said. "It is old, hard to come by, and the latter is only because I own literally all of it that still exists. The second is for us to share, though if any remains when we are done talking, I will certainly leave it behind."

Thaddeus produced two goblets from a cabinet and placed them beside the bottle.

"I am sensing," he said, "that this is more than a social visit."

"I regret that in all the years we've lived in this same city, those social visits have not materialized," Balthazar said, "but I think that you will, at the very least, find what I have to say interesting. I'm hoping you'll feel the same about it as I do, because it is likely to affect you, myself, the city, your daughter, and my apprentice."

Thaddeus opened the bottle, poured generous portions into the two goblets, and sat back.

"Ezra tells me," Balthazar said, "that someone here in the city has taken a rather dark interest in Noah and his compound. It seems that someone has managed a seeing aimed at gathering information. There are not many here who could manage that, and if I am to understand it correctly, they saw something at that compound that was able to break their spell. Ezra will not tell me what it is, though I can tell that he knows."

"And you believe that you know, as well," Thaddeus said. "In fact, I am going to guess that what we are discussing is confirmation of a very old rumor?"

Balthazar nodded. "That's what I believe. I can't prove it, of course, but we both know that if it's true, and if those involved have the proper backing, and by some strange twist of fate succeed, their first stop is going to be this very office."

"I won't pretend not to be curious," Thaddeus said. "About the creature, if it exists, and about how it would fare in the arena, or if it could even be contained to make the attempt. Of course, if there is truth in its existence, there is truth in so much more that I have ignored throughout my life that it makes my head hurt. For one thing, it means that rather than building new pens, I should be working on a boat of my own, and instead of overseeing events on the Sabbath, I should be at the temple."

Balthazar laughed. "Indeed, though, at this point I am

uncertain if you could find anyone in the temple who would be of much use. They have their own machinations, and even sorceries, going on. I believe your pack of Tooth Devils outnumbers the righteous in this city."

"No doubt you are correct," Thaddeus said. "But a Nephilim. These are truly strange times. And you are also correct that whoever is behind this must have had the same thought that I did, but with fewer concerns and scruples. The question is, will they approach me before they have actually secured their quarry or after they attempt it? If the latter, I may not be much help, though I can certainly get the word out for people to pay attention to rumors and watch for strange gatherings. Stranger, I mean, than what is normal in this part of the city. There are a great number of guilds and groups who might have the knowledge to attempt something like this, but it is always difficult to tell which have real power and what they are capable of from what they tell others they are capable of. Everything is mysterious, which is simply another way of saying they are both holding back information and putting forth false information."

"Games within games," Balthazar said. Then, watching Thaddeus carefully, he added. "I could do it. It would not be easy, but I have a certain silver bowl. The thing is, it has never occurred to me to use it. I have watched and studied others for centuries, and the one thing I have observed time and again is that any action brings a reaction. If one meddles with secrets, the problem is that they *are* secrets. There is no real way to know the cost or the consequence, until you make the plunge, and then, of course, it is too late."

Thaddeus nodded. He took a sip of his drink, then a larger gulp. "I have a thought," he said. "It may turn out to be nothing, but there is one man I have dealt with in the past who may have the contacts and ability to accomplish a feat of this magnitude. His contacts are not what you would call reputable, but they are powerful in their own circles, and recently I've heard rumors they have been meeting. Not far from here. I paid no attention, but do you know a man named Onan?"

Balthazar started noticeably, and Thaddeus smiled.

"I see that you do," he said. "Then you know the type of

person I am talking about, and the danger involved."

"That is worse than I'd imagined," Balthazar said, "and yet, now that you mention the name, I am not certain how it failed to occur to me immediately. It is exactly the sort of thing I would expect of him. Also, it occurs to me that despite the level of arrogance it would take to spy on Noah, let alone such a creature as a Nephilim, sorcery will not allow him to react well to being cut off so easily. He may have gotten the beginnings of the knowledge he was after, but I suspect he also got slapped down pretty hard. He won't take that well."

"And so," Balthazar picked up the thought, "he will escalate his efforts. He will try harder, will take risks. I will tell Ezra to be extremely careful of any new workers. He'll have to tell Ham, his brother, to be wary of new business deals, particularly if they seem too good to be real. And there is a further problem."

"What is that?" Thaddeus asked, pouring them both another round.

"We can't let Ezra, or your daughter, know that we *know* about the Nephilim. It was not something that was shared with me. I could, of course, just tell him that we've suspected this all along. That there is no way a family could live out where they do, with the beasts roaming, and thieves, and survive without being attacked, enslaved, or wiped out. It seems obvious, but I still believe they would be suspicious if they knew that I knew. I have my own problems with reputations and rumors. I don't want them to think I'm playing both sides against the middle, so this all has to be kept from them."

"Agreed," Thaddeus said. "I would hate for my daughter to believe I would condone such a thing, but I know there would have to be doubt if she knew what I know. There have been too many questionable decisions in the past."

"Then," Balthazar said, raising his cup, "it is you and I against whoever and whatever is to come. Assuming that the prophecy is real, here's to going out in style."

Thaddeus laughed, and knocked his goblet into his visitor's. "Indeed," he said. "They say life is too short. Here's to making the best of what is offered."

They both drank and sat in silence for a while, then Balthazar rose to leave.

"I will send word if I learn anything new, and I will await word from you in return."

"Thank you for the information, and the drink, and the challenge," Thaddeus said.

Balthazar only winked and turned toward the stairs, heading out into the night.

Chapter 25

The circle had decided that Ehsan would be the one to try and infiltrate Noah's camp. Being a merchant, he had valid reasons to visit, or could concoct them. He was also the best able to defend himself. They all had their strengths and weaknesses. He was often impulsive, prone to violent outbursts, but his power rivaled that of Onan himself, and coupled with his physical prowess, that made him the obvious choice.

There was also the fact that, among them, skills and abilities varied. Onan and Ehsan, through the use of various crystals and a pendant both would wear, would be able to maintain a sort of link. Some of what Ehsan saw, heard, and did would be visible to Onan, and could immediately be worked into their plans.

That was where the twins thrived. While their magical abilities did not stand against those of Onan or Ehsan, their wiles and machinations were without peer. They had ties to every guild and organization in the city, spies in half of them and holds on the rest. The logistics of what was to come would fall largely on their shoulders. That left Ghazalan and Hashir. Hashir worked for Thaddeus, who owned the arena. Ghazalan was a collector. He found things. When something was necessary for a spell or a trade, when a person needed to be located who could translate an ancient tongue, or the name of a particular creature came into question, it was Ghazalan who provided. He and Hashir had worked together for many years, using Ghazalan's knowledge to increase Hashir's influence, digging deeply into the entertainment network of the city. Most of those who lived within the great walls spent their lives in a constant effort to overcome ennui. Ghazalan and Hashir spent much of their lives making this possible. It was a practice that garnered favors on all levels.

The six were gathered at the table once more but this time there was plenty of light and wine. No magical workings were planned.

"We'll have to reach out to Thaddeus," Onan said, "and soon. If we have nothing in place to contain the creature, none of it will matter. And even if Thaddeus is on board, it's uncertain if we have the power or knowledge to pull it off."

"Now is not the time for doubt," Ehsan said. "Too much is already invested, and if Noah and his people don't know of our plans, it's only a matter of time. Secrets are not exactly safe in the city. I will be heading out this morning with the supply train. I've arranged to meet directly with Noah's son, Shem. I've recently managed to acquire a supply of construction materials that I know he is seeking, and I've let it be known my price will be more than reasonable. Of course, I will negotiate, but I will start low enough that he still feels he has come out on top. And I will have others with me."

"You must not let them act oddly," Akeem said. "If you try to learn too much, they will notice."

"I am not a fool," Ehsan said, frowning. "We will plant the crystals, as planned. We will do the work we are contracted to do, no more and no less. And I will make an effort to connect with the boy. From all reports, he is a shrewd businessman, and I suspect I will enjoy that. The rest of you need to prepare for tonight. Once everything is in place, we need to act before we are discovered."

Onan stood.

"Agreed. By tonight everything should be in place. We will have word from Thaddeus, and we will have a means to monitor the compound and the menagerie without worrying over direct connections going awry. They will be watching for us, expecting us, more than likely, but if we are careful this can be done before any of that matters. Once the creature is ours, there is little that Noah, or anyone associated with him, could do to stop us."

They rose, all but Onan, and departed in silence. Onan stood for a while once he was alone, then he too pushed his chair to the table, took a last sip of wine, and headed out into the street.

Thaddeus was not surprised by the knock on his door. No one could reach that point without passing the guards, so there were few men, and only a handful of women, who might call.

"Come in," he said, loudly enough for whoever it was to hear. In a sheath beneath his desk a short-bladed sword rested in a scabbard, ready to hand. After his talk with Balthazar, he was certain that whoever it was had no good news for him. If he were correct and Onan was involved, it would be Hashir. The man had worked with Thaddeus for years, but Thaddeus had always known he was not the only master the man served. Their dealings had always been profitable. Now, looking back, he wondered where Onan's hand might have been felt, had he been more cautious or paid sharper attention.

It didn't matter. He had an unexpected advantage this time, and it lent him vigor he'd not felt since he'd been a young man.

The door opened, and Hashir entered. He had to duck to clear the door frame, and he raised a hand reflexively to prevent his turban from slipping, though there was no danger. His brown eyes glittered beneath bushy brows. Thaddeus had always believed the man looked dependable, but in that moment, something shone through, something darker. Greed? Deception? Or was it just imagination?

"Hashir," Thaddeus said, rising and holding out a hand. The other he kept at his side, where he could reach the sword, if necessary.

The tall man crossed the room in only a couple of steps and clasped the offered hand.

"Hello, my friend," he said. "I hope the day finds you well."

"Well, and busy, as usual," Thaddeus said, returning to his seat. "What can I do for you?"

"I believe you have that reversed," Hashir said, seating himself carefully in the chair across the desk. He was too tall for it but was also used to being too tall for everything, so the motion was oddly graceful. "I have come across some news that you may find interesting. Big news. The sort of news that will fill the arena for a very long time, if all goes well…"

"That sounds like a description of a thing that might *not* go well," Thaddeus responded.

"There are variables," Hashir replied. "Nothing good comes without risk, as I've heard it said."

"And I have heard that risk is another word for careless-ness, when it comes to business," Thaddeus countered. "It always depends on what that risk might be, of course, the pos-sible upside and downside. I assume from your words that the potential profit is significant?"

"It is," Hashir said. "Indeed, it is. I am going to ask you a question, and when it sounds fantastical, I hope you will indulge me."

"I am listening," Thaddeus said, sitting back.

"Here is my question, then," Hashir said. "I know that you are aware of Noah, and his ark. I know you have heard the sto-ries, and the rumors. Do you know how he has remained safe for so long, how he has protected his family living beyond the safety of the city walls, with the beasts roaming the desert and swooping from the sky?"

"I have been told," Thaddeus said, "that Noah is a righteous man. He prays, and the Lord listens. There was a time when a great number of our citizens believed that same thing."

"But you are not one of them," Hashir said, leaning forward. "You are a businessman, and you understand how things work. I have no doubt that Noah has the ear of powers beyond the normal, but I don't think either of us believes it is the Lord look-ing out for him. There are rumors of giants. Of Nephilim, if you can believe it. The children of angels."

"You have possibly had too much wine for such an early hour," Thaddeus said. "The Nephilim never existed, or, if they did, it was long before our time, and they have passed from the Earth. I have no idea what security measures Noah may employ, but—"

"I can assure you," Hashir said, "that it is true. I have sources who have gained information from that compound. There is at least one such creature guarding Noah's family. I know of a group with the power to capture such a creature. Can you imagine what it might do in an arena? In your arena?"

"You are talking about fantasies," Thaddeus said, rising. "I am a busy man."

"You have nothing to lose by hearing me out," Hashir said. "What the parties I represent ask is simply that you prepare quarters. That you take into consideration what housing it might entail. Where it could be contained, and how. My party is willing to provide power to strengthen the containment. Spells, sigils, whatever it takes. The only real question is, are you interested?"

Thaddeus sat back and wiped all emotion from his expression. He'd known this moment was coming, and he knew what rode on his next words. He was thankful to Balthazar for giving him advance notice. He was aware that, without that, he'd be intrigued. Without having had the option to think it all through, this would sound like a wonderful business proposition that he'd be working over in his head, trying to find the most advantageous position. He needed Hashir to believe that was what he was doing.

"I know of no source of information that would guide me in creating such an enclosure," he said slowly. "We have some large stables, and we have contained a great number of dangerous creatures. A good part of how we have done that is with mild poisons or drugs. If, and I want you to understand, I don't believe for a second that you can prove your claim, but *if* there were such creatures, how would I, or we, know which drugs might be effective? What if nothing of this Earth would serve?"

"They are half human," Hashir said. "They have fallen from grace. It seems unlikely to me that they have been left with any spiritual immunity. At least, not a complete immunity. It would be foolish of me to claim they were just large men, but neither, I think, would they be gods, or even angels. I believe that my colleagues and I could strengthen any poison, or potion you might provide through certain rites. I know that you have great wagons at your disposal, large enough to move such a creature. A team of Reem could pull it, under cover of darkness."

"There is another flaw in your plan," Thaddeus said, meeting and holding Hashir's gaze. "If we travel by night, and under the very unlikely circumstance that we do so with this giant you mention, who will protect us on the road? How would we get through gates that will be closed until the morning? It is a fool's errand."

"We can handle the gates and the security," Hashir said. "Let me just say that my partners in this enterprise are not without connections and resources. We would not ask you to make that journey, only to be prepared to accept the cargo once it is successful. And, of course, to provide your expertise in the capture."

Thaddeus sat in silence. Another advantage of having been able to think this through was that he was prepared to ask questions that might provide important answers.

"Have you considered," he asked, "that if all you say is true, if Noah commands Nephilim, that the rest of it is also true? That there will be a deluge? A flood that wipes us all out? Are you so arrogant you believe you are beyond divine vengeance?"

"We have been hearing of divine vengeance for centuries," Hashir said. "Thus far, it appears to be another tale to frighten old women and children."

Thaddeus considered asking Hashir how old he'd been when Noah came to the city, but he held his tongue. Judging eternity on the span of a couple of centuries of debauchery and sin was an all-too-common trait of younger citizens. Hashir was not young, but neither was he an elder. Onan was a different matter. That one was old. No one knew exactly how old, because he'd come to the city later in life and clung to it like a leech.

"When would you be expecting to attempt this?" he asked.

"Tomorrow night," Hashir said. "If what we believe is true, there is too great a risk of being discovered before we can act to wait longer. We would need your poison, or potion, or whatever you would provide, by tonight in order to prepare it properly and provide a proper means of delivering it."

Thaddeus closed his eyes. Once more, he erased any emotion, then he stood and slowly held out his hand again. "I will have it ready," he said.

Hashir clasped his hand. "And the stable?"

Thaddeus nodded.

"I knew that I could count on you," Hashir said. "I will relay this news immediately. Shall I return this evening?"

"I will have it by late afternoon," Thaddeus said. "I will need the evening to prepare for delivery. I will have to handle this personally. If the wrong person were to hear—"

"Of course," Hashir said. "Of course. Until this afternoon, then."

He turned, and without a backward glance ducked through the door frame and was gone.

Thaddeus shook his head, and then he smiled. When he was certain Hashir was gone, he descended to the street and gave instructions to his guard to get word to Master Balthazar. The two of them would need to meet, and it would have to happen without anyone's knowledge.

"Have him come to the arena," Thaddeus told the guard. "To the lower pens, where the great beasts are housed."

The man nodded and was gone. Thaddeus returned to his office, then exited on the far side into the interior of the arena. There was much to do, and not much time to do it. He had a plan, but it would rely on timing, stealth, and not a little luck. Under his breath, though it felt like an empty gesture after so many years, he offered a short, silent prayer.

Chapter 26

Balthazar left the city two hours before sunset. He had a swift carriage, and he left from a gate seldom watched by more than a single guard. A guard he knew well, and who could be paid for silence. The carriage was unmarked, and he had remained within and concealed since exiting at the rear of his shop. He carried a pouch with a vial carefully packed in its depths. He'd gotten it from Thaddeus earlier that day, and now, bouncing across the desert, he cradled it carefully. A lot depended on its quiet, safe delivery.

The journey was a swift one, and once he'd entered the borders of Noah's compound, cloaked, he continued on to the menagerie, joining a group of others escorting a new troupe of creatures into the structure. He caught site of Ezra, who recognized him immediately and started forward, but he shook his head, nodding toward the door to the structure's interior. Ezra frowned, just for a second, and then turned back to the animals, calling out instructions and leading the group inside. Balthazar, without a backward glance, joined them and entered.

Ezra came to his side immediately once they were inside.

"Master Balthazar, what—?"

"Not here," Balthazar said. "Is there a place we can talk? Privately and safely?"

Ezra nodded, took the older man by the arm, and led him down a side passage toward the small space where they kept their records. None noticed their passing, and once they were out of sight and through the doors to the chamber, Ezra closed them and pulled a lock into place. He turned, then, eyes wide.

"What is it, Master? Why would you come here in secret?"

"There is no time for a full explanation," Balthazar said. "You know, I am sure, that there are those in the city who have become aware of one of your secrets."

Ezra started to speak a denial, and Balthazar held up a hand.

"Those of us who have known Noah longer than you have been alive have long suspected the existence of these creatures," he said. "It is only important that you listen, and that you act. My name cannot be connected with this, nor can that of Thaddeus. It could mean life or death. Do you promise?"

Ezra nodded again.

"Good, I knew that I could count on you. There will be an attempt tomorrow night to capture your giant. I know that he is powerful. I know that he is far beyond human. The men who will come have sorcery, and they have a potion that Thaddeus has provided that can render this giant unconscious. He had to make the potion real in case they test it first on one of the beasts. You understand?"

"You have come to tell me that you are facilitating a successful kidnapping?" Ezra said. His expression was serious, but there was a twinkle in his eye.

"Of course not. Do you take me for a fool? Here."

Balthazar pulled the pouch out of a fold in his robe and carefully handed it to Ezra. "Get this to your giant. I don't know who can communicate with him, or how, but it must happen just before dark tomorrow. Have him swallow the contents. It will not prevent the drug they will use from making him sleepy, but it will cause it to wear off. Swiftly. I do not believe they will have him out of the compound before he wakes."

"That will not end well for Thaddeus's partners," Ezra said.

"That is his hope," Balthazar said. "It will be a shame, of course, if he is unable to present this giant."

"Og," Ezra cut in suddenly. "His name is Og."

"Og, then," Balthazar repeated, rolling the name over his tongue and grinning. Such trust was a gift, and he realized it was all the more pleasant because it had been a long time since he'd received its equal. Trust was not something he took lightly. "It will be a shame if Thaddeus is unable to present Og in the arena. I believe it might be the first time his pack of Tooth Devils met their match. But at the same time, housing such a creature, containing him. So much responsibility."

At that moment, there was a knock at the door. Ezra slipped the lock and opened it, and Naḥlab entered the room.

"What's this about creatures?"

Ezra filled her in quickly.

"My father is a wise man," she said with a quick smile. "I can assure you, Master Balthazar, that there is no stall in the arena that would contain Og. I doubt they would even slow him down, and he is not alone. I've not seen any of the others, and they do not work with or for Noah, as he does, but they hover. At the edges of the compound. In the desert. They watch. I have not seen them directly, but you can sense such a being, their power, and something more. A deep, burning anger, or pain. I do not believe, even if their potion worked as they planned and they managed to get Og out of the compound, that they would survive the journey back to the city, or that Og would ever cross the desert."

"You are uniquely qualified for such an opinion," Balthazar said, "and I respect it. The important thing, from your father's perspective, is that if, or rather when, something goes wrong with their plan, these men will not follow that failure back to his doorstep."

"I don't know where the blame will be placed," Ezra said, "but I have serious doubts if anyone is returning."

"That is why I need for you to arrange for me to meet with Noah," Balthazar said. "He invited me back, and, under the circumstances, I believe he will be at least interested in what I have to say."

"I will get Ham," Naḥlab said. "He will be able to arrange it. You will have to spend the night, and I will see to it that you are well housed and cared for. We can get you out at daybreak and back to the city without notice."

"That is a great relief," Balthazar said. "I did not wish to attempt the return trip in the darkness. While I believe the Nephilim might forgive me my trespass, there are many other beasts, both wild and human, who would not."

"I will see you soon, I am sure," Naḥlab said. "For now, I will find my husband and see if I can arrange your meeting. Perhaps, in the meantime, Ezra could give you a tour of the menagerie."

Ezra grinned "This is a particularly good time for such a tour," he said, feigning nonchalance. "Most of the workers are on day shifts. Only a trusted few remain through the night."

Balthazar grew very still. "There will still be work underway?" he asked.

"There will," Ezra said. "I will be happy to show you."

Balthazar leaned on the bench beside him for a moment, and then nodded. As Naḥlab slipped out the door, he took a deep breath. "Amaze me, then," he said. "I have spent your entire life teaching you, or the greater part of it. Perhaps it is my turn to learn."

As they entered the gates of the menagerie, Balthazar fell silent. He studied every detail, checked every corner, as if some creature might be waiting, or some trap might be sprung. As they neared the passage leading downward, scents and sounds invaded his senses. He heard grunts, growls, and rumbling sounds that were simultaneously terrifying and oddly soothing. Far below, he heard thumps that actually shivered through the walls.

"How deep?" he asked.

Ezra glanced at him. "I'm not certain, without consulting the diagrams. There is no feasible manner in which we could expand upward, so we continue to dig. The last time I checked, there were at least ten levels, and it is wider below than it is here above."

They continued downward. In an odd parallel to Thaddeus's arena, one of the first pens they came to held a small group of Tooth Devils.

"There are more than two?" Balthazar said, surprised.

"Of course," Ezra said. "We have no idea how long it will be before the Ark is completed, less even of how long before the prophesied deluge. If we had a single pair, and one fell sick or died, or both grew too old to make the trip and sustain their species, there would be no point. There is no way to know, at this point, which individual creatures will be included. The strange thing is that the animals not only seem to understand, but to cooperate. They breed. They care for one another. Even species that should be feeding upon one another accept the meals we prepare. They don't make a pretense of camaraderie, but neither do they attack or threaten one another.

Balthazar felt his skin grow clammy and cold with sweat at those words. This was looking less and less like the crazy dream of a madman, and more like one of the prophecies of old, unfolding before his eyes. And there was that heavy thudding sound. He'd thought it was the stamping of feet, one of the great beasts uneasy in its stable, but it was too rhythmic. Too measured and steady.

Ezra led him downward. The halls were brightly lit by a series of torches, fueled by oil he realized must be replenished regularly. He glanced into pen after pen. There were cattle, rodents, reptiles, birds, both great and small. More than once he stopped, wishing that he had his journals with him, or a blank journal, so that he could record what he was seeing. He'd known the animals had been arriving in a steady stream, but had not, until that moment, thought about how long the period of time had grown between the wedding and this night. There had to be hundreds of pens, some split into segments with similar but different species. He saw creatures he'd never dreamed of, and others that he had not seen in so long that the sight of them raised memories that momentarily made him feel young.

"So many," he said. "All to be carried on a single craft, together, fed and nurtured by so few."

"I prefer not to think about that in too great a detail," Ezra replied. "I have been a part of the design of the Ark as well, and it is even more incredible than this place. The enclosures are more compact, sized precisely for two of each, but the logistics are staggering. Japheth and Ham, using our research and diagrams, have managed to create a great puzzle, the pieces of which will create a whole such as no man has conceived. If anything that I have seen in my short life could be described as miraculous, it is that ark."

As he spoke these words, they stepped onto a platform that allowed a view of the levels below. It stretched down farther than Balthazar would have believed, but he did not take notice. At the very bottom, huge pickax in hand, the giant Og carved away layers of stone, piling them behind him. There was a wagon there, as well, obviously the means by which the creature would haul the debris to the surface. Balthazar's breath caught in his throat.

"My God," he said.

"Possibly sent by him," Ezra said, his voice slightly teasing. "I can never get used to this sight. It never seems real, or even possible, but..." he spread his arms and spun in a slow circle, "you can see the proof all around you."

"Can he speak?" Balthazar asked.

"I have no idea," Ezra said. "I know that he communicates with Noah. I believe, at times, that he also communicates with Ham and with Naḥlab. I know he is aware of me, and of the work that I do, but I have never sensed any form of contact beyond that, nor have I heard him vocalize. He comes every night, he descends to the depths, and he works."

"But he is not always here," Balthazar said. "Unless there is some other creature who saved young Shem?"

"I have not been able to ascertain where he goes during the day," Ezra said. "There are many trees, and there are rocks and dunes. I have sensed his passing but have never seen him anywhere but here. And he has not missed a single night since I first arrived."

"Why?" Balthazar said. "Why would he work so tirelessly for one he knows will leave him behind? In the deluge, I mean?"

"I'm not certain he serves Noah," Ezra says. "It feels more as if he is a part of the prophecy, as if he serves that truth, or the God who created it."

"A very uncomfortable belief for anyone who is not a part of the family," Balthazar observed. "But fascinating. This place, the amount of work it must have taken to create it, and the ingenuity behind it."

"Yes," Ezra said. "Men could not have done in a century what Og has managed in only a few months. You'll see why I find it unlikely that, even if those you have reported are successful in locating him, they will ever control him. He is a force.

Like a great storm. He does not operate in the same way as the great beasts. He is old and wise."

"I have always believed that I was old, and that Noah was old, but I sense in this place, that I have no real concept of what old might mean."

"It is a difficult thing to wrap your head around," Ezra said. "We should be making our way back to the surface. Noah will be here soon, if he is not already."

Balthazar nodded slowly, but could not take his eyes from Og's figure, far below, swinging the great pickax. He turned, at last, and followed Ezra back toward the surface. He did not speak again.

Chapter 27

Just before sunset, Hashir returned to Thaddeus's offices and was allowed in past the guard. He ducked through the doorway with more confidence, as if sensing the day's transaction had somehow elevated his status. Thaddeus did not react. He sat and waited as the other man approached, no expression on his face.

"You have it?"

"Sit." Thaddeus said.

Hashir hesitated. It was obvious that he was in a hurry and his confidence was high. He was not in the mood for conversation or delays. Thaddeus held his silence and waited. After a moment of silence, Hashir folded his spindly frame into the chair across the table.

Thaddeus reached down to the floor, lifted a heavy glass flask from the floor and placed it on the desk. He did not release it.

"This is the strongest potion that I have," he said. "It has brought down every creature we have encountered, rendering them unconscious for an extended period. It has to be delivered into the bloodstream directly."

"Yes," Hashir said, too eager. "We expected this, and we are ready."

"Are you?" Thaddeus asked. "I have serious doubts. You are so confident but seem to be ignoring the bare truth. If you are correct, you are not dealing with a Mace Tail or one of the giant toothed beasts."

"We have planned for every possible difficulty," Hashir cut in.

"You aren't hearing me," Thaddeus said. "Listen. This is the strongest thing I have. You can test it on anything you like. What I am saying to you is, unless you arrive at my arena with a giant unconscious on a cart, this is the last time we will ever see one another. I want payment for this, regardless of the outcome. I can't guarantee it will work on such a being, and I won't be held responsible if it fails."

Hashir stared at him. "You would test it?"

"I will test it on any creature in my arena, but we will have to move quickly to do so."

Hashir bowed his head for a moment.

"There will be no test," he said. "You will be paid what you feel is fair for the potion, regardless of the outcome. I must tell you, it will not be me who pays you if we fail, but you have my word that the debt will be cleared."

"Who shall I call on, in that situation," Thaddeus asked. He did not release his grip on the flask.

"You know Master Onan?" Hashir asked.

"I know of Onan," Thaddeus said, ignoring the "Master." "I suspected he might be behind or involved with this. Very well. I believe he will honor your promise."

He released the flask, and Hashir snatched it up, gripping it tightly by the neck.

"Be very careful that does not touch anyone's skin," Thaddeus said. "Deliver it as deeply into the bloodstream as possible."

Hashir only nodded. He turned, ducked through the door, and was gone. Thaddeus stared at the door where he'd passed for a long time. Then he pulled out the bottle Balthazar had given him and poured a generous portion into a mug. Then he sat back, took a small sip, and closed his eyes. He hoped Balthazar had gotten through to Noah. He hoped that Onan's scheme would fail. He had no idea why he hoped that, and he was actually curious how his potion would stack up against a Nephilim. He almost wished he had not sent the antidote with Balthazar, but not really. He could not remember the last time he'd felt as if he'd done the right thing.

The others were already seated at the table when Hashir entered. He moved with confidence and slid into his seat with a very self-satisfied smile.

"You have it, then?" Onan asked.

Hashir placed the flask on the table and sat back.

"And it has been tested?" Ehsan asked.

"There was no time," Hashir said, "but he offered us freely the use of any of his creatures for a test. This is the strongest potion that he has available. It has taken down a Mace Tail. His terms are that, if the potion fails, he still expects to be paid. I suspect he is having doubts about the wisdom of trying to capture a Nephilim. I believe he *wanted* us to test the formula, so that he would not be held responsible if his best effort is not enough. He does not know the enhancements we will be able to provide, but his fear—his discomfort—was very real."

"It is well," Onan said. "It is better if he doesn't understand everything that we have planned, and if we fail, the cost of his assistance will not be our worst problem."

Ehsan stood. "I have the arrow," he said. He turned and strode to a shadowed corner. He reached into the darkness and lifted a large bolt, with effort. When he placed the butt of the thing on the ground, it stood a head taller than he was, and Ehsan was more than three and a half cubits in height. His shoulders were broad, but even he, holding this weapon, seemed small.

"But…" Akeem said softly.

Ehsan laughed. "It fits a very large crossbow, which I have mounted to a wagon. We will get a single shot, so we must make it count. There is a reservoir here, within an interior bladder made from a cow's stomach." He lifted a foot and nudged a thick spot near the base of the arrow. It is separated from a tube that runs the length to the blade. When there is sufficient impact, the tube will be slammed back into the reservoir, puncturing the bladder, which will close around it long enough to push the potion forward through the tube, injecting it into whatever the blade strikes."

"But where did it come from?" Ghazalan asked.

Hashir cut in. "Thaddeus himself has used these," he said. "It is how they bring down the strongest of the beasts for the arena."

"And it did not come cheaply," Ehsan said. "In fact, I do not believe that Thaddeus knows that it has gone missing, though I am certain if he learns of it, he will know why."

"I am equally certain," Hashir said, "that he will blame me, and if any harm comes to it, he will report it as stolen."

"Then we had better be successful," Onan said. "We have details to work out. You well know that, as strong as a Mace Tail might be, we are dealing with something much more powerful. I do not believe it would be wise to depend on Thaddeus or his potion, as effective as it might be. I have been studying some old scrolls. The Nephilim are not new to the Earth, and others have had to deal with them in the past. There are spells we can add to this potion, and sigils we can inscribe on the shaft of the crossbow bolt, that will lend a strength far beyond that of chemistry. It should be enough to render the creature helpless as we transport it. The same sigils will bind it if we apply them to the enclosure in the arena. There is no step in this process that does not require absolute concentration. We will need to embed a particular crystal on that shaft as well, to create a connection. Everyone who is not with Ehsan will be with me. We will form a circle, and we will connect to that crystal. What power we have we will lend to the strike."

"That will form a connection," Hashir said, "That will flow both ways."

"Then," Onan said, "we had better prove more powerful than whatever that weapon strikes."

"This is not the time to be timid," Ehsan said. "I will be there, wherever this creature can be found. Hashir will be with me, and others that I trust. We will be counting on the rest of you to do your part."

His voice dropped several octaves then, and he spoke very slowly. "If you fail, and I survive, it will not be good for you if we meet again…"

"There is no need for threats," Onan said. "We are all in this together. I would guess that whatever fate awaits us, for better or worse, we will share."

This time no one broke the silence. Ehsan placed the cross-bow bolt on the table, and they set to work, consulting a parchment that Onan had laid out beside the weapon. The potion in its flask sat safely near the center of the table. If anyone had been paying attention, they might have noticed a glow around the seam of the stopper. They might have seen lights dancing across the surface of the flask. As incantations were spoken and repeated, symbols etched into the long, wooden shaft, wisps of light and power slipped into the flask. Encased it. Changed it into something entirely different, and more potent.

Late that night, they disbursed in silence. Ehsan had to rest, and then gather his forces. Onan needed to center himself, study the spells and the rituals. It was one thing to effect changes on a sinful city and those who were easily manipulated. It was another entirely to confront a power born of a Heaven they only vaguely believed in.

Chapter 28

Noah had Balthazar ushered into his private study, a place even his wife, Na'amah, was not allowed within unless specifically invited. It was a place he went to study, to read scripture, and to pray. On rare occasions, he invited his sons there, or his daughter, but never more than one of them at any given time. It was private, and though he had no way of knowing all of this, Balthazar sensed he was being shown a great honor by the invitation. It was morning, and Ezra had explained that his father would be just back from his usual communing with the Lord. The two were to be brought their breakfast in that chamber, to share in private.

Most of his adult life, Balthazar had considered Noah to be something of an enigma. He came across as a crackpot, a man too caught up in his own version of reality to participate in that of the world. Recent events had changed his perspective. Balthazar had known prophets. He had heard them, followed more than one in his early days. Most of them had fallen from grace or proved to be charlatans out for their own gain. Some had died after centuries of life and teaching. Others had simply been slain for treachery.

Noah was not like any of them. He had been considered special by his parents, and the rumors surrounding his early years could fill books. They had, in fact, inspired a number of texts, some of which still remained, though in diluted form. Balthazar knew the stories. He had studied them, laughed at them, puzzled over them, and ignored them at various points, but now? Now he wished he had a direct line to the Lord to verify what he was nearly certain he already knew. Noah had been marked from birth. The deluge had been prophesied even earlier. All of it was true, and it had taken nearly six hundred years to come to pass.

All of this and more he tried to forget as he entered Noah's study. The other man held out a hand, and he clasped it.

"Welcome," Noah said. "We have known one another almost as long as we've been alive, so long that we have forgotten more than others will ever know. I never called you friend, and I am starting to believe that is one of the many failures of my life."

"I admit to similar thoughts," Balthazar said. "I have never quite known what to think of you. You know the oldest of the stories as well as I do. A man born, different from all others. A man—"

"Who did not need to be circumcised," Noah finished.

Balthazar nodded.

"My father got those words from Enoch himself," Noah said. "They have never meant anything to me. The stories have all seemed to be just that, until recently."

"And now you are building an ark," Balthazar said.

There was a moment of silence. Then Noah continued.

"I am having difficulty with the idea that my family and I are somehow more worthy than any others in the world. I have always tried to be a righteous man. I have led my family in that manner, and I have raised my children, as best I can, to believe it is the way. Now it feels oddly as if what I am being rewarded for is blind obedience, and that there is a lot of variety in men and women, and even angels, that is being pushed aside to fit a very narrow view."

"And yet," Balthazar said, "we are talking about forces beyond our ken. We are talking about the one source of life, of the Earth, of the animals you are gathering at an astounding rate, with equally astonishing ease. It is easy to try and second-guess such a thing, but having seen other prophecies through to their completion, I must reluctantly note that most of them, while often horrifying to men, have worked for the betterment of society."

"Perhaps," Noah said. "Perhaps you're right. It does not change how it feels."

"I am going to offer something," Balthazar said, "that I will be surprised if you accept, but my life is almost as long as yours, and I believe it to be appropriate."

He reached for his bag and withdrew a flask. He held it out and waited.

Noah stared for a long moment, and then something shifted in his gaze. Almost imperceptibly, he nodded.

"I did not bring goblets," Balthazar said, "or mugs. I was not sure how you would react."

"I think that the time for ignoring the world is far behind us," Noah said. "Things that have seemed so important to avoid, and to participate in, only seem ridiculous to me now. There is the coming deluge. There is the responsibility. There is the guilt."

"If you did not feel that guilt," Balthazar said with a soft chuckle, "I would not offer you the finest drink I've ever tasted. I do not believe that you have a choice, but I do believe that you wish that you did. That is the difference. That is why I will share this drink with you, and then I will return to my shop and my city, even though I believe the prophecy. Even though I know that my centuries on this planet are nearing their end."

Noah took the flask, opened it, and drank deeply. He closed his eyes, savoring the taste, and handed it back to Balthazar.

Balthazar drank, and waited.

"Tell me," Noah said, "of those who are coming, is it possible that they could defeat Og? That they could contain him?"

"I am uncertain if they might have accomplished it," Balthazar said, "but I am happy to report that they will not. Another reason I lean toward trusting your prophecy is how events have fallen into patterns. Your son married the daughter of Thaddeus, who is a good man, but a businessman. He would have welcomed the attempt to bring such an attraction to the arena under any other circumstances. Now, he has helped us set this plan in motion, and if I'm not mistaken, is taking a long, hard look at how he has built his fortunes. These are not thoughts he would ever have had without you. My presence here? Ezra befriending Ham, and making the one introduction that could lead to Naḥlab and her father? Surely, of all those who know of this sequence of events, you are most likely to see a hand other than that of *man* it."

"It is hard not to see," Noah said, "but at the same time that it is miraculous, wondrous, and powerful, it is also terrifying. I follow a God who provides everything that I might need if I am open to his gifts. At the same time, he is demanding in ways I can't fathom. He requires a price for his gifts that is either unbearably difficult or beyond my comprehension in its perfection. The temptation is to believe the latter, but I live with the former."

"Your family feels the same?" Balthazar asked.

"I can never let them know," Noah said. "If I am not comfortable with the price, I am less comfortable with the alternative. They are my anchor. If it were only myself, I believe I might welcome the deluge, after so many years of life, and take my chances on whatever comes next."

Balthazar drank from the flask and handed it back.

"Then you know my mind," he said. "Let us plan for the night to come. Do you have a way to communicate directly with…Og? Can you give him instructions or information? Can you warn him?"

"I can," Noah said. "I have no idea how it works. It is similar to communing with the Lord. It is a moment of shared thought that transfers both ways."

"If my sources are correct, a large crossbow, mounted on a wagon, has gone missing. There is a potion that Thaddeus has provided to them and I believe they will attempt to enhance it with sorcery."

"As plans go," Noah said, taking a more conservative sip from the flask, "this is not sounding good."

"The potion has an antidote," Balthazar said. "I gave it to Ezra earlier, but he gave it back and asked me to give it to you. It's not complete protection, but it will cause the potion to wear off long before they reach the city. We are counting on the fact your giant, even after being struck by a crossbow, can defend himself."

"But why," Noah asked, "allow them to attack at all? Why not stop them before they fire the crossbow?"

"They are powerful men. They will know of Thaddeus's betrayal, and likely of my own. And they will spread the word. Nephilim wandering free in your compound. Giants. I do not believe this would be a good thing. If we allow them to believe they are succeeding, and then to fail magnificently, possibly fatally, they will not breathe a word of it. I have other potions that might ease pain and help your giant to heal."

"He will barely feel the crossbow," Noah said. "I do not know why, but they do not feel pain the way that we do, and they heal very quickly. I suspect by the time he returns it will be impossible to tell he was injured. It is a good plan. Better, maybe, than you think. And you do this for me, for my family, knowing that I would build an ark and leave you behind to drown. Now, perhaps, you begin to see why all of this is hard."

"And there is no hope that your Lord will change his mind?"

"I do not believe so," Noah said, "but I will not stand by if there is a chance. When this is done and Og is safely back at work, I will come to the city. If you can arrange it, I will speak in the temple. I will try to get through to them. I will try to explain. It is the least that I can do, and possibly the most. I do not believe they will listen, but I know they will not if I do not speak."

"I will come, and I will listen," Balthazar said. "And I will speak to those who might listen, but I believe you are correct. In the end, a few will hear you. Some will be frightened. Others will be angry, and to the heart of that city, it will mean nothing at all. Despite that, I believe it is the right thing to do. Whether or not they will accept it, it is a courageous, righteous thing to reach out to them, to try and save them from themselves, or to call upon them to save themselves."

"Or suicidal," Noah said, then chuckled. He took another small swallow from the flask, and then handed it back. "That is all I dare," he said. "Of all the nights of my life, this would be the worst to fall victim to strong drink and fail my family. Would you like to come with me to commune with the giant? He is no danger to you, and after a life of self-imposed solitude, I suddenly feel as if things I have held close should have been shared. Much of my faith is based on direct experience, and I realize, particularly considering the plot we are about to defeat, that it could never have worked out differently than it did."

"The minute this is behind us," Balthazar said, "I will reach out to the temple. I will be certain they find it in their hearts to invite you to speak of the prophecy, of the Ark. Who knows, maybe we were brought together to save the world."

"Or," Noah said, sighing, "to verify the necessity for its cleansing."

Balthazar packed his flask away, and the two rose. Noah grabbed the second flask containing the potion. Together, they stepped out of the chamber and continued out the main door and into the compound beyond. It was beginning to grow dark, and not many were out. Those who were watched the two disappear into the trees and shared surprised glances. Whispered questions. The moon was bright overhead, but within moments the two were lost in the shadows.

Balthazar followed Noah into the trees. The only light was from points where the bright moonlight was able to pierce the branches above. Shadows stretched over the trail, if it could be called a trail, and every sound sent shivers up his spine. It was one thing to sit and drink and talk about giants. It was entirely a different thing to slip through shadows, far from anyone who might offer aid, to actually meet one.

The trail they followed curved, and after only a short time, Balthazar realized it was curving toward the menagerie. He thought they must be paralleling the more open trails of the compound, perhaps coming to the enclosure from the rear. There was not much sign of others passing, and he suspected Noah might be the only one who knew this way, or perhaps Noah's sons as well. It was also true that no one was likely to follow or to know where a person might have disappeared.

He shook this off. There was a sound out among the trees. Balthazar stopped in his tracks, but Noah was unperturbed. He continued as if he'd heard nothing, and after a few seconds, Balthazar followed. They broke out into a clearing. It was wide, stretching back toward the center of the trees. Noah stopped in the middle and stood still. Not knowing what else to do,

Balthazar stepped up beside him and stared into the shadows.

At first, nothing happened. Then a tremor rippled through the earth and vibrated up Balthazar's spine. It was weak—barely there—but he felt it. Then again, and again, and each time it grew more powerful. The ground shook. Not from a pounding, but just from the shifting of a great weight. The moon had risen behind the trees but was only a small crescent and provided little light. Still, it was enough to cause a huge, darker shadow to stand out against the backdrop of forest.

The shape was that of a very tall, very broad man. He could not make out the face or details, but the mass and the weight conveyed with each careful step the giant took. Trees shook and bent. The ground shivered. Balthazar fought the urge to turn and run. He also fought the urge to scream.

Og stepped into the clearing. Not fully, but far enough that his broad, homely face was clear. His shoulders and arms were massive, gnarled and roped with muscle. His eyes were huge and dark, deep in a way that Balthazar had never encountered. No sound passed his lips, but, though he did not understand it, Balthazar felt an energy—a communication—pass between Noah and the Nephilim. He could almost see it rippling in the air. He couldn't help himself. He stepped forward. Very slowly. Noah stood where he was and maintained whatever bond he was sharing. He made no move to stop Balthazar, or to hold him back. The huge, shadowy figure loomed closer.

Balthazar reached out. He was barely aware of what he did, but he lifted his arm and held his hand out before him. The giant moved, very slowly, but Balthazar held his ground. A great hand emerged from the shadows. As it neared, Balthazar's eyes widened. If it continued, it could press him into the ground like a twig or pick him up and break him. The corded muscles of that great arm rippled. Balthazar's legs grew limp, but he forced them to support him, forced his will into his aging bones until the massive fingers brushed his, and held steady.

The touch jolted him. He was afraid it would drop him to his knees, but instead he drew strength from it. And more. He shook his head, but it was too late. He saw a shimmer of light where his hand touched that massive palm. Images flowed, not words or conversation, more like memories that had somehow been suppressed. And emotion. It all came too quickly, like the deluge itself, he thought, just before losing himself in that flood. The pain was immense, the longing, the hunger. Images flickered through Balthazar's mind that were so wondrous, so unthinkably beautiful he had to fight for consciousness. Then shadow, and darkness. Loss. He wanted the images to return. He wanted to see the colors. The brilliant light...

And then, as suddenly as it had begun, it was gone. The giant pulled his hand back and slipped into the shadows. Balthazar crumpled, as if all strength had left his body. He felt his head strike the soft earth, but there was no pain. He closed his eyes and sank into comfortable darkness.

Balthazar woke in the tent that Noah had provided him. He saw from the light leaking in through the cracks around the windows and doors that morning was approaching. Groggily, he sat upright.

"You slept very soundly," Noah said.

Balthazar spun and found the other man seated in a chair. He had a scroll open before him, scripture no doubt. He rolled this carefully and tucked it into a fold of his robe.

"The morning meal will be served soon," Noah said. "If you join us, I will help you to find your way out of the compound quietly and out of sight of any prying eyes."

Balthazar closed his eyes. "What was that?" he said. "What did he show me? I can't get free of it."

"I suspect you have learned his secret," Noah said. "He shared a vision of what his father lost. The price of coming to Earth and breaking his sacred trust. His creation, you might say. Og's, I mean. His father was an angel, and—"

"I have seen Heaven," Balthazar said softly. "It was beautiful, and his pain..."

"He works constantly," Noah said, "so that he does not spend all his nights and days thinking of it. You've heard the stories of the Nephilim, how they kill and destroy. He does not want that. Despite his curse, he does not succumb to it. He works, and he dreams. He has shared that vision with fewer than a dozen people since his birth. You are blessed."

"I sense that is true, though the pain does not feel like a blessing, and the now-certain knowledge that my days are numbered has become an ache I feel every waking moment. Still, I would not trade a moment of the visions I was granted for double the years of my Earthly life."

"The great paradox," Noah said, rising. "There are always costs. There are always compromises, or losses, sacrifices that feel as though they are too much to survive. Measuring those against eternal rewards, weighing them on a scale against faith. What seem like simple choices of good and evil, faith and corruption, are complex, painful, and cut to the bone. My own faith would not be what it is if it were not for my family. If I have learned anything in more than six hundred years, it is that I am not a good enough reason for faith, but that those I love are. My family came to me later in life, and for too long I lorded it over them, self-righteous and full of arrogance. It has taken this prophecy, this huge pattern coming together like a child's puzzle with too many pieces, to give me a glimpse of the enormity of it all. I have been a fool, and I only hope I have recovered from that in time to play my part."

Balthazar rose, arranged his robes, and ran a hand back through his hair.

"Let us eat, my friend," he said. "I believe nothing any of us might do at this point would change the outcome. It is not a time to question, but one to act."

"And act we shall," Noah said. He left the tent, and Balthazar followed. The scent of food cooking and the murmur of voices led them down a wide path to a fork, and eventually to the family table.

"I believe it is fitting that you join us here," Noah said. "None but my family have eaten at this table since it was first placed here. Let this be one of many changes."

"I am honored," Balthazar replied, surprised to find that it was true. "Perhaps you will visit me one day, while there are still days for such moments. We have a lot of shared memory, some nearly forgotten, that I would love to rediscover. I am feeling a bit nostalgic."

"If I am allowed to speak in the temple," Noah said, "I will accept your hospitality. The logistics of such a trip, and an endeavor, within the safe bounds of travel would be difficult to arrange. I will be needing a place to stay, and for some reason I believe finding a priest I can trust in that city might be more difficult than it sounds."

Balthazar laughed. "That is one of the truest statements I've heard in many years. And the same would have to be said of inns and boarding houses. You are known to all, feared by many, and understood by few within those walls. Until very recently I might have said understood by none."

They continued in silence. Sunlight was just beginning to touch the tops of the trees, and both men knew it was going to be a long, strange day.

Chapter 29

The sun was dipping toward the skyline when Ehsan and his men rolled out the gate on the far side of the city. The guards were his, as well, and no alarms were sounded, despite the lateness of their departure. The cart was loaded and covered with tarps, creating the illusion, in case anyone was watching, that it carried nothing more than supplies. A small escort accompanied them on horseback. All were armored and armed. Anyone noticing the departure would think that some foolish merchant was attempting a late-night run for some insane profit, or that he was drunk or stupid. None of those would be a good enough reason for pursuit, or even for serious curiosity. And no one noticed.

Onan, Ehsan, and the circle had inscribed runes of protection on the sides of the cart. They had raised wards and done what they could to render the small party difficult to notice. There were other protections in place, but Ehsan hoped they would not be necessary. They were going to need everything to be in perfect condition for what was to come, and he did not want any distractions.

Those he'd chosen to accompany him were strong. They had battle experience, courage, and a certain quality, a lack of self-preservation, perhaps, that he felt would be necessary. They were not hunting a beast; they were hunting a legend. If it were a false trail, nothing would be lost, but if it was true, it changed the world as he knew it absolutely. Hashir, who was no warrior, rode on the wagon and tended the wards. None of the others were of any use with the sorcery, or even fully aware of it. Ehsan was grateful not to have to split his concentration between two worlds. He was going to have to be the point upon which both efforts pivoted, and he could not afford to be drawn one way or the other. It was not lost on him that this was a night that could make him famous, or that there were two wildly divergent ways in which that could happen.

He rode ahead of the wagon, watching the dunes and rocks and scanning the skies. He did not know if the flying creatures would hunt at night. It seemed unlikely, but he didn't want to be taken by surprise. He still had one of the teeth, sold by Balthazar, in his pocket for luck. It was as long as his finger, and the thought of being clutched in powerful talons and lifted to the skies to become a meal for flying lizards was not something he considered a part of his future.

Nothing stirred. The wards were holding, he sensed, but he never depended on a single source of protection. The weapons he carried, and those of his men, held their own power. He'd never known exactly why, but for years he'd collected them. Famous swords, bows that had belonged to warriors of legend, daggers that had slain monsters and kings. He'd spent a lifetime binding them to himself, learning, and bonding with their energy. He was confident that, even if the circle's wards failed, they would complete their mission, but he did not want to test it. Too much seemed to be riding on their success.

For one thing, there was this prophecy. Ehsan was not a stupid man. He knew that if magic existed, then denying deities and angels—and Nephilim—was a fool's game. One could not exist without the other, darkness and light. This might have been just another of Onan's schemes, but it did not feel that way. Time, a thing he'd never considered, seemed suddenly precious, and the idea that his life, even his world, might end, a thought he'd never spent an hour of his life considering, suddenly felt heavy as a great stone around his neck. This might be his last battle, and if that was truth, it had to be grand. The scale had to be worth the loss. Failure was simply not to be considered.

They rolled steadily into the growing darkness, and soon all they could make out of the city was a dim glow on the horizon. There was no light from Noah's compound. The trees surrounded them, and by night, they were quiet. There were no parties, no celebrations, or entertainments. Ehsan had detailed reports from workers moving in and out. He had paid dearly for fragments he'd combined into a rough map. There were several ways into the compound. The main road led to the gate where supplies were accepted. There was a second, to the left of that, where workers entered and exited, near the camps that held those felling the trees and cutting the planks for the Ark. Neither of these was going to work for his purposes, because they were guarded, even when there was no traffic.

There were two other ways into the compound. One was on the far side, a narrow trail out of the trees into a desert that led to somewhere other than the city. Ehsan assumed that it meant Noah dealt with distant cities and lands as well as those close by. That entrance was far too distant to reach and enter with enough time for their mission. That left the final way, a way that had been partially sealed off, and that was not even accessible from the interior. One of his spies had spotted what appeared to be a worn, open spot in the trees and had slipped off during his lunch break to investigate. About fifty feet in, the trail widened into an actual road, overgrown and pitted, but still passable. It ran almost to the edge of the trees. There was a thin line of saplings blocking the way, but a clear enough opening that if you came to it head on, you would see it clearly. It was not (apparently) guarded at all. Possibly it was forgotten, and Noah believed the trees would grow in over the entrance and remove it forever.

It was this entrance Ehsan sought. He'd led his party off the main road only a short distance from the city, angling to the right. If his source was correct, he would find the forgotten entrance about a quarter of a mile around to the right of the main road. If that source proved unreliable, it would not go well for the man who had provided the information. His followers questioned nothing. They were hard men, proven in battle, and loyal. They trusted his leadership implicitly, but had they not, they would have followed him for the pay. Ehsan knew the value of a good soldier, and he paid it gladly.

Their passage was without incident, and they came up to the tree line away from main road, and Ehsan sent a scout ahead to locate the entrance to the lost road. The man returned after only a short time, grinning widely.

"It was as you said it would be," he said. "A few minutes with a machete and we can roll straight on in. I followed it just a short way, then returned, but the road is wide. It is not in good repair, but still passable. I can guide us there quickly."

Ehsan nodded. He signaled for the wagon to move forward once again. The escort pulled in tight, everyone on their guard. Just before they reached the entrance, he halted them once again.

He directed two men to set to work on the saplings barring their way. Then he turned to the wagon.

"Ready the weapon," he said. "We have no idea what we will find once we are inside. Stage the second wagon out here. I want four guards. Remain alert, because if we are successful, we are going to need you to bring it in. If we are not, you will need to be ready to flee."

Men jumped up on the wagon, removing and stowing tarps, revealing the great crossbow and its massive bolt. Ehsan clambered up onto the wagon and pulled the flask from his belt. He'd waited to fill the reservoir until their arrival. If some large jolt or bump had punctured the seals, they would have no chance at success. As it was, he wasn't convinced their odds were good.

A good hunter needs one shot. That was a lesson he'd been taught over and over, by his father, by warriors, even by a sorcerer or two. The corollary to that rule was what bothered him, and that was that only a fool goes into a serious battle without a backup plan. These were good men, and he'd equipped them with weapons beyond anything they'd ever experienced, but there was just too much they didn't know about their quarry, and Ehsan feared they might soon learn they had never been the hunters at all. It didn't frighten him; it exhilarated him.

He poured the contents of the flask into the reservoir on the bolt and sealed it. He placed his palm atop the seal and spoke the words of power Onan had specified. His memory was nearly perfect. He'd honed it over the years, reciting chants and incantations. He did not have the raw power Onan possessed, and he did not have the resources, but his sorcery was more practical, learned only if it had a use that he believed to be important. When he was finished, he jumped down and walked to the front of the small caravan. He stared at the trees, trying to make out anything in the deep shadows. Nothing moved.

The last thing he did, as he returned to his mount and spurred it toward the trees, was to pull an object from a fold in his cloak. It was an intricate construct, a ring of crystals attached to a copper plate that bisected a larger crystal. All of it was held together by a rod pushing through the center and locked at both ends to hold it in place. He gripped the upper half of the sphere and spun it carefully three clicks to the right, one back to the left, four to the right and then spun it back to the original position. With a quick press of his palms to the top and bottom, it locked. There was a whirring sound, and a final, louder click. The sphere was attached to a chain. He dropped that around his neck.

"I have no idea if you can see or hear," he said. "I have done as you requested. Exactly. We are about to begin."

Moments later he and two of the escorts crossed the line of downed trees and entered the compound. The wagon rattled along behind, moving steadily, pulled by a team of three reem. For better, or worse, or eternity, it had begun.

Chapter 30

Og stood far back in the trees. He'd heard, or felt, the approach of the wagons long before. He remained still, like a great statue, waiting. He heard voices, and might have made out their words, but he seldom paid attention, and felt no urgent need to understand. He knew who was coming. He knew why they were coming. He understood what Noah wanted him to do, and he trusted the old man. Beyond anything in his long life, his father the angel, his long-dead mother, beyond prayer and beyond any logic, he trusted Noah. They had made a pact, and Og knew the inevitable was upon them. There was no turning from the prophecy. There was no turning from the events of this night.

He sent out a single silent thought to the others. Not his brothers, exactly, and not close to man, as Og himself had become. They believed they would be saved, in the end. They worked for the prophecy, but they did not understand. They believed, as their angelic sires had always believed, that in the end they would be called home. That they would be forgiven. That there was a place in Glory for the fallen. Og knew the bitter truth.

The God they believed in was vengeful. He would not bend, nor would He break. He would not show compassion, because the only thing He accepted was obeisance. Og would never grant that, so, while Noah believed in his Lord, Og believed in Noah.

The giant's simple message to the night was one of patience. He knew they would sense his pain. He knew they would hate the intruders. They hated all men and tolerated few. If they acted too quickly, the plan would be ruined. It was important, to Noah, that those who had brought news of this attack not be seen as guilty. The plan had to appear to succeed. Og had to fall and be taken. He trusted that it would not last.

Very slowly, he lifted the flask and examined it. It held the potion that the one called Balthazar had brought. Og had allowed the man to touch him so that he could read his intent. In return, he had shared just a glimpse of the temptation his own father had left to him. Memories of the heavens. The truth behind man's faith, or lack thereof. The exchange had been satisfactory. Og lifted the flask, opened his mouth, and popped it in. He chewed slowly, crunching the animal skin between great, grinding teeth until he felt the contents, the potion within, burst free and rush down his throat. He swallowed all of it, then dropped his hands to his sides and resumed his vigil. The sound of wheels turning had returned, and he knew they would soon draw near. He could not let them advance closer than he was to the compound. He would make his stand here, near the outermost ring of trees. Others would come behind, once he and the wagons were gone into the desert and had repaired the camouflage on the entrance to the road. Whether he lived or died, whether the potion did its job or failed, or whether the intruders had planned better or anticipated failure did not matter. What mattered was that the compound was safe, that the Ark was completed, and the prophecy fulfilled.

Onan and the others were gathered at the table. The scrying bowl was in place, and the wards activated. There was no discussion, because at this point there was nothing left to discuss. They watched the ring of crystals and they waited. It had been several hours since Ehsan and Hashir had departed the city. All of them knew that they were nearing the point in time where they would receive a connection from the caravan or they would not. The former meant the plan was moving ahead, and the latter could mean so many things, most of them bad, that, again, they did not think about it.

There was a flicker of light. It started on one bit of quartz near the center of the table, then, with a spark like tiny bolt of lightning, it danced to the next stone, and the next. Then, with a flash so bright it blinded them momentarily, it shot around the bowl, dimmed slightly, and pulsed. The crystals were linked by a thin thread of blue light. Onan leaned in and stared into the bowl. The surface of the water within shimmered like a mirror, then came to life. He saw trees and reem; he caught sight of Hashir to the right. Hashir turned, suddenly, staring back as if aware. The connection had been made. The image was rough. It moved with the lens that Ehsan carried, and he was mounted. The image focused just as he passed over the remnants of the trees hiding the road, and into the shadows beyond. The moon was high, and despite the trees, it trickled down through the branches and glittered on the ground.

"They are in," Ghazalan said.

"Indeed," Onan said. "And apparently without incident. I see no evidence of injury or damage. Hashir was able to hold the wards."

Akeem and Akbar rubbed their hands greedily. All of them rose and moved in behind Onan to watch.

The vision continued to waver, because the road was pitted with deep holes and ruts that Ehsan had to navigate around carefully. Progress was slow. The view shifted as Ehsan glanced from side to side, and occasionally up into the shadows. At one point, he turned, and the group saw that the great crossbow was loaded and taut. The tip of the great bolt angled up about forty-five degrees, and the warrior who manned it tested the controls of the makeshift turret he sat upon, swinging the weapon slowly from side to side.

"I hope Ehsan chose this one well," Akbar said. "We have only one shot. If it does not strike the giant cleanly..."

"Yes, yes," Onan said, irritated. "We are all aware. Perhaps we could make a joint effort to channel our energy to the wards, and possibly to the weapon, since it is also charmed, rather than repeating the possible dire outcomes. This is the time to focus. Return to your seats. Let us join ourselves to this connection and lend our strength."

They shifted their attention to the ring of crystals and drew in closer to the table, forming a smaller-than-normal circle.

Onan began the chant, under his breath and barely audible. The others joined in one by one, starting with Akbar and continuing around the circle until all voices were one. The image in the bowl brightened. It steadied, despite the fact that Ehsan was still mounted. They felt him, and then, moments later, heard his voice in their minds, echoing their own, joining. Ahead, the road widened slightly once more, and a darker shadow loomed to the left of the path. It moved deliberately, peeling slowly from trees.

Og stepped from the tree line into the road and turned to face the approaching men and wagons. He saw the weapon, saw the man behind it frantically spin the tip of the bolt around to face him. He saw the men on horseback pull up, another on a camel, all rushing to perform some act they believed would save them. To Og it happened very, very slowly. It was as if the men moved through heavy oil or deep water. He could have crushed them, reached out with a single hand, and swept them from the road, but instead he took a step forward, and then another. He concentrated on the crossbow and the bolt.

In his stomach, he felt the odd burn of the potion, and knew its potency. He heard their voices, as if from far away, drawn out and slow. The man behind the weapon locked his turret and stomped on the firing mechanism. The mechanism tripped and there was a loud, powerful *twang!* It reverberated through the night. Og saw the bolt shoot forward, but even that, driven by the pressure of the taut line, moved with the speed of a snail on a garden leaf. He watched its approach, and he shifted. It was not quick motion, at least not to Og. I was almost imperceptible, but it was enough. The bolt had been aimed at his heart. He knew that had not been the plan, but fear had ruled the shooter, and he had panicked. Og moved, and the bolt cut into his flesh just below his right shoulder, missing his heart. It drove in deep, and the weapon worked exactly as planned. The inner mechanism released the potion and it drove into his veins with incredible pressure, spreading through his bloodstream. He did not fight it. He could still have driven the small caravan into the darkness with a swipe of his hand, but he did not. He knelt, giving the potion time to take effect, and then, very slowly, as a deeper darkness claimed him, he rolled carefully, not crushing any of his assailants, until he dropped to the ground.

He reached out toward the approaching men weakly, and his hand dropped to the road.

Chapter 31

Ehsan sat very still as the giant crumpled. He'd seen the shot, worried it was too accurate, that all would be for naught and that the Nephilim would be killed. The worry proved unfounded, but it bothered him. His vision was good, and his instincts set his nerves on edge. Had the target moved at the last second, causing the bolt to miss its heart? Was it really unconscious? Would they approach, only to find themselves too close and trapped? It had simply been too quick, too easy. Not even a token response from the giant.

The others apparently suffered no such concerns. They surged around Eshan toward the fallen creature. He heard the rattle of the crossbow wagon being pulled to the side, and the rumbling wheels of the second, larger wagon approaching. Men swarmed. Moving a creature of this size was something they had done many times. These men knew their work, and they came with winches, ramps, and several unhitched reem trained to push, aiding them in rolling the giant into place. The symmetry of their actions and the efficiency behind it soothed Ehsan, but only slightly.

Hashir had no such concerns. He leapt from the wagon that carried the great crossbow and approached the fallen giant with mincing, almost ecstatic steps. Ehsan watched, careful to position himself so that those in the city could also watch. He did not approach the giant, but instead sat still so the image would be clear.

He had come to the compound expecting violence. Capturing a Nephilim was beyond the accomplishments of any hunter in his lifetime. The danger should have been intense, but everything had happened, instead, as if scripted. It should not have been this easy, and he could not shake the idea that something was wrong. That they had miscalculated in some way that was not obvious. He watched as their crew bound and rolled the giant onto the cart, mesmerized at the knowledge behind it. He knew they had brought in Mace Tails and other creatures larger than the Nephilim. He had no doubt they could manage to get their quarry loaded. It still felt wrong.

Ehsan was a warrior first and a sorcerer second. He'd honed his instincts over two centuries of battles, sieges, mercenary wars, and revolts. He had not survived by being stupid, or by ignoring his instincts, and those instincts were screaming at him that it was just too simple. There had been no battle at all. The Nephilim had walked into the bolt blindly. Or had he? That sudden shift—Ehsan could not get it out of his mind. No plan ever goes exactly as expected. He wanted to reach out to those in the city, to call it off. He wanted to tell the workers scurrying around the wagon, attaching great ropes and pulleys, to roll the giant into the road, turn, and run, but he knew he could not. His instincts were enough to warn him, but they would not be enough to sway the others.

Two things were possible. Either the giant was a bumbling thing with little thought and little likelihood of drawing more than a curious crowd once or twice in the arena, or they had known this was coming. It was possible that the Nephilim had surrendered himself without a fight because he knew there was no real danger. In his heart, Ehsan felt that this would be the answer. What he had to figure out, what he had to know to survive, was why. The creature was clearly not faking unconsciousness. He was being loaded like a piece of dead meat with no reaction at all.

Could there be others? Could there be a force waiting in the desert, aware of their intent, ready to attack? Ehsan turned his attention from the activity behind him. He rode through the ranks and picked out several men, then rode to the wagon where Hashir sat, wide-eyed, watching the others work.

"Hashir," Ehsan said.

At first, Hashir did not respond. Ehsan drew his mount

closer, reached out, and slapped Hashir on the shoulder.

"Wh... what?" Hashir said.

"Something is wrong," Ehsan said. "Very wrong. Does it not seem odd to you that we rode in, saw this all-powerful giant, and a few moments later he's defeated, and we are declaring victory?"

Hashir glanced at him in shock. "But you see it, yes? He is being rolled onto the wagon. We will be on our way back within moments..."

"Exactly," Ehsan said. "How did you see this before we arrived? Did you not believe there would be a struggle? Did you believe a being half-angel, half-human with immense strength that had lived for centuries would just stumble into our hands, or were you afraid for your very soul?"

Hashir started to answer, and then held his silence. He glanced uneasily at the wagon bearing Og's inert form.

"We have to be prepared," Ehsan said. "I believe that we were betrayed in some way, but that does not mean we can't succeed. The giant seems to be out of the picture. It is up to the two of us to find a defense. If you want to see the city again, you will use every resource at your disposal, and you will stay close to me. I don't know what is coming, but I know it's not good."

Hashir hesitated, just for a moment, glanced one last time at the fallen Nephilim. Then he turned back and nodded.

"You are correct, of course. Even if you were not, caution should be our plan. This is not a beast from the desert, and it *has* happened with unlikely ease. There are different wards I can set. For one, I can monitor the trance. If I detect signs of consciousness during the trip, I will let you know. We can also monitor our surroundings to a point. A patrol from Noah's camp, or something worse, would cause a disturbance that I can sense. Thank you for returning my focus."

"We will get through this," Ehsan said. "There was no battle here, but it is a long journey to the city."

Hashir nodded, and Ehsan turned his mount, trotting to where he'd left the group of men that he'd culled from the crowd to give instructions. They would have a different formation for the return trip. Scouts and guards would be set, and a regular system of reporting in place. These were trained warriors. They believed his warnings without question and accepted their part in what was to come. The uncertainty that had gripped him eased. Ehsan did not fear confrontation, he only feared being unprepared.

He glanced over his shoulder at the fallen giant and grinned fiercely.

"Sleep well, my friend," he said softly. "Before this night is through, we'll know who was the wiser and the stronger."

Then he turned and spurred his mount toward the desert. The wagons were moving again, and he wanted to make a quick scouting trip to check the road ahead. They were ahead of schedule, and he wondered how the others, hearing his words, and watching his progress, were reacting. He hoped they would lend their energy, but, if they did not...he was ready.

Not far from where the hidden road entered the trees, Noah, Ham, Naḥlab, and Ezra stood, draped in shadows, watching. They had been there when the young trees were felled and the wagons rolled through. They had heard voices, cries of fear, the resonating thrum of the great crossbow. At that sound, Naḥlab had started forward, but Ham wrapped her in his arms and held her still.

"It will be fine," he said. "I trust Balthazar, and I trust your father. We have to let it play out."

Naḥlab spun, her eyes wet with tears.

"He is our friend," she said. "He has done so much, with so little in return. To just let them shoot him with that weapon and drag him off like a piece of meat..."

"He is a warrior," Noah said softly. "They have no idea what they are tampering with. Do you know their story, the Nephilim?"

"I have heard stories, of course," Naḥlab said. "Most of them contradict other stories. Many of them are more about you and your connections to them than they are about the giants themselves."

Noah turned and smiled.

"The simple truth," he said, "is that the Nephilim exist because men, women, and angels have more in common than scripture would lead you to believe. Before there were men, there were angels. The Lord created this place, and the won-drous Garden we will never be allowed to experience. He created Adam and then Eve, and even then, at the very least, Lucifer was jealous. I am not certain the truth of the fallen, and the Garden, has been adequately recorded. There is Lilith to consider, and the broken relationship between Lucifer and the Lord. One thing I know—Adam and Eve left Eden, and they brought the world of men to life, branching out until there were cities and armies, kingdoms and temples, and all of that time, the angels watched, and grew more jealous.

"Our world is a beautiful place. The Lord created it for us and denied it to his first children. There was discord. Many of the angels wanted to visit this place, to enjoy the beauty and wonder of it. He did not want to allow it, but, in the end, they convinced him that they could resist the temptations of our world, that they would come and then return, and all would be as it had always been."

"Clearly," Naḥlab said, "That was not the case?"

"They had not counted on women," Noah said simply. "The angels were struck by the beauty of the women they encoun-tered on the Earth, and they strayed. They used their power and their heavenly beauty to seduce the women who were already seducing them. There were children. Og is one of the oldest, but there are many more. Some of the angels returned to heaven, but those who had succumbed to the pleasures of the flesh were left behind. They joined the fallen, though not exactly accepted there, either. Their children grew huge, wreaking havoc in the cities of men, killing and destroying. They were not immortal, and many were killed. Some fought among themselves. Others were killed in shame by their own celestial parents. The angels themselves have been imprisoned or rendered powerless, but the Nephilim are among us. There are more here than Og. Sometimes they help him, sometimes they leave and return, or do not. They help to prevent the beasts from reaching us, but they do not communicate with me. They don't trust me. I have known Og most of my life, and he has followed where I've traveled. Though he has never reached out to my family, only to me, he has protected us. He is like a part of the family, and,

whatever the consequences, if I can find a way to save him from
the coming deluge, I will do it and face the consequences.

"I will tell you this, though. That bolt will only hurt him in
the way a splinter would hurt one of us. The potion might have
contained him until he reached the arena, but he would have
torn that place apart and likely wrecked one of the gates or walls
of the city on his way out. They believe that they understand,
but their sorcery is a creation of men. Og is a being beyond their
comprehension. Beyond my own, in truth. He has survived battles that would curdle their blood. That group will never reach
the city. They will be lucky if any of them survive to report the
failure. He does not need our help, and it's entirely possible that
his brethren will feel compelled to act. If that happens, it will
go very, very badly for those involved. Their best hope for any
mercy lies in Og awakening, and even that will be bloody."

"The city will have a thousand stories about what happened," Ezra said. "There will be rumors. Priests will cry out
in the temples. They are going to say you are communing with
demons if they learn of this."

"I am aware," Noah said. "And they will learn of it. I sense
a connection between the city and at least one of those on the
wagons. If the one they call Onan is involved, he will know, and
it won't take long for them to figure out that they were tricked. I
suspect your father," he turned to Naḥlab, "may wish to request
asylum here at some point. I have no idea what these events will
bring about. I will be speaking at the temple tomorrow, to get
ahead of it. I will be asking them to see the signs, to remember
their Lord. I will be trying to prevent what is to come by changing their hearts. Sadly, I am certain that I will fail. I say this
because, if I were wise enough to change the prophecy of the
Lord, I would be creating my own prophecies, and they would
not include so much death."

Before he could continue, the wagons rolled back out of
the forest, and they all turned to watch. Og, unconscious, lay
bound to the larger wagon. Despite the size of that conveyance,
he draped over all the sides. His arms were bound to his stomach to prevent them dragging on the ground, and the wagon
bowed in the center from the weight. It was pulled by a team

of reem, powerful beasts with massive horns and huge chests, and they snorted and struggled with the effort of getting the wagon up to traveling speed. Despite the difficulty, the invaders rolled out into the desert and moved steadily away from the trees, undisturbed.

Onan quieted the others after their initial burst of enthusiasm. They'd all witnessed the bolt striking home and seen the giant loaded onto the wagon. A few moments later, though, their view changed rapidly and repeatedly. Ehsan was not watching their captive. Briefly they saw him converse with Hashir, saw the sorcerer's expression shift and grow serious. There were others in rapid succession, and a small group of the guards escorting the caravan rode out through the trees and into the desert. It was not how they had planned it.

"What is wrong?" Akeem asked.

"There is no time to discuss that," Onan said. "Hashir is clearly attempting something, as is Ehsan. We have a connection to Ehsan. We need to focus. If we can channel our combined strength through the crystals, it will lend Hashir strength. Whatever has happened, or that Ehsan believes might happen, we must do what we can to assist."

They sat back and closed their eyes, reaching out to the bowl and the connection Onan maintained. Light rippled along designs etched into the table. The color of those lights varied slightly as they passed by and through each of those at the table, until, where they met the tips of Onan's fingers, they blended to a brilliance.

The surface of the liquid in the bowl rippled. The image, the desert sky beyond the trees as they caravan rolled back out into the desert, winked out, leaving a strobed echo in their minds. Then, there was nothing but the connection and the steady ebb and flow of energy.

In the desert, Ehsan started suddenly. He glanced down at the pendant and caught its glow. He smiled, realizing the significance. He was glad for their strength. He only hoped it would prove enough.

Chapter 32

For the first couple of miles, the caravan moved steadily. The drivers were experienced, and even the reem pulling the load seemed energized, as if something in the air had passed the urgency of the moment to them. The importance of crossing safely. Maybe it was just that they knew they were heading back to their stables, where on any normal night they would be bedded down and resting. There was danger in the desert, even by day. The number of times they might have been driven at night was limited.

Ehsan rode ahead with his chosen scouts. They maintained a greater distance from the wagons than they had on the way across. They covered more ground, and they rode with weapons at the ready. There was no sign of beasts, but he did not trust this silence either. The wards were strong, probably stronger with the others lending their strength, but it was strange that they had seen nothing. No sign of aggression or even a distant shadow. Nothing. The desert was a desolate place, but on this night, it was a wasteland.

Far in the distance, the faint glow of lights from the city beckoned to Ehsan. His nerves were on fire. He had to still his thoughts several times to prevent being drowned out by the pounding of blood in his ears. He felt as if he could hear things for miles.

Far behind, the wagons rolled forward. The first had been covered with the tarp that had concealed the weapon during the crossing. The larger wagon rolled on behind. They had covered the giant as well, though there was no way to disguise his bulk or modify his shape. He might have been any number of species of beast, but there was no mistaking that something alive, or recently alive, was being moved. They would need stealth and luck to get him from the rear gate to the arena. It was not something they had spent much thought on. When they reached the city, people would know what they had done and what they had returned with. Even if it only spread as a rumor, it would work in their favor. There was no time to worry over that at present. The focus had to be on the crossing. Other than Ehsan, Hashir, and the men he'd shared his concerns with, optimism was high. The journey was going safely and without a hitch. None of them noticed when, almost imperceptibly, the weight on the wagon shifted.

Beneath the tarps and ropes, very slowly, Og opened his eyes. His mind was still foggy, but it was clearing rapidly. He felt the roll of the wheels, heard the grunts and heavy breaths of the beasts drawing the wagons. He heard the voices of the guards and the drivers, those who had loaded and bound him. He felt the pain where the bolt from the great crossbow, still protruding from just below his shoulder, had pierced him. That pain brought red anger, washing through him, but he suppressed it. Powerful as he was, he understood caution.

When his thoughts had cleared, he began working his uninjured arm free. They had not been particularly careful in binding him, and it did not take long. Then, careful not to shift enough to alert the drivers, he dropped his arm over the side the wagon. At first, he just let his massive fingers scratch over the ground. The wagon shivered. Several of the reem grunted and struggled. The drivers shook their reins and called out to them, but no one was concerned. They did not react. Og took a deep breath. He closed his eyes for just a second, and then, with a sudden, powerful jab, he drove his fingers into the road. He gripped, and the wagon skewed. The reem cried out in fear, dragged by their reins and the collars binding them to the wagon. The drivers fought for balance and then flailed as the wagon spun, flipping them through the air and dropping onto its side. The guards scattered, trying to make room between themselves and the wagon. Og, with a shrug of his shoulders, snapped his bindings and rolled off the wagon. He gripped the crossbow bolt by its shaft and ripped it free. As it tore his flesh, he screamed, and that sound carried across the desert to Noah, to the city, and to Ehsan.

Hashir, on the first wagon, sensed the giant's energy before it was unleashed. He stood and turned. Og drove his fist into the road to offset the pain from his wound and rose to his feet. His back was still to Hashir, who knew he had moments, maybe seconds, to react. He stood, raised his hands, and called on the energy he had been channeling into the protective wards. He gathered that energy and focused it. He released it from the protective boundary it was providing and drew it into himself, knowing it was a risk taking on such a huge burst of power, knowing, as well, that he had no skill, no talisman or weapon through which to project it. He drew it into himself, and then, when he felt he would burst, or die, or simply melt from the heat, he swept his arms toward the screaming giant, and joined his own voice to that sound. He felt the energy burst from his hands, saw the brilliant flash of multi-colored light drive into the Nephilim's back. The creature staggered, and Hashir laughed. He raised his arms and released himself to the light, to the attack. His skin grew hot. Sweat rolled down his cheeks, and his eyes were bright.

Then Og turned and straightened. He returned Hashir's gaze and spoke a single word. It was not a word that any who heard it could comprehend. It was not spoken with force, but almost a whisper. The power that had burst from Hashir grew brighter, and then brighter still. Then, with a sound like a clap of thunder, it shattered. Those near the wagon dropped as if they'd been struck on the head with great hammers. The beasts lost consciousness and lay still. Hashir, eyes still bright, lost his grin. His eyes widened, and he scrambled to draw the power back, to use it to form a ward or a shield. He was unable to control it. There was a connection now between himself, the others in the city, and the giant, and they were no longer in control of it. He felt power building. He felt the creature's rage. He tasted its pain. Then, in a flash of white-hot light, memory, vision, and revelation, the direction of the power shifted. Hashir barely had time to gasp before his earthly form burst from within. One moment he stood, wide-eyed and defiant, and the next he simply ceased to exist.

As the guards scattered into the night and the driver of the first wagon urged his beasts to rise and move, Og reached down and retrieved the crossbow bolt that had struck him. He focused on Ehsan and his men. They were gathering and, having seen the utter destruction of the caravan, were readying themselves to flee to the safety of the city. Og waited. As the horsemen settled into a formation, with a last cry of rage and pain, the giant drew back his arm and launched the great bolt through the air. Without a second glance, he turned, and slowly, favoring his wounded shoulder, he began walking back toward the trees.

The throw was not like a shot from the bow. The shaft spun, rotating, and flying so fast that the air it cut through in passing caused a deep thrumming sound. At first no one heard it, or they thought it was the pounding of hooves, or perhaps the rush of blood through their ears. At the last second, maybe out of instinct, Ehsan turned. The wooden pole sliced into the rear guards, driving them outward, and crashed into the center. Ehsan did not even have time for a quickly breathed prayer. The center of the bolt struck his neck dead on with such force his body continued riding, but his head flew free, broken and mangled. It bounced off an outcropping of stone, glazed eyes flashing to the darkened sky.

Onan felt the sudden drain as Hashir called on them for power. The others leaned closer, held by that connection and feeding it. The table and the bowl wobbled, then shook crazily. Onan watched. He stole a single moment to speak a ward under his breath, and he waited. The rings of light that had flickered around the table brightened steadily. The heat was intense, not quite burning, but near the limit of what Onan could stand without crying out and pulling away.

He wished that the image in the bowl were still clear, that he could witness what was happening directly. There was a flash of energy, and the heat lessened. Their combined energy flowed, and just in that instant he saw what Hashir saw... what they all saw. He saw the light strike the wounded giant. He saw it stagger. He felt Hashir's exultation and realized he was screaming, that they were all screaming. The sensation was incredible, the channeling of power so far beyond a single man. It was so intoxicating that he almost missed the shift. Almost. He felt tension, resistance, and then he felt something sifting back through the light, through the power. Something unfamiliar. At first it was a trickle, but very quickly that grew to a rushing flood. Again, he sensed Hashir screaming. Onan called on the one thing left to him, called on the ward he'd spoken, and it freed his hand, just for a second. With a quick swipe he drove his palm into the bowl.

It did not move. Not at first. His hand burned and he screamed, again, but that scream, and that pain, freed his mind from the connection. In his absence, it grew uneven. He drew his arm back again and, ignoring the pain, crashed it into the side of the bowl. It tipped. The liquid spilled onto the table, ran along the lines of energy. Onan staggered back. He saw Akeem fall back. The others, rather than pulling away, were drawn into the lights, now spinning and whirling crazily. They leaped from the designs and the sigils onto the bare center of the table and became a small cyclone of light, drawing in toward a circular point in the center.

"No!" Onan cried out. He leaped for Akbar, and then, before he touched the other man, he stopped himself. Something was wrong with Akbar's skin, his face. He had become translucent, fading, and then returning to clarity. Onan turned and saw that Ghazalan was the same. The center of that glowing whirlwind brightened again, and Onan turned, diving away and covering his head. "Down!" he screamed. "Get down!" He had no way to know if Akeem had heard him.

There was a great flash of light. His hearing and his sight left him. For a long moment it felt as if he floated off the floor, hovering, and then, with the strength of a charging bull, an explosion of energy rippled out from the table, lifted him, and slammed him into the wall. As his mind fell to darkness, he saw the light sucked into a smaller and smaller point, then disappear into the center of the table. Akbar and Ghazalan shimmered, whirled, and along with the light, flashed out of existence as the room joined Onan in darkness.

Chapter 33

When Og came into sight, staggering slowly toward the trees, Ham started forward, as if to go into the desert and help in some way. Noah put a hand on his son's shoulder. Ham spun, but Noah shook his head.

"Watch," he said. "There is nothing we could do to help him."

Ham tried to shake his father off, but then grew still. Peeling from the trees on the far side of the now-open route into the compound, a tall shadow stepped into the moonlight. Then another. They moved with ponderous grace across the sand, and Og, aware of their presence, slowed, and at last stood still. The others approached him, turned to stand on either side, and waited as Og wrapped his great arms across their shoulders. Og winced as his wounded shoulder stretched, but when his escorts began to walk, he fell into step, and they guided him carefully, drawing him into the trees. There should have been great, booming steps. There should have been crashing as they pushed through the trees. There was nothing. Not a ripple of sound. The three huge creatures were simply swallowed by the shadows. A moment later it was difficult to believe that they'd been there at all.

"You knew they would come?" Ham asked.

Noah nodded. "They do not communicate with me, as he does, but they are always nearby. I do not pretend to understand why they watch over us or why they help him. They are close, and they will heal him. They do not injure easily, unlike men. I have seen Og hurt before. It's as if their flesh is called back to its original shape. It can be disrupted, and I assume sufficient energy could disperse them permanently, or for a long period of time, but they draw back into themselves very quickly. I've seen a tree fall on Og's leg. It was clearly broken. He sent me away, and the very next day I found him standing in the trees. He made no mention of pain or healing. He was simply there."

"As he will be tomorrow," Ezra said softly.

"Do not be surprised," Noah replied, "if you find him in the menagerie, working, before morning."

"What of the men who tried to take him?" Naḥlab said. "Are they—"

"Dead? Probably," Noah said. "As I've mentioned, we do not exactly speak, but I know that Og realizes any of them reaching the city would bring others, perhaps an army. No one will care that these men came here in the dark, trying to capture a creature they had no right to attack, from a place they had no right to be. They would hear only how a giant, something they could not understand, own, or control, had killed men, and brutally. And they would tie that knowledge to this place—to me. They would say I have called up demons to aid me. They may still do that. There are others in the city who are involved, and I do not believe those who crossed the desert would have done so without some means of communication—some connection. Og may have handled that as well. He is as far beyond my understanding as the Lord himself. My heart tells me we have enemies now in the city. Men who believe, despite the dishonesty of their endeavors, that we now owe them something. They are not going to let this pass. From this day forward, we will need to bolster our security, and keep a wary eye on one another's backs."

"Then you will not be speaking in the temple?" Ham asked.

"I will speak," Noah said. "I have come to a point where I cannot proceed with our plans, with our salvation, without honestly presenting the citizens of that city with an alternative. I don't know that changing their ways at this point would be enough, but I know that *not* changing means their certain deaths. I could not live with all of them on my conscience, but if they make the decision of their own free will, I will, perhaps, be able to sleep, and to do my part in the coming trials. Even with the Ark, what we face seems beyond the realm of possibility. The notion of faith will be tested, destroyed, and tested again. I have been told that we will survive, and still, I have a hard time believing it. For all our piety and righteous speech, we are men and women, and we have never faced anything like the coming days will present. Perhaps, if we can pull such a thing off, we *are* worthy."

"But," Naḥlab said, her expression troubled, "is it safe? After what happened here tonight? Considering that some very wealthy, very powerful men have been hurt so directly? Won't they try—?"

"To kill me?" Noah said. "I would be surprised if they did not, or, if they did not at least try to stir the masses to do it for them. That is if any of them survived whatever happened in that desert. We'll never really know. I will have men go out tomorrow and bring in any evidence of it, and I think Og will see to closing off that road again. The truth is, if it is real, if I am not a crazy, very old man, and we are building a great boat to save us from a deluge that will cleanse the Earth, I should be safe. If I am spreading my Lord's word, trying to save these people's lives and divert disaster, I believe that I will not be harmed."

"A test, then?" Ezra asked.

"No," Noah replied. "I would never test my Lord. I may be testing myself. There is certainly danger, but who among us could board that ark knowing we did not do everything within our power to save others? I have to speak. I will travel to the city in the morning to speak with Balthazar. He is working to make the proper connections."

"I will go with you, if you will have me," Ezra said. "I may be of some help. I have connections still, and I would not mind seeing Master Balthazar, truth be told."

"I would enjoy the opportunity to get to know you better," Noah said. "We will leave after the morning meal. Be prepared to stay the night in the city, if necessary. I'm uncertain what to expect."

Ezra smiled, and nodded. "I will be taking my leave, then. I will need time to explain to Yalith, and to pack for the journey."

"I believe we could all use some rest," Noah said. "I will

see if I can contact Og, to be certain he is well, and then I will be retiring for the night. I suggest the rest of you do the same."

"We will check the menagerie," Ham said, pulling Naḥlab close. "I don't know if he will return to the work or to commune with the beasts. If he does, I will send word. Then we will rest as well."

Uncharacteristically, Noah hugged Ham, then the others, one after the other. Then they turned and retraced their path to the compound in silence.

Chapter 34

Noah managed to slip through the gates in one of the merchants' wagons. He pulled his cloak up and over his head, wrapped it tight, and headed straight to Balthazar's shop. Though it was early, the door was open, and he stepped quickly inside. Balthazar heard the bell and exited the back room. He smiled, crossed to the door, and locked it. It would not be the first time customers found him closed, particularly since Ezra had moved out to the compound. He'd thought several times of searching out a new apprentice but held back. Anyone with access to the shop, and to him, might hear or see something they should not. They were all living in strange times, and he believed that, worthy or not, he'd become a part of it.

"I wasn't sure if you'd make it here without drawing a crowd," he said. "Rumor has it that there are fewer mercenaries in the city, and that Thaddeus is looking into the theft of a wagon and one of the weapons he uses to bring in the great beasts. There are others missing, though they are not very public and are likely not to raise many eyebrows."

"Would I know them?" Noah asked.

"Perhaps. Hashir, Ehsan, Akbar, Ghazalan, all members of Onan's circle. No one has heard from them or seen them since yesterday. Is all well at your compound? The menagerie?"

"All fine," Noah said. "Og heals remarkably quickly. The road they used has been sealed, and I sent men I could trust to the desert to clean away the wagons and any other sign of that battle, if you could call it such. I saw it from a great distance. I could not make out details of what took place but I felt the energy in the air, and heard the screams. I heard those. I recognized two of them. Hashir was there—he was the one who concentrated the attack on Og. I think he hurt him, for a moment. He was already weakened by the potion—"

"I did what I could to lessen that," Balthazar cut in.

"I know that, and so does he," Noah said. He placed a hand on the other man's shoulder. "You are the reason things did not get truly ugly. In some way, they were connected to the others in the city, the circle. The thing they did not consider, because men are arrogant, is that the magic and sorcery they possess, potent as it might be, is not a match for the child of an angel, no matter how corrupted. When Og retaliated, Hashir, at least from where I stood, ceased to exist. Ehsan tried to retreat. He gathered the survivors and headed for the city, but Og used that great bolt he'd pulled from the wound in his shoulder and used it like some sort of whirling blade. He threw it with such force it burst through the entire party. There was little left to clean up, and by the time my men arrived, the beasts had cleared most of it away."

Balthazar shook his head. "So foolish," he said. "I would say that it is a waste, but I am not certain the city is not better off without all of them. I'm beginning to feel the world will not be a worse place with all of us gone."

"You have spoken to the priests in the temple?" Noah said.

Balthazar nodded. "Believe me, it was not difficult to convince them to let you speak. Their seats will be filled, and they will collect money—to do the Lord's work, of course—enough to build new golden idols and fill their coffers. People do not flock to the temples unless there is a show. I'm afraid that is you, this day."

"We expected no less," Noah said. "I have communed with my Lord but received no specific instruction or inspiration. I believe that this is my own to do. I have no sense of whether He approves, or is indifferent, His mind made up and the future sealed. It does not matter. I will do what I can."

"I will be there to listen," Balthazar said. "I will also spread the word of what you say, and relay to you how the citizens react. I wish I believed that the priests would stand behind you, that they would raise the standard, even if for their own gain, and work for change."

"You are an optimistic man," Noah said, "if you believe that's a real possibility. We will both do what we can then. I am nothing if not a champion of lost causes."

"I don't know what to believe any longer," Balthazar said. "At the same time, for once in a very long life, I sense I am close to belief. Close to understanding what that means. Not reading the scriptures or showing up at temple. Not eating the right foods on the right day or tossing stones at those who worship false idols. It's not about showing how righteous you are, denying yourself joy, or inordinate hours of prayer. The notion of faith is bandied about quite freely, but the simple truth is, as I have heard many say, 'to see a thing is to believe in it'. I touched a giant. He spoke to me in my mind. I have seen animals, creatures great and small, walk docile into your menagerie for no logical reason other than—it is all true. For better or for worse. If He is a loving God, or a monster, a fair deity, or a very powerful child too far removed from this world to see the horror being unleashed—He exists. Your ark exists. There is a cleansing on the horizon, and I have been given a glimpse of what is behind it, following on a lifetime of warnings against what brought it about. I am not optimistic, but I am self-preserving. It is in my best interest if the people listen to you."

"I do not like your chances," Noah said, "but I will do my best. It is a powerful message, and I will try not to spend my words on rules and law and piety. There is magic in this world. It is not necessary to profit off one another, to war...so many things would be better if men and women simply listened to one another."

"It's not our strength. Listening, I mean."

"It's a shame we can't tell them all that occurred in the desert," Noah said. "As you say, it's one thing to hear priests crying out of doom and eternal damnation. It is quite another to know that the spawn of angels walk among you, that they have powers we can barely conceive, and in no way match."

"They would not react as they should," Balthazar said. "If they knew, they would be afraid. If they were afraid, they would lash out. Things that cannot be understood and controlled, even if it's only the very rich and powerful who can do so, will cause them to react violently. The only good that might come of them knowing of last night's failed kidnapping might be that they would be too frightened to attempt such a thing themselves."

"You are probably right," Noah said. "And for all we know, they have already heard. We don't know for sure that none of those involved survived. I would be surprised if that were true. The men involved are foolish, but they are all intelligent, shrewd, and in possession of power most don't really believe in. If they take their story to the streets to stir the citizens against me, this could be a difficult day indeed."

"I have seen to your safety," Balthazar said. "Thaddeus helped. We will have men in the crowds, and we will have a means of getting you safely from the temple and out of the city. I have said that I believe, but I am also cautious. If my part in all of this is simply to keep you alive until that ark is afloat, I mean to fulfill it. Not surviving in this world need not be the end, after all."

Noah laughed softly. "You are a very surprising man," he said. "If we both get through this intact, you will have to bring more of that drink to the compound. Perhaps you should simply stay. I would never promise something I cannot deliver, but I feel as if your part in all of this is far from complete."

Balthazar blushed, slightly, and turned away. Then he rose.

"Come," he said. "We must find our way to the temple, and if we wait much longer, it will be difficult to do so without drawing notice."

Noah stood and followed Balthazar into the back room, then out a door that led to the alley behind the shop. The sun had risen fully as they spoke, and the streets were quickly filling. The two hurried off in the direction of the temple, Noah with his cloak pulled about his features once again and Balthazar leading the way.

Ezekiel smoothed his robes and sat up straight in an ornate chair behind a huge, polished wooden desk. For probably the hundredth time, he scanned the hall outside and re-arranged himself. It was a big day. It had been a long time since the temple had been full, but there were lines forming in the street, and all of the temple servants had been assigned guard duty at the doors. Acolytes roamed the halls, polishing, dusting, setting out candles and incense.

And the worst of it was, there had been no sign of Noah. Balthazar had promised the man, or prophet, or however he styled himself, would appear. In all the years that Ezekiel had known Balthazar, the man had never lied to him. Most of their discussions involved mutual profit, and this was no different, except it was strange. Noah was a very private man. He had not entered the temple in a hundred years. When he spoke of any of the priests in the city, it was with disdain. For him to make a full turn and agree to speak was so far out of character that it made Ezekiel uneasy.

Then, far down the hall, he caught a ray of daylight as the doors were opened. Moments later, an acolyte rushed ahead to tell him that Balthazar had arrived, and that Noah was with him. Ezekiel rose, straightened his robes, and walked slowly toward the door of his chambers. He wanted to meet them in the hall and usher them in. His mind raced. He didn't want to say or do anything that might deter Noah from speaking, but at the same time he had to find a way to maintain distance. He had no idea what the man would say, or how those gathered might react.

As Noah approached, he removed the cloak that had been wrapped tightly about his head. His hair was gray, but full. It flowed over his shoulders. His eyes were bright, intelligent, and intense. He walked with confidence and authority. He did not appear crazy in the least, and it threw Ezekiel off. He had been prepared for wild eyes, a shifty appearance. He had not seen Noah in many years. His memories had been filtered through stories and rumors, and he felt unprepared for the man who now stood before him.

"Ezekiel," Noah said. "It has been too long."

"I was thinking the same," Ezekiel replied. "I have been tied to this temple for many years. I don't get out often, and when I do it's related to temple business."

"It's a business now, then," Noah said. "That would explain a lot."

Ezekiel blushed. "What I meant is, there are a lot of people I have lost contact with, and you are one of them. Things have changed since we last spoke, and I can't say I believe for the better. The people have to be won over. They no longer fear the vengeance of a Lord they long ago broke ties with. They want to gather and be entertained, and that means the temple is in competition with the arena, the brothels, the gambling halls, and any number of other enterprises more suited to gathering crowds. I remember a time when fear of falling out of favor with the Lord was enough to bring them in, when they actually felt guilty as they disobeyed the commandments. I am sorry to say it's a dim memory."

"It is easy to believe a thing does not exist when there is no direct contact," Noah replied. "It is simple to disobey commandments when there are no repercussions, when nothing forces you to obey. And it is the hardest of things that I know to believe that you have been given freedom of choice, but that this choice is governed by guidelines you must either abide by or be destroyed. There has never really been a choice."

"It's always been the catch, hasn't it?" Ezekiel said. "It's easy to have faith in a supernatural being. It's so much harder to maintain that faith without constant reassurance. What does it say about our character? Our strength? I have heard the stories of your ark and the deluge. I have read the prophecies. I remain uncertain whether I am frightened or relieved by the possibility it is all true. As a priest, I have failed. As a man, I have also failed. I am as guilty as anyone in this city, more because I am trained to know better, and to put others before myself, but have not felt that was the case in over two centuries."

"One of the things the Lord has told me," Noah said, "is that men will no longer bear that burden. The length of a life will be limited to one hundred and fifty years."

Ezekiel met his gaze. "I think that is wise. I think, also, that beyond small things that have meant the most to me, remembering anything further back than that is difficult. Perhaps we are already allowed only so many years of memory, and then they are overwritten with the present, the things that matter the most."

"My own memory is slightly better," Noah said, "but that may be because I have been isolated. I have done the same things, spoken the same truths, followed the same rules for so long that remembering one day is much like remembering a year. The only things that vary are those around me. My wife, my family, and now this prophecy. If you are correct, so much change so quickly and completely is likely to erase the world as it was before long. I wonder if that is a good thing or a bad thing. When your situation is dire, and that has been caused by centuries of mistakes, it seems unwise to lose track of those mistakes as you move forward into an uncertain future."

"It is good to speak with you," Ezekiel said. "There are so few who even care to do so, let alone possessing the experience, knowledge, and intellect to make it interesting."

"Maybe a few will come forward when I speak," Noah said. "Though I will count it as a good thing if no one shoots an arrow from the back of the temple or rushes the stage with a dagger. It is not a happy message I am bringing, and I do not intend to weaken it to ease the hearts of those who will listen."

"We have guards in place," Ezekiel said. "Balthazar and I have arranged to get you out of the city if things go badly. I have a feeling, though, that they will listen. The reaction after they do so is anyone's guess, but they are coming to hear what they have only known in rumors from the one man who truly knows what is taking place at your compound. They have been watching, gossiping, and wondering for a very long time. They may not believe, but they will listen."

"That may be the most frightening thing of all," Noah said.

Footsteps sounded in the long hall, and they all looked up.

"It seems that it is time," Balthazar cut in. The others looked at him, as if just realizing he was there. Balthazar smiled.

"I will be in the audience," he said, "but near a door. Mark my location, if you can. If things go badly, make your way toward that exit. That is where we will depart if there is trouble. I will pray—yes, I remember how to do that—that there will be no trouble. But just in case, be certain before you speak that you know where I am. It is on the right as you look out from the stage, near the front. Now you know why I am wearing this brightly colored robe."

"I will look for you," Noah said, rising. "And I admit...I did wonder."

Chapter 35

Onan had grown tired of Akeem's grief. They had both lost allies and friends, and he knew that Akbar, being Akeem's twin, would cause a deep wound. The connection between the two had been so strong they'd spoken in unison, one answering questions asked to the other. It was eerie and potent. Together, joined, the two were powerful, intuitive, and the sort of ally one needed to achieve any true power in the city. Now, though, everything was a shambles. It had been up to Onan to clear away the backlash their failed abduction had created. He'd also had to fabricate stories to explain the absence of several powerful men and have those rumors circulated in ways that had no connection to himself or the circle. Thankfully, the one thing it was easy to pass off as truth in the city was a rumor.

Thaddeus had sent men around, looking for information on his missing weapon and wagon. It seemed he had not seen his employee, Hashir, in several days and was looking for anyone who might know or have information about the man's whereabouts. Of all those in the circle, the one Onan had closest ties with, unfortunately, was Hashir. There was nothing direct, but Thaddeus was no fool, and he had provided the potion. He knew something had gone wrong, and the attempts to find Hashir were a signal that he also knew of the theft and the failure. He would have to be bought off, or dealt with, and that was another thing for which Onan had no time or patience to spare. He needed Akeem to regain control of his emotions.

To that end, he had a plan. For absolutely obscure reasons, Noah was said to be coming to the city. Not only that, but the man intended to speak in the temple, to address the public about his prophecy and his ark. The minute he'd heard, Onan had summoned Akeem, and now he waited. If anything could get the man to return to his life, it would be revenge.

The door opened, and Akeem entered. He moved slowly, shoulders slumped, and he nearly forgot to latch the door. He turned, and Onan waved to him to hurry.

"We have things to talk about," Onan said. "I want you to sit, and I want you to listen. You have lost your twin, and I won't pretend I understand that particular pain, but there are things we have to attend to."

"Our attending to things cost Akbar his life," Akeem said pointedly.

"And the things I am speaking of will offer you revenge," Onan said, not letting his voice rise in pitch or tone. He needed Akeem to hear him out. "Noah will be in the city today. He plans to speak in the temple, to explain his prophecy. If my sources are correct, he plans to offer a route to safety. He will tell the people that if they return to the law, to the temple and the ancient teachings, there is a chance. I can't believe he actually thinks any will listen, but then, I did not believe we would fail, yet here we sit. We did not capture the Nephilim, but we survived. I believe there is a reason, and I believe that reason begins to be important this very day."

"He is coming here?" Akeem asked.

Onan nodded. "I believe he will only be protected by the temple, and we both know that those guards can be bought. We may have lost our friends, but we have an opportunity to do something about it. We have been granted access to the man responsible for our friends, and your brother, being taken from us."

"I believe some of the blame for that falls on us," Akeem said, his eyes more focused than Onan had seen them since the attack. "It was a fool's errand, and if anything, proves that whether we believe it, or like it, some force is protecting Noah and his family."

"Say that you do believe," Onan said. "Does that change anything? I am a man who has lived his life for his own pleasure and gain. I do not believe any sacrifice, or prayer, is likely to change my status with angels or the Lord. I believe you are in a similar state. I do not care if the deluge is coming. I do not care if we are all to be wiped from the Earth, I have nothing to lose, and I am not a forgiving man. I propose that we gather as many of those who follow us as we can, and we storm that stage. I suggest that we take Noah, and tie him between two great beasts to be torn apart. I do not care if the world ends, but I find that I do care whether he survives."

Akeem stared at him for a moment, and then nodded. He said nothing, but Onan had seen, just for a second, a spark of something more useful than grief in the man's eyes.

"We have little time," Onan said. "Gather those that you can and make your way to the temple."

"When will we move?" Akeem said.

"You will know the moment," Onan said. "I will give you a sign that will be impossible to mistake."

Akeem nodded again, rose, and was gone. Onan took a deep breath. He rose, turned, and made his way back through the halls beyond that chamber and down to the streets. Two men waited there, and he waved them close.

"It is time," he said.

The two men disappeared so quickly they might as well have never been there.

Onan walked out to the main street, turning toward the temple. He had plenty of time, but he wanted to be early. It was important that he get a good seat, and that he have an idea where the others would be located. One way or the other, it was going to be a remarkably interesting day.

Noah heard the crowd long before he saw it. As he walked through the corridors behind the altar with Ezekiel, his mind replayed days in the past. Some where he'd spoken, others where he'd listened. He remembered when the first stone of this temple had been set into the ground. It was strange to have returned because everything felt different. He sensed the bones of the temple, but it felt distant. Like an echo. In his mind, he remembered the words, the chants, the rituals, but so much had changed. It was as if someone had recreated the building and the finery, but removed the soul.

The halls and rooms were dingy. The finery had been neglected, too few priests, too few donations, and so many turning away completely. He felt as if one moment he walked through his own past, and the next he passed through nightmares, things he could not change, rot strong enough to infect solid stone.

Ezekiel remained silent. It was impossible for Noah to tell if the man sensed what he felt or shared in any of his dismay. Surely it was something that the priest had remained with the temple, but the utter failure of faith and righteousness was palpable. The closer they came to the great chamber and the altar, the heavier the weight of it all grew. Instead of the hope he'd felt as he spoke with Balthazar, each step was more ominous than the last. Just before they stepped through heavy curtains and into the open space behind the altar, Noah closed his eyes and offered a short prayer. There was no time to search for an answer or acknowledgment.

The room was alive with sound. It had been created so that those who spoke from the front could be heard, but the acoustics were fickle, and it also magnified the sound of the crowd, which in solemn ritual would be silent. Noah heard laughter, high-pitched chatter, and angry shouts, barely contained. He wasn't certain if he could raise his voice high enough to quiet them, or that they would listen when he tried, but there was no going back. To return through those curtains without speaking would show a weakness in his faith he was unwilling to consider. They might not want to hear him, they would almost certainly not listen if they did, but he would speak. He owed it to them, for all their faults, and to his Lord. That last thought flickered through his mind and disappeared, but it left a calm and a rush of strength. Without glancing at Ezekiel, he stared out into the crowd before him and stepped to the altar. He placed the palms of his hands flat on its surface and waited.

He scanned the crowd and saw Balthazar far to the right. There was no missing the man's brightly colored robes. Noah made no sign that he'd recognized his friend, but his heartbeat slowed, and he was able to take deeper breaths. As bad as this might get, he was not alone. That in itself was enough to make this day unique.

Slowly, almost miraculously, the chatter faded. The laughter grew muffled, and then died. The angry voices stilled, and the eyes of every man and woman in the crowd fixed on the altar and the tall, gray-haired man standing behind it. Still, he held his silence. When it felt as if a tiny pebble could have dropped to the floor in the rear of the temple, and he would hear it, Noah began to speak.

"You know me," he said. "Some of you know me personally, have known me for centuries. Others know of me. The crazy man. The prophet in the desert. The deluded madman building a boat that will forever rest on land."

There was a soft murmur. He paused, then went on.

"You also know of my faith. I remember when the first cornerstone of this temple was laid. Some of you were there, others have known this place all of their lives. When it was new, this was a place of worship. Sacrifices were offered to our Lord and the temple. Its ritual and sanctity was the center of our lives. We were warned, even so long ago, that we would stray. We were offered a path to salvation, but at the same time, another offer was presented.

"I could go on at great length about the greed. I could mention the idols by name, and their followers. I could speak of drunken orgies and drug-induced rites. The arena you are all so proud of, where you pit creatures against one another to their deaths, not in any way to honor the Lord, but to belittle His gifts.

"I will not do that. I will tell you what I know to be true. There is a cleansing coming. A deluge. The oldest of you will remember the original prophecies, the youngest have heard the stories repeated to frighten you at night. I have been given the task of building an ark, a vessel to save the creatures of the world, and granted the gift of my family. I do not believe it must end this way."

There was a second ripple of sound, but he spoke over it.

"It is not too late for you to repent of the sins you have fallen into. It is not too late to cleanse the city of the idols, the sorcery, the vile entertainments. You can dedicate your lives to the Lord. You can make this city whole. I believe, if you do this, you can be spared. We can all be spared."

A voice rang out from the crowd then, loud, angry, and filled with spite.

"He lies! Tell us, oh prophet, of your Nephilim. The fallen who do your bidding!"

Noah paused. He stared straight into the eyes of the man who had risen. He recognized Onan, though it had been many years since their paths had crossed.

"Shall I tell them how you sent men to invade my home?" Noah asked. "Shall I mention that, in the dark of night, you opened the gates of the city to send a caravan of stolen weapons into the desert for your own gain? I know of the stories told here in these city walls. None of you, not one," he swept his eyes across the gathered crowd, "bothered to come to me and ask if they were true. I have never made a secret of anything in my life. I do not offer up things that are not mine to share in casual conversation, and, in truth, until very recently I have not had a conversation with any of you that involved more than handing over wealth for supplies. So no, I do not believe I will be telling tales of my life, or those I care for. That is not why I am here."

"He is here to draw us all in," Onan cried. "He is here to lull us, to distract us. He is planning on escaping with his loved ones and leaving us all to drown."

A murmur rolled through the crowd. Men and women shifted in their seats, and a number of others rose. Noah studied them. They did not seem as if they were present to hear a speech or to visit a temple. Each of them stood poised, as if preparing for some action. He glanced at Onan who met his gaze and grinned.

"I have come to prevent that very thing," Noah cried. "I have come to say that I do not believe it is too late. It is not my choice, it is yours, but I can help. The city must be cleansed. The temple must become the gathering place of the faithful that it was meant to be. The Sabbath must be celebrated. So much has been lost, but it is not beyond your reach."

His words were cut off as a piece of rotten fruit smacked

into the altar, just in front of him. He scanned the crowd, try-ing to see where it had come from, but as he did so a second hit him on the shoulder and nearly spun him around. Then more, and more. People rose, crying out. Some voices, very loud and clear, fueled the sudden madness, and before his eyes what had been a silent, curious crowd became an angry mob. He spun to his right and caught a flash of color. Without a word, or even a glance back at Ezekiel, he leaped to the floor and ran toward the exit near where he had seen Balthazar.

The crowd surged, hands reaching for him, faces alight with anger or fear. As he ran, he tried to watch for those he'd seen, those who'd disrupted the speech. The crowd was dangerous, but he knew that if that group captured him, it would likely be his last day on Earth. Someone grabbed his shoulder, and he turned, ready to strike out. It was Balthazar. He was flanked by three big men. None of them smiled.

"Go," Balthazar said. "They will get you to my place by the back ways. I will do what I can to slow those who are following. There are, by my count, ten, plus Onan."

Noah clasped Balthazar's hand very briefly, nodded, and turned. He fled into the streets, flanked by two of the three men Balthazar had brought and followed by the third. It had been a long time since he'd had occasion to run, but he found his strength had not deserted him. Or, more likely, his Lord lent what he needed. The four turned a corner, rushed down an alley, and disappeared into the heart of the city.

Chapter 36

Onan stood tall and gestured for his and Akeem's men to follow Noah out the door. The crowd had surged, a much more powerful reaction than he'd expected, and there was no clear way through it. He rushed toward the door himself, tossing men and women to the right and left. He was tall and powerful, but it took far too long. By the time he and the others gathered in the street, Noah and those who had aided his escape were nowhere to be seen.

"Balthazar will take him to his shop," Onan said. "Go there, find them. Do not let him out of the city."

Five men ran down the street; Akeem stopped beside Onan and watched them.

"They will not find him," Akeem said.

Onan spun. "Why would you say that? Of course they will."

"No," Akeem said. "We have made a mistake, Onan. We have not pitted ourselves against a man. We are not fighting Noah. We are standing in the way of a true prophecy, a thing I never believed I would encounter in my life. Think of the power we spent on trying to capture the giant. Think how strong, experienced, and powerful Ehsan was. Think about that bolt, and that potion. It was a solid plan. It should have worked. Everything we have done, everything we have thought and tried has worked against us. We are fighting a battle we cannot win, and one that will probably secure our place in whatever awaits the fallen. We will not win."

Onan stared at his friend for a long time. "You may be right," he said. "You may be wrong, as well. Either way, my course is set, and I believe yours is as well. We aren't going to cross the desert to apologize to Noah. We have lost friends, comrades we have shared power and dreams with. I am going to follow those men to Balthazar's shop. I am going to use any power or means left to me to prevent Noah from returning to his home. If I fail, I will turn my efforts to the people, whisper in the right ears, speak in the right public places. I will rouse them to burn that ark to the ground, or I will die trying. If I am wrong, I will still die, so my path seems clear."

Akeem only hesitated a second. He nodded. "For Akbar, if for nothing else, I am with you. Come, I know a shortcut to Balthazar's shop, and it will cut off the easiest escape from the city."

Onan grinned. They turned and hurried into the city. Behind them, the temple was alive with shouts and scurrying bodies. They spilled into the streets and spread in all directions like a rising flood.

Ham and Ezra had not been in the crowd. They had waited outside, out of sight. Ezra spotted Onan as he entered, and noted those who looked furtive, studying their surroundings as if planning something. He'd lived in the city long enough to know that more than a simple public sermon was about to happen. When the shouts broke out, and the crowd rushed toward the exits, he pulled Ham back against the wall.

"What is it?" Ham asked.

"I don't know," Ezra said. "That was Onan who stood and shouted. It can't be good, and he won't be alone. Master Balthazar is near this exit."

As he spoke, Balthazar and Noah rushed through the door. There were three gigantic men with Balthazar, and, after exchanging a few words, Noah left with them and Balthazar dove back through the mob into the temple. There was a scuffle and commotion inside.

"Balthazar must have paid someone to help stall them," Ezra said.

Ham started forward, but Ezra pulled him back. "I know those men. They will get him away safely. We should wait. When Onan and his men fight their way out of there, someone should be ready to follow. Balthazar would be too obvious, and too slow. I don't believe they will give up this easily."

The two stepped into the shadows by the wall and watched as the crowd continued to spill through the door like a human flood. Onan appeared with a short, round man. They leaned close, seemed to discuss something, then the shorter man nodded and led Onan down the street and into an alley.

"They are taking a shortcut," Ezra said. "They believe Noah will be in Balthazar's shop."

Balthazar appeared at that moment, in time to hear Ezra's statement.

"They will be disappointed," he said. "Thaddeus has made arrangements to get Noah out of the city. They will not go near the shop."

"Then we should let them go?" Ham asked.

"Of course not," Balthazar said, laughing. "I believe we should make our way back to the shop ourselves. I have my own shortcuts, and more entrances than others are aware of. I also have tricks up my sleeve that Onan will not expect. I'm a little tired of them, and I think it's time they knew it. This day in the temple could have saved lives. Maybe my life. We will never know, but I suspect Noah will not be coming to speak in the city again anytime soon, and despite what the hedge witches will tell you, there is no way to know when it might start to rain."

"If what Onan shouted spreads," Ezra said, "people will be frightened, and then angry. Getting Noah out of the city might be only the beginning of much worse things to come."

"Then we had better see to it that we prevent as much as we can," Balthazar said, turning. "Come, I am not fast, and we have little time."

Noah was glad he'd kept himself active over the years. His three escorts did not slow or stop. They took him on a winding track that he realized after a few moments was not leading toward the center of the city, or Balthazar's place, where he'd left his things.

"Where are we going?" he asked.

At first there was no answer. As Noah slowed, one of the men took his arm firmly.

"We are to get you to Thaddeus," he said. "We are not to be seen, so you must hurry."

Noah allowed himself to be dragged into a run. Balthazar must have expected they might need to escape. Another thing he owed the man who had, until recently, seemed as far from a friend as was humanly possible. Noah concentrated on running. They had long outdistanced the crowd, and he did not believe anyone had witnessed their route, but he had seen the hatred in Onan's eyes, and he was taking no chances.

They rounded a corner, and he could suddenly make out the outer wall of the arena rising above the other buildings. His escorts led him through streets surrounding the place, avoiding all main entrances, to what must have been the supply entrance at the rear. There was a wagon there, loaded with barrels and crates. A robed figure sat, reins in hand, a team of two reem in harness. As they approached, the man turned, and Noah saw that it was Thaddeus.

"I figured you'd be along eventually," Thaddeus said, "but I honestly thought it would take them longer to lose control."

"It was Onan," Noah said, slowing and breathing heavily. "He rose and accused me of trying to lull them into complacency while I escape with my family."

"A lot of citizens already believe that," Thaddeus said. "I wish they had listened, but I knew in my heart they would not. Climb aboard and put this on."

He tossed a long, dark robe to Noah, who caught it and slipped it over his head and shoulders. He climbed up onto the wagon beside Thaddeus.

"You are driving?"

"I thought it was about time I paid my daughter and son-in-law a visit," he said. "Possibly, it is my one chance to speak with you myself. I did not attend your speech because I feared the outcome, not because I did not want to hear what you had to say. Like Balthazar, I am coming to understand that knowing so little about you for so long has been a mistake."

"There is nothing special about me," Noah said. "I will be

the first to tell you that I have lived many years of my life as if there was, but the weight of all of this is greater than it should be."

"We can talk as we cross the desert," Noah said. The three men climbed into the back of the wagon, donning brown robes of their own to hide their bulk, and the weapons belted to their waists. "We have enough time to reach your home before it is late and more dangerous. We will be leaving by the same gate Onan's men used to try and capture your giant."

"I know you had a hand in protecting him," Noah said, "and I am grateful. I am sure Og is grateful, as well. I am uncertain whether he actually needed the help, yours or mine, but everything worked as planned. The battle took place away from my compound, with no witnesses. Only those involved are aware that it happened at all. Until today."

Thaddeus glanced at him. "Until today?"

"I may have mentioned, before fleeing from the temple I helped build, that Onan and his men had opened the gates at night, put the city in danger for their own gain. I had time to say enough, I think, to make things a little more difficult for them if they try to organize."

"Maybe," Thaddeus said, shaking the reins and setting the wagon in motion, "but don't count on that. People are more easily swayed to hate and anger than to change. Given a choice of blaming you for the end of the world and giving up the things they believe give them pleasure, they will choose their pleasure every time, and one of the things that gives them pleasure is having something to hate."

Noah turned and stared ahead, and they both fell silent. A few minutes later, the rear gates swung open, and Thaddeus guided the wagon out onto the road and away from the city. The gates closed behind them, and Thaddeus brought the team to a trot, leaving the tall stone walls, and all that lay within, behind.

Chapter 37

Ezra, Ham, and Balthazar reached the old shop very quickly, and slipped in through the rear. Balthazar wasted no time. He grabbed a bag beside the door as they entered and headed for the front.

"Lock the door," he said. "Ezra, the seals!"

Ham watched, confused, as Ezra nodded, then turned and slammed the bolt home on the sturdy wooden door.

"Quickly," he said, tossing a small bag to Ham. "It's a flint and steel. The candles. You'll find them at regular intervals along the wall. Start by the door and light them, quickly as you can."

Then Ezra grabbed a second flint and started around the far side of the room. Ham did not stop to ask questions. He did as he'd been directed. The candles were placed in sconces along the wall. A variety of colors, and, when lit, a variety of scents as well. His hands shook, but it seemed that no matter how ill he struck the flint, the sparks jumped, and the wicks of the candles flamed greedily. The two met at the doorway to the front of the shop.

"It's the same in there," Ezra said. "Hurry."

They crossed into the main chamber of the shop and worked their way quickly and steadily around the walls. The light from the candles danced. Shadows slithered and stretched to touch in the center of the floor and the arch of the ceiling. Balthazar stood in the center of the room. He held the bag he'd grabbed steadily. He was chanting softly and drawing on the floor with some sort of powder. Ham lit the final candle on his side of the room. He turned then, stared, and was about to ask a question, but caught sight of Ezra on the far side of the room waving his hands and shaking his head. Ham held his silence.

Balthazar closed the circle on the design he'd created and stepped back. He looked worn, tired in a way that made no sense to Ham. Ezra hurried to the older man's side and steadied him. Not knowing what else to do, Ham took Balthazar's free arm and helped. After a second, Balthazar shook them off. He stood very still for a few breaths, and then opened his eyes and smiled.

"That should do it," he said. "Quickly, to the back room."

The three stepped back into the rear of the building. Ezra leaned and gripped a metal handle in the floor that had looked to Ham as if it were part of the design in the tile. It opened, and Balthazar grabbed a torch from the wall. He lit it from one of the many candles.

"Come," he said. "We must get as far away from this place as quickly as we can. I believe, if we hurry, that we can catch up with Thaddeus outside the gates. If not, we will follow them to the compound. There will be nothing for us here, but I believe, at the very least, I have bought us time."

He stepped through the opening in the floor and descended. Ezra gestured for Ham to follow, and he did. Ezra closed the hatch behind them and tugged a long, hooked clasp into a ring embedded in the stone foundation of the building. They descended stairs that led to the floor of a passage cut through the very stone of the city at a depth about twice the height of a man.

"Where are we?" Ham asked.

"Catacombs," Balthazar said. "They run all beneath the city, but very few remember they exist, and fewer still have access. This will get us to the gate, and I have arranged for us to be met there. There will be a transport that will get us free of the city. I believe that will be for the best. If Onan and whoever is with him survive this day, he is going to be most unhappy. I believe that I may have to put myself at your father's mercy, Ham. I don't think that I will be welcome in the city after today, and Thaddeus may be in the same situation."

"I don't think that will be a problem," Ham said. "You are

the closest to family that Ezra has. But there is a lot about what is happening that you are going to need to explain, either on the ride to the compound or when we reach the wagon with my father. I sensed power back there, but nothing like what I feel when Noah is caught in a vision. Nothing like when we pray."

"I have met your giant, you know," Balthazar said softly. "I think you will find that what you sensed is close to what you feel when you communicate with him. The lines of power, faith, and the world are not as immutable as priests and scripture would like you to believe."

Ham stopped in his tracks. "Og? You have..."

"Not now," Balthazar said. "We must hurry."

Balthazar hurried off down the passage. Ezra and Ham followed.

Onan and Akeem reached Balthazar's shop and stopped outside. There were flickers of light within, something Balthazar would never allow if he were not present. Too many things in that place were flammable. Too many things were valuable.

"They are here," Onan said.

Akeem said nothing. He did not look convinced. Several of those the two had brought to the temple stood arrayed behind them, waiting for a sign or an order. The streets were barren. Everyone was at the temple or fleeing from it. They were not coming to the center of the city but racing for their homes.

"I have known Balthazar a long time," Akeem said. "If he is in there, it is not going to be as simple as opening this door or breaking a window to get inside."

"Agreed," Onan said. "But we must try."

He stepped forward and placed his hands on the door frame. Then, closing his eyes, he pressed inward with his mind, trying to sense what lay beyond. Akeem stepped up beside him and placed his own hands on the far side. He slid his foot across the ground until it contacted the taller man's. There was a jolt. The men behind them took a step back, because a glow had formed around both their hands, rippled down their arms and backs and joined in the dusty street.

"Do you feel it?" Onan asked. He didn't open his eyes.

"Yes," Akeem said. "There is a circle. They must be within, but..."

"But what?"

"There is a flaw," Akeem said, suddenly excited. "The design is perfect. It would keep a demon at bay, but—"

Onan concentrated, and then he sensed it. "Yes! There is a break. It is not complete. He must have hurried."

"Concentrate," Akeem said. "We can break that circle from here. Once we do, the door will be the only barrier remaining."

The two joined their energy and reached out, worrying at the small gap in the circle Balthazar had drawn. It was not easy, but the weakness was real, and they forced their joined wills through it. They were already parting the outer circle when they realized their mistake. As they broke that line of powder, the inner circle came to light. Flame from the candles surrounding the room flashed and met in the center of the room, then shot down to the smaller inner circle. Onan and Akeem tried to retreat, to pull their minds free, but the faster the small circle of light spun the tighter it gripped them.

"No!" Onan screamed. His body still stood, palms flat against the outer door, but his mind, the energy that drove him, drained faster with every beat of his heart. He tried to connect with his body, tried to give his men a sign. He quit fighting the circle and the flames, even as they licked at the tendrils of his thoughts and began to search along them for his tortured mind.

Beside him, Akeem fought a similar fight, but he was not as old, and not as strong without his brother. He was fading quickly. Onan tried to communicate with him, to join more deeply. Akeem allowed it, and Onan dove in with every ounce of power remaining to him. Without hesitation he bonded with Akeem's energy and, with a whispered apology he did not feel and scream of triumph, he ripped that energy free of his companion, drew it into himself and threw himself back to his body. He began to pull free, felt the scream finally reach his lips, but it was not enough. He felt pressure building, and knew that any second, he would snap back inward like a bolt shot from a crossbow, and he would be gone.

Strong arms gripped him. The men cried out. The energy

flowing through him burned them, but they were big, and they were loyal, and they wanted to be paid. They wrenched Onan from the door, and he staggered back, only remaining upright because they caught him and held him. Akeem's body shook, just for a second. Then, like a wine bladder being emptied, he shriveled and collapsed. Within seconds there was nothing but skin covering a vaguely human shape, bones poking out at odd angles. The lights inside the shop grew incredibly bright, and then, in a single flash that blinded them all, snapped to darkness.

Onan slowly opened his eyes. He blinked, and the front of the shop came back into focus. He shook his head and stood, steadier than he'd been.

"Get me to my quarters," he said. "I will pay you, and I will have more work."

Without a word, the men supported him and started off down the street. Behind them, Balthazar's shop stood dark and empty. Abandoned by all but the cadaverous remains on its doorstep.

Chapter 38

Thaddeus drove the wagon onto the main road leading to Noah's compound. The three men had pulled back their hoods and spent the trip going over the events of the day, speaking of times long past, of their children. Just before they passed out of the desert, Thaddeus turned to Balthazar. Ham and Ezra had arranged to come later, with one of the supply wagons.

"Do you think they will come after us?"

"Someone will," Balthazar replied. "I will be surprised if Onan and Akeem survive their visit to my shop, but I have learned that it is a bad idea to underestimate one's enemies, particularly when they are absolutely without scruples."

"I suspect we will know soon enough," Noah said. "I don't believe we have seen the end of this day. I should not have gone to the city. I should not have presumed to know better than my Lord who would listen."

"You did the only thing you could have done," Balthazar said. "It was inevitable that the city would turn on you. At least, assuming your prophecy is correct. It's easy to ignore such a thing until it starts to rain."

As they rolled in toward the center of the compound, shouts rose to the right. Thaddeus turned and glanced at Noah.

"Stop," Noah said. "We should go and see what is happening. That's the direction of the menagerie."

Thaddeus stopped the wagon. Noah called out to two young men hurrying down the road toward the distant cries.

"Tend to this wagon," he said. "Take care with the animals."

There was no hesitation. Those who lived and worked in the compound did not question Noah's orders. One of them took the reins before Thaddeus could move to hand them over. Without a word, Noah, Thaddeus, and Balthazar ran toward the menagerie. The cries were louder, but they did not seem to be angry or threatening. The closer they came, the clearer it became that they were hearing cries of amazement.

As they approached the doors of the menagerie, they slowed, and then they stopped.

In the small yard outside the main doors, two horses stood. They were a hand taller than any they'd seen before. Their coats glistened and their bodies rippled with muscle.

"What?" Noah said, starting forward again.

At that moment, the beasts turned. All three men caught their breath and stood very, very still. As the horses turned, they saw they had been mistaken. The creatures were magnificent. One was pitch black and a full hand taller than the other, which was silvery white. Their manes were full and flowed about their heads and shoulders, blowing in the breeze. None of this mattered. Both of them sported a long, spiral horn that jutted from the center of their forehead. Light caught on each horn, rippling and twinkling, suggesting power beyond the deadly-sharp tips. They were breathtakingly beautiful.

"I thought," Balthazar said, "that they did not exist. They are in my journals. There are drawings, but not from actual sightings, just descriptions."

Thaddeus only stared, but Noah started forward, moving slowly and carefully, crossing the distance separating him from the waiting creatures. As he approached, he held out his hand. The larger, black unicorn stepped up to meet him. He held out his hand, and the creature leaned down, offering the tip of its horn. As Noah touched that glittering spiral, it began to rain.

The unicorns would not be led through the doors of the menagerie, but Ham and Naḥlab were able to coax them into one of the pens behind the structure, and when presented (not without trepidation) with hay and oats, they seemed content to feed, drink, and watch. No one was under any illusions about whether or not they were trapped. They could have cleared the fence and been gone before anyone watching knew they'd begun to move.

But they stood, and they watched, and they waited.

At first, crowds had gathered, pressing up to the fence laughing and pointing, but Noah quickly put a stop to it. Visitors were allowed, if they were quiet and respectful, to go in small groups to see the creatures, but no one was allowed close enough to the fence to cause a disturbance. There was something magical about the unicorns, and it did not seem right to allow them to become a spectacle. Over time, those who visited began dropping to their knees and offering prayers. The unicorns paid no attention to this, but remained quiet and content.

Off to the side, near the menagerie, Naḥlab stood with Ham, watching them.

"Do you see?" she asked.

He glanced at her. "I see them, yes. They are—"

"No," she said, "the mare."

Ham looked again. He studied the smaller, silver-white unicorn carefully. It was odd to say smaller because his head barely reached the height of the mare's shoulders. He started, because he could not help himself, at the horn, and swept his gaze back over her. And then, he saw.

"Oh," he said simply.

Naḥlab grabbed his arm and pulled him closer. "She is in foal."

"How far, do you think?" Ham asked.

"Not far," Naḥlab said. "It is barely noticeable. It does not affect her motion, but there is no doubt."

"We will have to tell Noah," Ham said. "It is a wonderful thing, like a sign."

"It is wonderful, to be sure," Naḥlab said, "but it means we will have to be even more cautious with her care. They look like horses, but it is clear that they are far more than that. I trust that they will guide us, but..."

"It's all so new," Ham said. "We will figure it out. *You* will figure it out. I think it is why you are here. I didn't even notice. No one noticed, but you looked, and you saw."

There was thunder in the distance, and lightning struck the desert sands. It was raining lightly, still. It had been since Noah had touched the unicorn's horn. Not a deluge, yet, but steady, and without end in sight. There was little sign of the sun, and the moon was too pale to break through.

"It is time, I think," Ham said.

Naḥlab nodded. "We must speak with your father. We have to get the animals onto the Ark, get them settled, and load as much food, as many supplies as we can carry."

Ham leaned in and kissed her on the forehead. "It is all so strange," he said. "Like a dream that won't end."

"But it will," Naḥlab said. "How it ends? That is up to us, now, I think. It may be a long time before we rest."

Chapter 39

The rain had started shortly after Onan returned to the sanctuary of his chambers. He lived several stories above the chamber where he'd met with his circle. The floors between were lined with books, collected art, weapons, and treasures he had accumulated over a long life. Most of it was meaningless, other than its monetary value, but there were objects of power sprinkled in, books that had belonged to sorcerers and priests. Objects that traced back to ancient prophets and beyond.

Not all of it was real. He had ways of knowing. Some of it came with provenance that was so fantastic that he'd not been able to resist having it and passing on the lies. He stumbled up the stairs, glancing into the darkened rooms and grimacing from the bruises and cuts he'd sustained being dragged from the door of Balthazar's shop and then the explosion.

There had been so much power unleashed in that final moment. He had misjudged the man. He had always considered the shopkeeper to be a clever trickster, a dabbler in so many arts he could not possibly have mastered any of them. It had proven so far from the truth that the circle was destroyed, and only Onan remained to exact revenge.

He heard the patter of rain on the roof as he entered his chambers. He lit several lamps, poured himself a tall goblet of wine, and sat behind his desk. It could just be rain. It was not common, but it did rain in the city. It could be a coincidence, but Onan was not much of a believer in coincidence. It had begun. He had saved himself, or, rather, his men had saved him after he cast Akeem into the abyss, but it was all for naught. The rain would not stop. The deluge was coming for them all, and everything he'd lived for, acquired, dreamed of, and coveted would be washed away forever. As he sipped his wine, he found that this did not frighten him. It angered him. It angered him that they had failed, twice, confronting Noah. It bothered him that the Nephilim had killed his comrades, and that that Balthazar had taken the last of them. It bothered him that the Ark was in the hands of another, and that the lives of animals would be considered before his.

He thought others would feel the same. The rain was steady, but not yet any sort of downpour. It was a harbinger of the flood to come, a warning bell. There was time. He would go into the city, and he would speak. He would tell them that a man in the desert was going to float away with his family and a bunch of animals and leave them all to drown and bloat and rot. He would tell them that there was room on that ark for all of them, if they were careful, and enough cattle and food to see them through any flood. He would work them into a frenzy, arm them, and lead them across the desert. He might have to wait for the rains to strengthen. They might not take his word, but when the water began to rise, and the truth became their reality, they would follow. They would be frightened for their pathetic lives. They would become an army. Onan would lead them.

He knew there was nothing he could do to prevent a divine flood, but he was a student of scripture as well as sorcery. He understood that men and women had been given freedom of choice, and that, at the same time, if they made any choice other than that ordained by their "Lord," it would end badly. Not a choice at all, just a test. He thought, just maybe, he could make that other choice. He was probably going to die. The choice that would not lead to direct conflict with the heavens was clearly to sit back, have a drink, and await his fate. The other? If he could not find a way onto that ark and make it his own, he could burn it to the ground and be certain no one escaped. He did not believe Noah's "Lord" would postpone the cleansing of the earth if the boat weren't ready. Couldn't he just start over?

Onan sipped the wine and leaned back heavily in his chair. It would have to wait for a couple of days, at the least. Ne needed to recover, and he needed to gather the most powerful of the artifacts he possessed. He would need a new circle, or, at the very least, men with military experience who would not back down from a fight. Others would follow, if they were angry enough, but he needed a core of strong men who understood their lives depended on winning against impossible odds and accepted the challenge.

Onan glanced to the sky and winked raising his glass. "I choose my one chance at life," he said. "It was your greatest gift. I trust you will understand why I value it."

He finished the wine slowly, placed the goblet on his desk, and rose. He needed rest. The next day, and those following, would be the most important of his life, and if he spent them poorly, among the last. He snuffed all but one lamp and carried that with him to his bed chamber. He knew he would dream of giants and endless pouring rain.

Chapter 40

No one at the compound was under any illusions about the rain. It had fallen steadily for three days and there was no relief in sight. The clouds darkened the skies, occasionally lit by flashes of lightning. Thunder rolled in the distance. They felt like warnings, not of slashing rain and trees exploding into flame at a lightning strike, but something far more ominous.

No one slept. Work parties ferried feed and supplies into the holds on the Ark. Smaller animals were moved into their quarters on board, but after meeting with Thaddeus, Naḥlab, Ham, Ezra, Balthazar, Shem, and Japheth, Noah had determined it was best to keep the majority of the animals in the menagerie until it became clear they had no time left and had to board. Cleaning the stalls and the extra mess on board would add a burden during a time when all of their energy was needed to load the Ark, to move what they could of their belongings on board, and, under Shem's supervision, make as efficient use of the interior of the great craft as possible.

The women had been a miracle. Noah's wife, Na'amah, had joined Shem in moving their household, listing, and solving issues of food, cooking, storage, and arranging their quarters to put each person as close as possible to the things that they would be required to manage. She did not often speak up in gatherings, but when she did, all listened. As he watched the work happening around him, Noah realized it had not always been so, and wished he had paid more attention. A lot of things were changing in his heart, and his mind, things that he would not have expected to change so late in life. He was finding that he did not much like the man he'd been for many years. He should not have had to learn to the talents and strengths of his own family through necessity.

The animals also sensed the change. They were uneasy. They were restless, and at times more difficult. Japheth had brought workers to build a shelter for the unicorns, and others for the cattle and animals used to free grazing. The water posed health issues that Thaddeus was invaluable in pointing out and in offering solutions. Since the Ark itself was basically complete, Japheth had consulted with Shem and Ham on where the workers he still had at the compound could be put to the best use.

When the main work, the felling of trees and construction of the Ark had ended, he had let the majority of those who traveled out daily from the city go. There was simply nothing for them to do. When the rains came, others left, as well, but there was a core group content with the pay, the quarters, and the food. Some of them had taken to building their own boats in their off hours. There was plenty of material left over, and it would not leave with the Ark, so Japheth had not discouraged it. He did not believe it would do them any good, but it seemed to calm them. Like his father, the weight of the deaths of so many he'd worked with day after day darkened his dreams and became more and more difficult to justify through faith.

There was an energy running through the compound, an awareness that had not existed before the rain. It was one thing to work toward a prophecy, and a different thing altogether for that prophecy to pour from the sky in a steady rain, blocking the sun and reminding them all drop by drop that a great cleansing was imminent. It was no longer possible to scoff. It was only possible to come to whatever peace was possible with the reality.

At first the rain only raised the level of water in pools and ponds, muddying the soil and wetting the sand. Then those same waters rose beyond their boundaries and stretched, eating up the solid ground and crawling steadily toward the center of the compound, the Ark, and the menagerie.

When there was a sheen of water across the roads, Noah gathered the family and the workers, everyone who remained in the compound. He sensed that Og was nearby, and that he too was listening and aware.

"Tomorrow," he said, raising his voice to be heard, "we will begin to move the animals to the Ark. I know that daybreak is no longer a thing, so I will say, rest. Get the sleep that you can. Tomorrow, a few hours from now, we will rise, and we will work. We will move the animals and the beasts, all of the creatures, to the Ark. Nothing this grand, this impossible, has ever been attempted. It must happen as quickly as possible. I expect by the end of the day we will have completed this task, and we will seal the Ark. I am thankful for all who have assisted in this great task. If the prophecy were my own, and were not guided by my Lord, I would bring you all on board. I know many of you have built your own crafts, and I truly wish you the best. I hope that your efforts on our part will be noted. I hope that we will meet again when this is ended. For now, rest. Sleep. Spend the evening with your loved ones. Drink, if that is your solace. Tomorrow, we will begin the final stage of all of your efforts."

No one spoke. It wasn't a time for speeches. First one, then another, and finally groups of those gathered rose and departed. There was nothing left to say. There were no secrets. The prophecy had been the impetus for all their labor, and it had not been kept a secret. It was simply harder to live through such a reality than to ignore it and profit from it. The rain fell steadily, dripping from tarps and roofs, soaking the ground. After only a few moments, everyone but Noah and his family had departed. He waved at the rest.

"You, too," he said. "Take this night. It is likely to be the last in a long time you can claim as your own."

Then, turning to where Na'amah stood at his side, he wrapped his arm around her shoulders and led her toward their quarters, holding her close. He knew that, ritual or not, he would not be greeting the sunrise any time soon.

When all of them had left, a great shadowy figure emerged from the shadows. Og stood for a long time, staring in the direction of the Ark. Then, as suddenly as he had appeared, he drew back into the shadows and was gone.

Noah, despite the rain, continued his morning ritual. He sat, cloaked and dripping, staring out into the clouded skies. There had been no real sunlight for several days, but the rain, while steady, was still light. It was everywhere, affecting everything, but there was the sense that something was hanging over them, like an executioner's blade.

He closed his eyes, stretched out his senses, and waited. He had done this exactly this same way for weeks and felt nothing. Now he felt the storm. He felt the wind, and each flash of lightning sent shivers of energy through the hairs in his beard, down his arms and back, but they brought no visions. They brought no contact.

Still, he came. Every day. He sat, and he prayed, and he waited. This day seemed no different, and after the appropriate amount of time, he started to withdraw and rise.

Two things happened simultaneously. He spotted lights, many lights, on the road from the city, and he heard a single word in his mind.

"Now."

The word faded instantly. The presence in his mind was simply gone. The world felt empty. The lightning paused, just for a moment, and the wind died. In that instant he heard cries, voices from the road. He saw that the lights were bobbing and bouncing, moving steadily closer, and he knew. Without another word, he ran back to the compound. As soon as he thought it was possible and was within earshot, he began to call out.

It was time to load the animals, and somehow, they would have to simultaneously defend the Ark. He didn't know how he knew, but those lights in the desert were the people of the city. Somewhere at the front would be Onan, or one of his followers. They should not have survived, but even if they had not, the city had seen the rain. They knew what was happening in the compound, and they were coming to be part of it, or to stop it.

The closer he got, the more others heard him, and by the time he'd made the final turn to the menagerie there were men, women, carts, and animals scurrying in all directions. He found Ham and Nahlab at the menagerie gate. They were already directing a steady line of creatures, carefully monitored and controlled, moving efficiently toward the Ark. The two turned at Noah's approach.

"We can handle this," Ham said. "You need to find Og. We need you to protect the gates."

Noah had never received an instruction from any other member of his family. He almost drew himself up and reprimanded Ham, but he saw what they were doing, what they were accomplishing, and he knew the boy was right. He nodded.

"I will do what I can. It seems that most of the city is out on the road. The rain will slow them, and most of them have no experience in any sort of conflict. We have prepared for this, but not for such a crowd, and not during the loading."

"Then," Ham grinned, stepping forward and giving his father a sudden unexpected hug, "we will have to have faith."

Chapter 41

Onan rode in a wagon at the front of the caravan. Behind him rode guards, soldiers, citizens, even a few priests. The city had divided into two camps. One chose to remain, move to the highest stories of the buildings with supplies and their families and wait out the storm. The rest had chosen a more direct approach. That there would be a deluge was no longer in question. Who would survive it, though, that was a different question. If man had been given a choice, it seemed that choosing to take the Ark and save as many as possible was viable. If not, it was not a worse way to die than drowning.

Onan did not care about the deluge. He was not concerned with the people of the city or the Ark. He did not expect to survive, but he had a debt to pay. He knew that Balthazar, and probably Thaddeus as well, were in that compound. He knew that the giant who had killed Ehsan was also there. He was not naive enough to believe he could kill them all, but that no longer mattered. What mattered was that he release the anger and hatred eating him away on the inside. He hated to lose, and the past weeks had seen him defeated again and again. The worst of it was that he suspected he'd not been defeated by men. Not by Balthazar, Noah, Thaddeus, or even the giant. He was fighting a prophecy and understood the futility. It did not abate his anger. It did not change his path.

Those who followed him were of no importance to him at all. They gave him opportunity. He had to be certain he made that count. He'd brought the most powerful of his amulets and spells. He'd prepared as never before in his long life. He did not expect victory, but he did expect to leave a mark.

The animals seemed to understand the urgency of the moment. They moved in a docile, well-controlled line from the menagerie to the Ark. All of those who had cared for them were involved, coaxing, calming, and pushing them to greater speed. There were other creatures as well. Many of the animals had arrived as families or had become families while in the menagerie. As if controlled by some force beyond understanding, only two would join those being herded to the Ark, and their human guides had no say on which it would be. No one tried to argue or change this. The other beasts either backed off or slunk off into the compound. They did not attack those rushing about to secure the Ark.

Ham and Naḥlab seemed to be everywhere at once. They encouraged the others, they calmed animals, and directed last-minute supplies. They were on and off the Ark, directing the creatures to the proper levels and containment, securing the cages, and ensuring that there was water available to all. There would be time for feeding after the Ark was sealed, and the rain complicated it all. The rain and the imminent threat from the desert.

There was no time to think about the implications of what they were doing. They opened cages, emptied pens and larger enclosures, keeping enough space for separation from one group to the next, but not much. If there had ever been a time to trust the prophecy, this was it. The beasts would board the Ark, or they would not, but any hesitation at this point would cut them off before they were finished, and any altercation would likely disrupt the entire operation.

In the distance, they heard shouts. They heard the clash of metal and the sounds of others—beasts pulling wagons or mounted. Torches bobbed and weaved, remaining lit in the steady rain, but hissing, sending steam and sparks into the air.

Onan had added his own charms to the torches. They would have burned in the steady rain, but he had made them burn strong and bright. He had little power left to give, but he intended to use every bit of it this night. What would be the point of conserving? If Noah was right, he was going to die anyway, but if it won him a place on that ark, whoever was in charge, it was the only course that made sense.

The entrance to Noah's compound was close. The mob was on fire with anger and fear, and there were a lot of them. More than Onan had hoped for, and surely more than Noah had to guard the Ark, though there was the giant to consider. And there was Balthazar. Of all the strange things happening, the merchant's siding with Noah and his family felt the strangest. Thaddeus could claim to be supporting his daughter, but Balthazar? He would die with the rest of them, just to see his apprentice survive. It seemed surreal and wrong. It worried Onan because, if it was actually true, it meant Balthazar had come to peace with his own death, and that he believed. Balthazar was older even than Onan, and he was not a fool. It worried Onan to be opposed to such a man. Noah he could write off as crazy. Balthazar was an entirely different story, and the man had bested him once already.

The mob surged toward the compound. Those who were mounted took the lead, brandishing bows, swords, scimitars, and sabers. Whatever they'd been able to grab and bring at short notice. There was no plan to this attack. They would break into the compound and take the Ark by force, or they would die trying. Most of those who had followed him did not really believe in the Nephilim or the prophecy. They thought this would be easy. They believed they would attack a strange old man and his family, a few workers, and storm the Ark, sealing it behind them and survive, defying the Lord they'd turned their backs on so many years in the past. Onan knew it would not be easy, but he was still hopeful that superior numbers could win the day.

As they drew within sight of the road leading in through the trees, it seemed they would pass without opposition, but as they surged forward, arrows flew from the trees. Those who had led the charge were struck down, falling from their mounts, and crying out in pain and shock. The mob fed off this fear and drove inward. More fell, but many did not. For every man or woman who died, four more followed and took their place, and slowly they hammered their way into the compound.

Onan rose and called to the others to back off and regroup. If they all died before they reached the compound, it would be in vain. Stretched out behind him were clearly superior numbers, but he needed at least the semblance of a plan.

Those who had not died immediately fell back, drawing in close to the wagon. Onan stood, gripped a large crystal he had been holding in his lap tightly, and raised it over his head. He began a slow chant, his eyes fixed on the trees. At first nothing happened, and arrows continued to fly toward him, but then the shadows at the base of the trees began, slowly at first and then with increasing speed, to rise, taking the shape of men and beasts, growing substance and gaining voice.

Onan closed his eyes, imagined an army of shadows invading the trees, and sent his vision through the crystal into the night. The arrows faltered, and then stopped. There were shouts, and then screams. The shadows dove into the trees, releasing a high-pitched, shrill screech born of the sorcerer's anger.

Behind and around him, the men and women of the city gathered, watching and waiting. They felt the tide turning in their favor, but none wanted to move while those shadow nightmares invaded, and the guardians of the compound screamed.

Chapter 42

Noah gathered the workers who were not involved in moving the animals and armed them as well as he could. They were not used to conflict, but the possibility had always been real. The city considered him a pariah, a crazy man. There were thieves, and only the rumors of Nephilim and the dangers of the desert itself had prevented them from invading sooner. No one in the city, at least not until recently, would have stood by him. If an invading force had come, it would have been up to Noah, his family, the few who worked for and with them that were faithful, and Og. With that in mind, he had cached weapons. There was armor, not a lot, but enough to outfit a small force. He took charge of them himself, unwilling to put another into the position of the danger the coming conflict was sure to create.

He already heard screams near the road. The invaders were showing no mercy. They were killing anyone they came near. It made no sense. They were crazed and determined, and not spending thought on the consequences of their actions. They believed, at this late hour. They knew a reckoning was coming, and they did not care about anything but the Ark, getting aboard it, and surviving. Every cry of pain stabbed into Noah's heart, and he wondered, just for a moment, as he grabbed a helmet and a sword and ran for the road, how much deeper the pain would be once they were sealed into that vessel, and the Earth became a mass grave. He wasn't certain he could bear it, but he knew that the choice was not his own.

Then, shattering all other sound, a screeching, high-pitched scream erupted through the trees.

As he rushed forward, he heard a snapping sound and turned. A great tree, broken off to a stump, rose into the air, and he saw Og gripping the trunk like a club. Noah stopped and met the giant's gaze. He saw images of the mob approaching, shifting from Og's mind to his own. He saw Onan, slightly behind the front of the mob, eyes blazing. He knew this was the source of the anger, the heart of the invasion. The others might believe they acted in their own self-interest, but they would not have known, and could not have come so far so quickly, without direction and leadership.

"Protect the animals," Noah thought, directing it to the giant. "Protect my family. Onan, the sorcerer, is for me to deal with. I will put an end to this, and I will meet you at the Ark."

Og did not respond, but Noah knew the message had gotten through. He turned, and though they stared over their shoulders in awe at Og's sudden appearance, the small force he had gathered turned, and followed him at a run. They were armed with a variety of weapons, wielded clumsily. They were not warriors, but Noah thought, if they were going to die, that they intended to do so with a purpose, not drowned in a deluge, but protecting something that mattered. Protecting the future of mankind. Better to be a willing sacrifice to a higher purpose than simply ceasing to exist.

He felt lighter of foot than he had in years, felt strength he had believed long behind him. He did not want to hurt people. He did not want to do battle with the invaders, but he would protect his family, and he would do anything in his power to see the prophecy through to its end. He needed those who had supported him, those who had spent long, thankless hours making this prophecy a reality, to know they had not given their time, their sweat, and in many cases, their lives, in vain.

The others gathered around him, almost protectively.

"There is a man leading them," he cried. "His name is Onan, and some of you will know him. He is the one I am after. Without his direction, they will lose focus, but he will be protected. We need to cut into the trees and come out beside them, or we will never reach him."

No one answered, but when Noah swerved off the path,

they followed. They slipped between trees like shadows. No one made a sound. It was surreal, men and women who had cooked, cleaned, carried supplies, and cared for the beasts, armed and wild-eyed, running into the desert and almost certain death.

Noah held his silence, but he stretched out his mind as he did during his morning meditation. He did not try to converse. He did not wait for a vision or a message. He simply thought, "Help us."

The trees thinned and he hit the sand at a run. His rag-tag band of would-be warriors fanned out around him. What he saw chilled his heart. There were too many. It seemed as if most of the city had crossed the desert, hoping for a spot on the fabled ark, hoping to save themselves or their families. He saw Onan almost immediately. The sorcerer stood on a wagon with a crystal clutched in his hand that seemed to pour a stream of darkness onto the sand.

Noah felt a darkness nearby. He heard claws scrabbling and footsteps. He heard whispered voices. The air grew suddenly cold, and his heart felt as if it skipped a beat. He ignored it. He knew Onan had power, and he knew that the sorcerer would use it in any way possible. Closing his eyes, he mouthed a silent prayer, and drove forward into the desert.

The mob was focused on the road ahead and the compound, but many noticed his approach and spun to defend Onan. Noah did not hesitate. He had to stop this or cripple it. He had to do what he could to buy time for his family, and for the animals and beasts. It would not matter in the end, he saw. There was no way the small force in the compound could withstand an attack of this magnitude. They would be overwhelmed and the Ark lost. Ignoring this, Noah renewed his speed. He saw the shadow creatures Onan was forming materializing around him, but he ignored them.

"They are illusions," he cried. "Follow me. We must stop the sorcerer before he reaches the Ark!" After a slight hesitation, his followers broke from the trees and headed into the desert at a run. They saw something disturbing the sorcerer on the far side of his army and took full advantage to drive straight at Onan's wagon. Men were screaming, and there was a loud, wailing cry, but they paid it no mind. Whatever happened, they were committed, and they were closing fast on the front ranks of Onan's force, who had not yet even seen their advance.

Balthazar and Thaddeus had not returned to the city. They had chosen, instead, to man the front chamber of the menagerie, helping to usher the many creatures up and out the doors, releasing those that would not be taken aboard, and doing what they could to speed the process. Thaddeus had years of experience with a variety of creatures, and Balthazar had been studying them all of his life. Despite the message sent by the relentless downpour, it felt wrong to abandon them, and some of the largest had yet to be freed. In the depths of the menagerie, so far below ground level, it was only a matter of time until the water broke through the doors and seals and turned it into a watery grave.

"We have to open the containments as we go," Thaddeus said, hurrying downward. Most of the upper levels had already been vacated, but when they reached the very lowest level, where some of the largest and most difficult beasts were housed, there were stragglers. One group was the last of the Tooth Devils. A young, healthy pair had followed, almost docilely, as the rest were cleared, but one pen held the first pair that had arrived. They'd grown. The male was slightly lame, and his mate had refused to be parted, even when their child was moved to a different containment.

"This is what one calls a moment of truth," Thaddeus said.

"What do you mean?" Balthazar said.

"When I release them, they may just take off for the surface as the others have done, but these creatures have always been different. They are smart, possibly on the same level as men. They hunt, and they are viciously clever. The prophecy does not protect either of us from them, so I believe—much as Adam and Eve in that Garden so long ago, when they are free, they will have a choice."

Balthazar turned and stared into the shadows beyond the gate. Then, with a chuckle, he shrugged. "I am uncertain that it makes a difference, all things considered, though being clawed and shredded to death has never crossed my mind as the best way to die."

Even where they stood, far below the ground, the rain pounded, and, in the distance thunder rolled. Thaddeus took a deep breath and opened the gate. He stepped back and stood by Balthazar, waiting.

At first, there was nothing. Then, glittering in the torchlight, two pairs of eyes, about the same height as their own but large and reptilian. A large head poked through and turned quickly, like a great bird. The Tooth Devil stepped into the hall, head tilting one way, and then the other. It glanced at Thaddeus, and then at Balthazar. Its mate exited behind and also watched them.

Then the female turned. She lowered her head and emitted a screeching roar in the direction of the surface, as if she'd heard or sensed something. The larger Tooth Devil spun, and, without a glance back, took off with incredible speed, a slight hitch to his gait the only indication he was lame. His partner glanced a last time at Thaddeus, chittering loudly, a sound that chilled both men's hearts, and followed.

"What," Balthazar said, "was that?"

"Something is happening," Thaddeus said. "They are being called, but I have no idea why, or by whom. Come with me. We have two more to release, a Mace Tail and a nearly full-grown Three Horn. He will be almost too large, and it will take our combined concentrations. And a small wagon. I think there are melons down here still."

He turned and hurried on to the lowest level. Balthazar shook his head, and then followed.

The Mace Tail proved no problem whatsoever. He was not old and not much bigger than a bull, and he'd been led to the surface to forage many, many times. When they opened his containment, he turned his head to them, gazing at them and looking for food. Seeing none, the beast turned and lumbered up the passageway and toward the surface.

Thaddeus hurried to a small alcove and returned pulling a wagon. It was loaded above its edges with sweet green melons, almost past ripeness.

"I will do my best to lead him," Thaddeus said. "The Three Horns are trained to certain commands. They are the most domesticated and useful as working beasts. This one has had training but has not been worked. I will need you to move ahead of us with this wagon. He may not listen to me, but he will follow the fruit."

"What if he wants the melons more than he wants to listen to your commands?" Balthazar asked, glancing dubiously at the wagon.

"Then you had better be a bit more spry than you appear to be," Thaddeus said. "Just keep it moving steadily. I have the sense that our part in all of this is not done, and in any case, there is something I have always wanted to do that I believe I will share with you once we reach the surface."

"What is that?" Balthazar asked.

"Just start pulling the wagon," Thaddeus said. His grin was wide and his eyes sparkled. Balthazar took the handle of the wagon and started toward the surface at a fast shuffle. Behind him, he heard the sound of a great bar sliding free of its latch. He did not look back.

Chapter 43

Onan stood, gazing ahead at the road leading into the compound. He held the crystal high. He sensed Noah and his followers at the tree's edge, but he was not concerned. There were hundreds, possibly a thousand men behind him, all eager to surge forward. He knew they could keep him from harm long enough to reach the tree line and turn toward the Ark.

He also didn't believe Noah had many men with him. Most of the workers had returned to the city. Some of them were with Onan's troop. There would not be enough armed men to provide more than a distraction once they moved, but there were other things to think of. The giant, for one thing. If Ehsan's trained guard could not bring the giant down, Onan had no illusions about his own chances. He needed a distraction, and he needed the overwhelming numbers of his followers to give him the protection he needed to get close enough. The Ark was the goal. Everything else was secondary or meaningless.

Then he heard a crashing to his right and nearly faltered. Trees shivered and the ground vibrated slightly. The giant? He could not turn. If he lost his concentration, the shadow creatures he'd sent out into the woods and the compound would falter and fail, and he would be left with nothing but human assistance. Behind him, he felt the masses shift. Some moved to the right and seemed to be forming some sort of defensive line. The rest were actually turning and backing away. Sweat poured down Onan's face and into the front of his robes, but he held his concentration.

Not the giant, he thought. *They would all run. But what?*

The Three Horn burst from the trees with a loud snort and a rumbling wail. Onan stared in disbelief as it lowered its armored head and shot forward toward his force at a rolling gallop.

It wasn't the beast that startled him, though. He'd expected to run into many, though he had no idea what to expect from them. It was the two figures, one clinging to the massive frill surrounding the creature's face and the other with his arms wrapped around the first. Onan turned fully and squinted through the fading light.

"Thaddeus," he said. "And—Balthazar."

He saw that a number of the city guards had formed a line, burying spears in the earth and lining their shields, but he also felt their fear. He could taste it. They were not going to stop that charge, and there was no time to form a new plan. He turned to the driver beside him.

"Now!" he cried. "Get to that road and get us to the Ark!"

As the driver complied, Onan turned and screamed to those behind. "Follow me! To the Ark!"

Thaddeus took in the scene ahead of him in a second. He turned and screamed into the wind and thunder of the Three Horn's huge pounding feet.

"We have to split them!" he cried. "If all of those men make it into the compound, it will be overrun. Even Og will have his hands full."

Balthazar, bounding crazily and fearing that any moment he would slip and fall to the sand passing far too quickly beneath them, nodded. He tilted his head toward the rear of Onan's wagon, and Thaddeus grinned in answer. Turning, Thaddeus raised a hand, and then, with a hard, chopping motion he hoped would be enough to get the beast's attention, drove his hand down into the beast's shoulder. He struck a second time, and slowly, almost reluctantly, the Three Horn swerved. They were no longer driving straight at the wagon, Onan, and his flimsy guard. They were headed directly at the following crowd and picking up speed.

Even across that distance they heard the cries of fear. Men broke and ran, mounts whirled, causing a confusion that became a mob, turning clumsily. Nearly three-quarters of Onan's force spun and fled back across the desert toward the city. They did not turn back to fight. Moments later, the small force that had been unable to flee quickly or would have simply been too confused, were directly in front of them and Thaddeus closed his eyes. The Three Horn plowed into them, tossing men and beasts aside with its massive horns. The creature was in a frenzy, completely beyond his control, and all he could do was to hold on and hope not to fall and be crushed.

The remainder of Onan's force surged toward the trees. On its own, the Three Horn turned toward the city and thundered on. It seemed intent on running until its breath gave out, and they swiftly gained on the rear of the retreating forces. Thaddeus glanced back at the compound, but, just at that moment, an archer, one of those who'd lined up to defend against their charge, released an arrow. Thaddeus tried to call out. He released the beast's frill and reached for Balthazar, but it was too late. The arrow flew straight and true. It cut through Balthazar's throat and continued on, driving into Thaddeus's chest and slamming the two together. They toppled from their mount in what seemed like a slow-motion vision of stars and flashing lights.

The two hit the sand, bounced, and rolled. The shaft of the arrow broke off, and they pulled apart, blood shooting from their wounds. As they rolled to a stop in the sand, Thaddeus found himself staring straight into Balthazar's gaze. The other man could not speak, and Thaddeus felt his life pouring out and soaking into the sand. He managed to open his suddenly dry mouth and to speak.

"You were right," he gasped. "This...was a much better way to die."

Then he closed his eyes, and darkness consumed them both. As the wagon leaped forward, Onan sensed another disturbance, and he turned. He had forgotten Noah. He'd thought his shadow-creatures would send the man's small force scurrying for cover and turned all of his attention on the charging beast. It was too late by the time he heard the screams and pounding of feet. He turned, just as Noah burst through his closest ranks. His eyes went wide, and he opened his mouth to speak. Noah did not allow it. With a great cry of pent-up anger and frustration, Noah leaped to the side of the wagon and swung the sword he carried in a clean arc. Before Onan could speak, his head leaped from his shoulders and bounced once on the wagon before rolling among the feet of his followers.

They all turned, but it was too late. Where Onan had sat, they saw Noah, eyes wild, hair and beard waving in the wind where it flowed out beneath his ill-fitting helmet. Blood pumped from Onan's corpse, and Noah's followers also leaped to the wagon. One of them, less shocked than the rest, grabbed the reins and urged the reem forward. The wagon cut a swath through the unsuspecting foot and mounted soldiers, driving toward the road ahead. There was no way they could make it—no way they would break free. What remained of the mob had turned and had begun closing in. Then the earth shook. And again.

Noah glanced up and saw Og step from the forest. The giant held a tree in one great hand. His eyes, normally calm and thoughtful, blazed. The remaining men split like water running into a large stone in a river. Some turned and curled back toward the city. The rest, eyes bright and crazed with the lust of battle, followed the wagon. There were soldiers and mounted guards, and their steeds quickly outpaced Noah and his wagon, driving through the entrance to the road leading to the compound, and the Ark. Others continued forward, and Noah followed them. They would not make it, he knew, but he might. He might reach the Ark. He might save his family.

He sent a single thought to Og. "Thank you."

Then he leaped up beside the man who had taken the reins.

"Get me to the Ark," he said. The man nodded and shook the reins for more speed. As the giant swung his club, the night erupted in screams and blood. Noah closed his mind to it and focused on the road ahead. He only hoped he was not too late.

Ham heard the shouts and clashing of weapons drawing closer. They had most of the creatures loaded. They had saved the larger ones for last and had freed all of those that were not part of the pairs. The animals seemed to understand. Those that were not meant to board the Ark milled about. Some of them shied back from the approaching mob, others turned and formed a line. The line slowly became a wall. The larger beasts—the predators—moved to the front. They did not look at one another, and they did not fight among themselves, though many were mortal enemies.

Ham stopped and stared. The last of the animals were loaded behind him, but he barely noticed. Nahlab stepped up beside him.

"What are they doing?" she asked. "Why...?"

"They are protecting the Ark," Ham said simply.

At that moment, as if cued by his words, the two unicorns brushed past so closely the two felt their manes tickle their faces.

"No!" Nahlab cried. "You have to go to the Ark. You have to get on board."

The mare turned and glanced down at her, snorted, and continued on until the two stood near the front of the grouped animals. Though some of the beasts towered over them, they moved aside, as if in deference. Then, moments later, the first of the invaders broke through from the road, turning toward the Ark. Some were mounted, others ran, swords and bows and clubs in hand. Their eyes were wild and they screamed. It was the most chilling sound Ham had ever heard. He pulled back, closer to the gates leading into the Ark. Ezra was there with Yalith.

"Where are Japheth and Shem?" Ham asked. "Where is mother?"

"They are safely on board," Ezra said. Japheth is moving and loading supplies. Shem is helping and organizing. Mother and Sedeqetelebab are settling the beasts and giving them water. But Noah?"

"He went to help at the road," Ham said. "We have not seen him since—"

His words were cut off by a thunderous roar. They all turned and saw that the elder lion from the pride they'd kept had stood up. He would not be on the Ark, the younger male and female would make the journey, but he was strong, and his eyes glowed with reflected light from the torches. He lunged toward the approaching mob, and, as if following some sort of order, the remaining creatures charged. They hit the first line of men and scattered them. A few took swings with unfamiliar swords, but they were no match for the speed, fury, and surprise of the attack. They parted, fleeing into the trees to either side, with wolves, big cats, bulls, and the Tooth Devils cutting them down one by one. The two unicorns charged up the center with the lions. They were focused, and after what seemed the longest moment of Ham's life, he saw a wagon thundering through the mob. The driver was one of the workers who had left with his father, and Noah sat at his side, a helmet holding back his wild hair and his beard flowing around his face. They moved up from the rear, even as the beasts attacked from the front, and it seemed they would simply drive straight through, making it to the Ark safely.

Then Ham saw it. He turned; the others turned. A small group of men from the city, probably guards, had formed a line. They had shields and spears, and they stood shoulder to shoulder. One of them stabbed the old lion through his throat as he attacked, and though the big cat took down two men as he slammed into them, he fell, and there was a small opening. Behind those men, a tall man with a bow stood very still. He had an arrow leveled at the approaching wagon, aimed directly at Noah's chest.

"No! Ham screamed. He started forward, but Ezra grabbed him.

"It is too far," he said. "You can't—"

For the second time in what seemed only seconds, the air filled with sound. The unicorns had turned, and the mare, lifting her hooves in the air, threw back her head and screamed. It was like no sound they had heard before. Men and beasts froze, and turned, just for a second, and, in that second, she moved. One moment she stood, rear hooves planted, and the next she shot across the short space the creatures had cleared for the wagon, directly at the line of guards. The man with the bow saw her approach. He released the arrow, but he was too slow. She leaped, moving so fast her white pearlescent coat glittered like a bolt of lightning. She left the ground and flew, and the arrow, flying straight and true at Noah's heart, pierced her shoulder and dug deep.

She stumbled, just for a second, then turned and aimed her long, deadly horn at the line of guards. The bowman reached for a second arrow, but again, he was too slow. She burst through the shields, stumbling only once from the pain, and drove her horn into him with such force he was lifted from the ground and driven back. The unicorn swung her head, and the bowman slid free, tumbling through the air, bow dropped and forgotten. One of the men, not quite knocked from his feet, swung his spear and plunged it into her side. She screamed again and ripped free, but her wounds were spilling blood far too quickly. She turned to strike her assailant down, but the stallion, with a scream of his own, drove in, impaled the man and threw him into the air with a quick toss of his head. He rose, hooves flashing, and battered the others, striking two on their makeshift helmets before lunging in again and skewering a third. The mare tried to continue the fight, but she'd lost too much blood. After a few stumbling steps, she dropped to her knees, shook her head, and slowly rolled to her side.

The stallion saw this. He turned to her, moving closer. Two of the remaining men, rather than run, instead rose and gripped their spears. That was when the ground shook, and everyone looked up. Og had returned, smashing trees out of his way as if they were small twigs. He took in the scene at a glance and drove a massive hand down. It struck the two spear men and drove them into the ground with such force that when he withdrew his fist, there was only earth and a stain of blood. The giant glanced at Noah, who held his gaze for a moment, then dove off the side of the wagon and ran for the Ark.

Naḥlab saw everything in a surreal, slow-motion wash of color and movement. When the unicorn mare went down, she cried out. When Ham tried to rush out and help the creature and Ezra pulled him back, she barely noticed. She heard the unicorn scream, and then she heard the stallion scream in return, saw him throw himself into the fight, protecting his mate, sending the remainder of the guards fleeing into the trees. He stood his ground, snorting, great eyes flashing with anger and hate. And then that fist, that giant, impossibly powerful fist. It had slammed into the two remaining men so hard and so fast they simply did not exist. Naḥlab barely noticed. She saw only the blood and the fallen unicorn.

The return of the giant, Og, had robbed the final courage from the men of the city. They fled into the pouring rain, disappearing like shadows. The road was clear, and Naḥlab rose, stumbling out toward the fallen unicorn. Ham tried to grab her by the arm, but she shook him off. He followed, glancing over his shoulder at the Ark and then at the road, where Og stood, staring back toward the desert.

"She's hurt," Naḥlab said. "We have to help her. We have to get them onto the Ark."

Ham followed, but his heart sank as they neared the two creatures. The stallion had dropped to his knees beside his fallen mate, oblivious to the growing pool of blood. The mare gasped for breath. Her eyes were wild and her chest heaved. The stallion turned at their approach and started to rise, but Naḥlab ignored him. She dropped to the ground on the far side from him and reached out to the wounds. The arrow could easily be pulled free, and the wound would heal, but she'd been moving when the spear struck, and it had carved a gash in her chest. It was impossible to tell just how much internal damage there might be, but there was far too much blood.

"We have to get a wagon," Naḥlab said, turning to Ham. She saw his expression and her eyes grew fierce. "We have to!"

Ham shook his head. He knelt beside her, and, though she struggled, he held her.

"It's no good," he said. "She only has a few minutes. If we moved her at all, that would be the end. You know it's true."

Naḥlab tore free again and wrapped her arms suddenly around the mare's neck, burying her face in the soft mane. The unicorn shivered but was quiet. The stallion leaned in, careful to keep his horn averted. He nuzzled Naḥlab softly and snorted. She glanced up and met his deep, liquid gaze. He was so beautiful, so impossibly powerful, and she felt his sorrow and his pain as if he'd sent his thoughts driving into her heart.

The mare shivered again. She arched her back and stiffened, and then she was gone. Ham felt Naḥlab stiffen at that same moment and held her tighter. The stallion pulled back. He stood. He nuzzled the still body a last time, still wrapped in Naḥlab's arms, then he turned away. He did not look back. He trotted slowly over to where Og stood, guarding the road from the desert. He turned so that he stared, just as the Nephilim stared.

"We have to get him onto the Ark," Naḥlab said, rising.

Ham shook his head. "We can't. Only mated pairs. I don't even know if it would be possible for him to enter if you could make him, but I suspect that you cannot. Look at the others. All of those who know they are not chosen. They guarded the Ark. They offered themselves as a shield, but they will not enter, and he will not enter."

"But he is the last."

"And he would be the last when the storm passes. I don't know if it would be possible for him to mate with one of the horses, but it would be a lessening if he did, a new thing."

Naḥlab was about to speak again, but at that moment Noah called out from behind them.

"The storm is strengthening," he screamed. "Get inside, quickly!"

Ham turned and stared up at Og. He sent his thoughts, his love, his gratitude. He sent them to the unicorn as well. He had no way to know if that were possible, but he knew Og would hear, and that he would know.

The giant turned, just for a second. He met Ham's gaze, and then he turned away. At that same moment, the unicorn spun, rose its rear hooves, and screamed. The sound was different this time. It was filled with pain and anger, but it felt more like a communication. It felt like a release. Ham grabbed Naḥlab and the two ran for the Ark. They climbed the long ramp, even as the water around them that had been puddles only a short time before had now reached the lip of the wooden gate. Before they had even passed into the interior, the great hoists began to lift. The gate rose slowly from the muck, dripping water and mud.

Japheth and Ezra manned the handles of the winch, Japheth's design, that allowed them to bring the huge weight up, quickly, until the gate closed with a huge thundering *slam!* They hurried to work the bolts, sealing the gap. There were barrels of pitch waiting, and they all fell to work sealing the cracks where the gate had once opened. Someone had lit torches, and they worked hard and steadily in the wavering light and dancing shadows. No one spoke, but beyond the walls of the Ark, they heard the crash of lightning and the roar of thunder. It had begun.

Chapter 44

The waters rose at an impossible rate. The great craft rocked on the supports holding it upright, and Noah feared that it would topple. At one point it wobbled unsteadily, and he clung to a beam, clutching Na'amah tightly to him. Then, even as it began to rock to the side, it stopped. Not gently, but as if it had fallen against a wall. A moment later, they righted, and as the water level rose and the keel lifted from the ground and from its supports, they floated. The stone and sand they had added for balance kept them upright and steady.

Noah pushed off the wall and turned. He hurried to a ladder leading up to the next level, gripped the rungs, and began to climb.

"Where are you going?" Ham called. "What—?"

Noah ignored him and continued to climb, his hair waving crazily about his head. In a moment, he was gone.

"I'm going after him," Ham said. "Check to be certain we have all of the stables and stalls closed properly. Look for anything not tied down. If the weather turns rough—"

"They will fly about like weapons," Ezra called out. "Yes, I know. I was there when you learned that from Master Balthazar's journals."

His voice broke at the end of this, as the realization of what had just happened, so suddenly and so violently, hit them all. Finally, Ezra found his voice again.

"Go," he said.

Ham turned and climbed. His father was out of sight, but there were only so many places to go. Each level had a long, central passage, and the containments for the creatures. A quick glance to either side showed Ham that the lower levels were empty, at least of men and women. He climbed, and when he was certain he knew where Noah had gone, he climbed faster. All about him he heard the nervous or frightened cries of animals and beasts, and the scrabbling of claws, hooves, and feet in search of balance. He ignored them all.

There was a narrow chamber running the length of the Ark at the very top level. No creatures were housed there. There were supplies. There were no windows, but Ham knew that Noah had made changes. He did not know why, and he didn't know exactly what, but somehow he knew he was about to learn. He wasn't sure if he feared it or was thrilled by it. The Ark shuddered then. It was fully afloat, but something had shifted. The rear of the boat dipped. It stayed that way, sending things just slightly off balance, and then they righted, but not quite as they'd been. Ham clung to the ladder, just until things evened out, then he climbed the final ladder to the upper chamber and clambered up.

He felt a mist of rain, something he had not expected. Something that should not exist within the confines of the Ark. He saw flashes near the rear, and he turned that way to find his father, gripping the edges of a small hatch that opened to the skies. There was a plan; it was not this. That hatch was to have remained closed and sealed until the storms fully abated.

"Father!" Ham cried. He crossed over carefully, holding on to a rail that ran along the wall. They had intended this for tying down supplies, but it also came in handy to steady him against the unfamiliar roll of the rising waves. Wind and rain whipped through the open hatch, and Ham pulled himself up beside his father. Noah remained silent, so Ham followed his gaze.

Nothing could have prepared him for what he saw. They floated at the tops of the trees. Waves crashed, white-foam-tipped, and crashing over one another, and over the bow of the Ark. But there was more. Bits and pieces of the wagons rolled over the waves. Here and there, heads bobbed. Dead men, or drowning? Many of the creatures who had fought to defend them struggled atop the swelling waves.

Two things fixed his gaze. The first was the unicorn, the

stallion. It fought the floodwater, head held high, legs churning. There was no high ground anywhere near, but he fought. The second was Og. The giant, so huge on the ground, was dwarfed by the Ark. He clung to the aft end of the craft. His expression was the same as always, but Ham felt something akin to fear.

"Help me," Noah shouted.

Ham shook his head and saw what Noah was doing. He had a long, braided rope in his hands, and he was struggling to get the end of it out onto the top of the Ark and down to Og. Ham didn't hesitate. He grabbed the rope and helped his father feed it out through the hatch, He nearly tripped and fell through the hatch when he felt his father's mind reach out to the giant in a mental scream.

"Tie it around your arms below your shoulders. We will secure it here. Rest when you can. Do not fear. We will find a way to feed you. We will carry you through. If this breaks the prophecy, we will die with you. Do you understand?"

Og made no response. He reached, stretched, and grabbed the end of the rope in one hand. He turned and wrapped it around himself, surprisingly agile for such a huge creature. He drew it around, only causing a small wobble to the great ship, and tied it tightly, still clinging with first one hand, and then the other, to the Ark.

Noah and Ham checked their end. It was already looped and knotted to a great ring in the deck. It was meant as an anchor, and it was solid. Without wrenching great chunks out of the Ark, or something severing the thick rope, Og would travel with them. If he were strong, and if they fed him, he would survive. Ham was torn between fear for his family and joy at not losing yet another. He was still trying to wash the words Ezra had spoken from his mind, and to not think of Master Balthazar. To not think of the men and women he'd met in the city, the workers, those who had cared for the beasts and helped to build the menagerie.

He saw Og lurch suddenly. It shifted the Ark, but not much. The giant was reaching for the unicorn. Ham thought he might catch it, lift it up to the upper deck, and save it. He prayed it would be so. But then, from the skies, a brilliant flash of light.

It was like lightning, but at the same time not. Brighter. One moment he saw the light glimmer on the unicorn's slick black mane, then it was too bright. Too intense. He closed his eyes and ducked his head. When he finally dared to look, Og had withdrawn his hand, and the unicorn simply was not there.

"No!" he cried, but he felt his father's hand on his shoulder.

"It is well," Noah said. "He has been taken. I do not know where. I don't know why or how. I know it is not the end for him. Now, quickly, we have to seal this hatch before the waters begin to wash over us and soak down to the lower levels. Og will live, or he will not. We have done what we can."

"Ham stared into his father's crazed eyes and felt a reflection of his own pain at the incredible loss. He nodded and the two set to work. The hatch slammed with a crashing, thunderous sound, and was sealed. They tied it off, being careful with their knots. Then, together, father and son descended into the Ark. They had their families, and all the beasts of the world to care for. They shared the pain of a loss beyond comprehension.

Outside, the rain continued to pour.

And thus, the Earth was cleansed...

About the Author

DAVID NIALL WILSON has been writing and publishing horror, dark fantasy, and science fiction since the mid-eighties. He is an ex-president of the Horror Writers Association, and multiple recipient of the Bram Stoker Award. His novels include *Maelstrom, The Mote in Andrea's Eye, Deep Blue,* the Grails Covenant Trilogy, *Star Trek Voyager: Chrysalis, Except You Go Through Shadow, This is My Blood, Ancient Eyes, On the Third Day, The Orffyreus Wheel,* The DeChance Chronicles, including *Heart of a Dragon, Vintage Soul, My Soul to Keep, Kali's Tale,* and the stand-alone spinoff *Nevermore – A Novel of Love, Loss & Edgar Allan Poe*–which culminates in the latest volume in that series, *A Midnight Dreary.* His novels in the O.C.L.T. series include *The Parting, Crockatiel,* and the novella *The Temple of Camazotz.* He is also the author of the memoir/cookbook *American Pies: Baking with Dave the Pie Guy,* and editor of the well-received anthology *Voices in the Darkness.*

David can be found at: www.davidniallwilson.com

Curious about other Crossroad Press books?
Stop by our site:
http://store.crossroadpress.com
We offer quality writing
in digital, audio, and print formats.

CPSIA information can be obtained
at www.ICGtesting.com
Printed in the USA
FSHW010341301121
86558FS

9 781637 899342